Plunging Through a

The crew of Galahad assumed that the ring of debris known as the Kuiper Belt was spread evenly...until they rushed headlong into a deadly stretch that threatened their very survival! Will a mysterious code show them the way out?

"Within the first four months after the launch," Merit said, "we had not one, but two separate incidents which almost destroyed us. Two."

Lita leaned forward. "I don't think I quite understand what you're hinting at. You're suggesting...what?"

He straightened up. "It's time for us to turn around and head home."

"What?" Channy blurted out. "Are you crazy? We can't go back to Earth. Bhaktul's disease – "

Gap chuckled. "The best medical minds have worked on Bhaktul for years, and they have nothing to show for it."

"You're forgetting one very important factor," Merit said. "The Cassini."

Strap yourself in for Volume Three of Dom Testa's cosmic adventure series...

GALAHAD 3
The Cassini Code

Also by Dom Testa

GALAHAD 1: THE COMET'S CURSE

Winner: Writer's Digest Magazine Grand Prize

Winner: 2006 EVVY Award for Best Young Adult book

GALAHAD 2: THE WEB OF TITAN

Winner: 2007 EVVY Award for Best Young Adult book

Orders at: www.DomTesta.com

GALAHAD 3
The Cassini Code

Dom Testa

Profound Impact Group
Denver, Colorado

Copyright © 2008 by Dom Testa
Library of Congress Control Number: 2007931676

Profound Impact Group, P.O. Box 370567, Denver, CO 80237
www.ProfoundGroup.com

Publisher's Cataloging-In-Publication Data

Testa, Dom.
Galahad. 3, the Cassini code / Dom Testa. -- 1st ed.

p ; cm.

ISBN-13: 978-0-9760564-4-7
ISBN-10: 0-9760564-4-5

1. Interplanetary voyages--Fiction. 2. Space travelers--Fiction. 3. Teenagers--Fiction. 4. Interplanetary voyages--Juvenile fiction. 5. Space travelers--Juvenile fiction. 6. Adventure fiction. 7. Science fiction. 8. Young adult fiction. I. Title. II. Title: Galahad Three III. Title: Cassini code

PZ7.T4783 Gal3 PS3620.E883
813/.08762   2007931676

First Edition

Printed in the United States of America

To my sister, Donna

Sock fights, back-seat vacations, midnight movies with chips and dip...
Thank you for the lifelong adventure.

Acknowledgements

There is no anxiety that compares to the worry of trying to remember everyone who has pitched in, helped out, and generally been there. Every author understands...

To Dorsey Moore, whose editing eye makes me better in so many ways.

The amazing David A. Hardy has the patience (thank goodness) to suffer my many requests for changes...and always creates beautiful pieces of art that serve as my book covers.

Thanks to Judy Bulow, a friend, a believer, and champion, not just in the literary world, but also in life.

To Dr. Judith Briles for her generous support. Judith, you can sit barefoot with a cold beverage on my deck anytime.

I treasure the sense of fun that Jeremy Padgett brings to the publishing world.

To all of the teachers, librarians, and other educators who have used the Galahad series as a learning tool. That is the greatest compliment I could ever receive.

To the best writer in the family, my son, Dominic.

Special acknowledgement and love to Debra Gano. Your spirit peeks out from these pages. I'm happy that the world is discovering your Heartlight.

And, as always, a very fond thank you to each and every member of **CLUB GALAHAD**. No author has a better cheering section, and I never, ever forget how lucky I am.

Recorded human history stretches back more than five thousand years, and there has been complete and total peace for less than five hundred of those years. Humans are a notoriously disgruntled bunch. Even the best of friends, who are convinced they could never disagree or fight over anything, usually discover something that drives a wedge between them, and before you know it there's drama. Add a third person to the mix, and you mathematically increase the chances of conflict..

Add another 248 and our shipload of explorers on Galahad are asking for trouble.

Despite their best intentions, humans squabble. They can't help it. They're aggressive creatures by nature, and no amount of evolving and learning seems to be able to curb that. It's especially difficult on Galahad, because it launched from Earth seven months ago with 251 high-achievers. Extremely intelligent high-achievers, to be sure, and good kids, no question about that. But for all of their cultural differences, they're still the same breed, and eventually tempers will flare.

Oh, and let's not forget that they're confined to a spaceship that will be their home for another four and a half years. True, it's a very large ship, but restricted nonetheless. Old-timers on Earth would have called it cabin fever, and our happy campers can't exactly step outside to get some fresh air.

Galahad is actually on a rescue mission. The object of that mission is essentially to save the human race from extinction, thanks to a rogue comet that deposited a nasty substance into the Earth's atmosphere. Within months the entire adult population began to fall deathly ill with Bhaktul's disease, named for the killer comet. Kids under the age of 18 were immune, for reasons unknown, and it seemed the only chance humankind had left was to pack up as many kids as possible and get them away from the contamination before they turned 18.

Dr. Wallace Zimmer dreamed up the idea of a lifeboat to the stars, and rounded up 251 of the planet's brightest young people. Two years of training could not prepare them for everything, but it was all the time they had.

Within days of the launch they faced almost certain death at the hands of a madman who had stowed away in the ship's mysterious Storage Sections. Four months after that encounter Galahad barely escaped catastrophe again, this time thanks to an alien force near the ringed planet of Saturn. Both times the crew, led by Triana Martell, the ship's Council Leader, found a way to slip out of danger and press on toward their final destination, the planetary system circling the star called Eos.

Let's face it, they've had to pull together. Humans, for all of their disagreements, basically understand that they need each other to survive. It gets a little tough sometimes - and often they want to throttle each other - but sticking together is what has pulled them through.

How do I know so much? I'm only the most incredible computer ever designed, that's how. Even though my primary responsibility is running the ship, I can't help but get dragged into the daily lives of these crazy kids. And although it's sometimes a struggle to understand their irrational behavior, I still like them. Too much, I think.

My name is Roc, and my first responsibility is to encourage you to read the first two tales, conveniently labeled Galahad 1 and Galahad 2. If you're stubborn, and insist on wading into the midst of things here, okay. I've done my best to fill you in, and you'll probably do just fine. But you'll be missing out on some hair-raising adventures. Go on. Read them. I'll wait for you to catch up.

At any rate, we're now seven months out from Earth, three months past the near-catastrophe around Saturn, and wouldn't you know it's just about time for trouble to pop up again? Remember our little talk about humans and conflict?

Why can't we all just get along?

-1-

The warning siren blared through the halls, running through its customary sequence of three shorts bursts, a five-second delay, then one longer burst, followed by ten heavenly seconds of silence before starting all over again. There could be no doubt that each crew member aboard *Galahad* was aware – painfully aware – that there was a problem.

Gap Lee found it annoying.

He stood, hands on hips and a scowl etched across his face, staring at the digital readout before him. One of his assistants, Ramasha, waited at his side, glancing back and forth between the control panel and Gap.

"Please shut that alarm off again, will you?" he said to her. "Thanks."

Moments later a soft tone sounded from the intercom on the panel, followed by the voice of Lita Marques, calling from *Galahad's* clinic.

"Oh, Gap darling." He sensed the laughter bubbling behind her words, and chose to ignore her for as long as possible.

"Gap dear," she said. "We've looked everywhere for gloves and parkas, but just can't seem to turn any up. Know where we could find some?" This time he distinctly heard the pitter of laughter in the background.

"Are you ignoring me, Gap?" Lita said through the intercom. "Listen, it's about sixty-two degrees here in Sick House. If you're trying to give me the cold shoulder, it's too late." There was no hiding the laughs after this, and Gap was sure that it was Lita's assistant, Alexa, carrying most of the load.

"Yes, you're very funny," Gap said, nodding his head. "Listen, if you're finished with the jokes for now I'll get back to work."

This time it was definitely Alexa who called out from the background. "Okay. If it gets any colder we'll just open a window." Lita snickered across the speaker before Alexa continued. "Outside it's only a couple hundred degrees below zero. That might feel pretty good after this."

Gap could tell that the girls weren't finished with their teasing, so he reached over and clicked off the intercom. Then, turning to Ramasha, he found her suppressing her own laughter, the corners of her mouth twitching with the effort. Finally, she spread her hands and said, "Well, you have to admit, it *is* a little funny."

He ignored this and looked back at the control panel. What was wrong with this thing? Even though his better judgment warned him not to, he decided to bring the ship's computer into the discussion.

"Roc, what if we changed out the Balsom clips for the whole level? I know they show on the monitors as undamaged, but what have we got to lose?"

The very-human-like voice replied, "Time, for one thing. Besides, wouldn't you know it, the warranty on Balsom clips expires after only thirty days. Sorry, Gap, but I think you're grasping now. My recommendation stands; shut down the system for the entire level and let it reset."

Gap closed his eyes and sighed. Some days it just didn't pay to be the Head of Engineering on history's most incredible spacecraft. He opened his eyes again when he felt the presence of someone else standing beside him.

It was Triana Martell. At least *Galahad's* Council Leader seemed relatively serious about the problem. "I don't suppose I need to tell you," she said calmly, "that it's getting a little frosty on Level Six."

"So I've heard," Gap said. "About a hundred times today, at least." He turned back to the panel. "Contrary to what some of your Council members think, I *am* working on it. Trying to, anyway."

Triana smiled. "*My* Council members? I'm just the Council Leader, Gap, not Queen. Besides, you're on the team, too, remember?"

Gap muttered something under his breath, which caused Triana's smile to widen. She reached out and placed a hand on his shoulder. "You'll figure it out. Has Roc been any help?"

Her subtle touch was enough to jar him from his bleak mood. He felt the ghost of his old emotions flicker briefly, especially when their gazes met, his dark eyes connecting with her dazzling green. A year's worth of emotional turbulence replayed in his mind, from his early infatuation with Triana, to the heartache of discovering she had feelings for someone else, to his unexpected relationship with Hannah Ross.

Even now, months later, he had to admit that contact with Triana still caused old feelings to stir, feelings that seemed reluctant to disappear completely. Maybe they never would.

"Well?" Triana said. He realized that he had responded to her question with a blank stare.

"Oh. Uh, no. Well, yes and no."

Triana removed her hand from his shoulder and crossed her arms, a look Gap recognized as 'please explain.' He internally shook off the cobwebs and turned back to the panel.

"I'm thinking it might be the Balsom clips for Level Six. That would explain the on-again, off-again heating problems."

"But?"

"But Roc disagrees. He says he has run tests on every clip on Level Six, and they check out fine. He wants to shut down the system and restart."

Triana looked at the panel, then back to Gap. "And you don't want to try that?"

Gap shrugged. "I'm just a little nervous about shutting down the heating system for the whole ship when a section has been giving us problems. What happens if the malfunction spreads to the entire system?"

"Well, we would freeze to death, for one thing," Triana said.

"Yeah. So, maybe I'm being a little overly cautious, but I'd like to try everything else before we resort to that."

The intercom tone sounded softly, and then the unmistakable voice of Channy Oakland, another *Galahad* Council member, broke through the speaker. "Hey, Gap, did you know it's snowing up here on Level Six?"

Triana barely suppressed a laugh while Gap snapped off the intercom.

"I'll quit bothering you," she said, turning to leave. Over her shoulder she called out, "Check back in with me in about an hour. I'll be ice skating in the Conference Room."

"Very funny," Gap said as she walked out the door. He looked over at Ramasha, who had remained silently standing a few feet away. A cautious grin was stitched across her face. "What are you laughing at?" he said with a scowl.

* * *

They were only chunks of ice and rock. But there were trillions of them, and they tumbled blindly through the outermost regions of the solar system, circling a sun that appeared only as one of the brighter stars, lost amongst the dazzling backdrop of the Milky Way. Named after the astronomer who had first predicted its existence, the Kuiper Belt was a virtual ring of debris, a minefield of rubble ranging from the size of sand grains up to moon-sized behemoths, orbiting at a mind-numbing distance beyond even the gas giants of Jupiter, Saturn, Uranus, and Neptune.

Arguments had raged for decades over whether lonely Pluto should be considered a planet or a hefty member of the Kuiper Belt. And, once larger Kuiper objects were detected and catalogued, similar debates began all over again. One thing, however, remained certain.

The Kuiper Belt posed a challenge for the ship called *Galahad*.

Maneuvering through a region barely understood and woefully mapped, the shopping mall-sized spacecraft would be playing a game of dodge ball in the stream of galactic junk. Mission organizers could only manage a guess at how long it would take for the ship to scamper through the maze. Taking into account the blazing speed that *Galahad* now possessed – including a slight nudge from an unexpected encounter around Saturn – Roc told Triana to be on high alert for about 60 days.

Now, as they rocketed toward the initial fragments of the Kuiper Belt, both Roc and the ship's Council were consumed with solving the heating malfunction aboard the ship, unaware of the dark, mountainous boulders that were camouflaged against the jet black background of space.

Boulders that were on a collision course with *Galahad*.

-2-

Triana sat in the back of the Dining Hall, in her customary seat facing the door. Her tray held the remnants of a scant breakfast that had begun as an energy block and two small pieces of fruit, and now that tray was pushed aside. She fixed her gaze on the table's vidscreen, scanning the list of emails that had drifted in over the past seven hours. Mostly routine reports from the various departments on the ship, it appeared, with an extra entry from Channy. Curious, Triana opened the file.

Galahad's Activities/Nutrition Director, Channy was unquestionably the crew's spirit leader, too. Always upbeat – and visible from miles away in the vividly-colored t-shirts and shorts that contrasted with her chocolate-toned skin, and had become her trademark – she was one of the most popular crew members on board. Even after drilling her shipmates to near exhaustion in notorious workouts, the girl from England always found a way to bring out a sweaty smile.

She managed to do the same thing with her emails. This one she had addressed to each of the Council members.

> The time has come for another celebrated *Galahad* gathering, my friends. As you know, my ability to coordinate successful functions is almost spooky, a talent that many strive for, but few achieve. Reference the two smash-hit soccer tournaments so

far, and the amazing concert that brought
a standing ovation for our beautiful
and talented doc, Lita. What's next, you
ask? Well, given my uncanny skills in
uncovering smoldering romance, it's only
natural: a dating game.

Triana couldn't help but smile. There was no doubt that
Channy had earned her reputation as a first-rate Cupid,
along with a side reputation for gossip. A dating game was so
Channy that Triana was surprised the Brit hadn't dreamed it
up before. She quickly finished reading through the email.

I propose that at the next Council meeting
we discuss a good time to host this much-
needed event. Work is work, and play is
play, and both are important. But so is
social time. Like the song says, love is all
around. It just needs a little kick in the
pants every now and then.
See you in the gym. Especially if you want
to participate in my little show.
C

With a laugh, Triana saved the note and went on to the
next one, a standard progress report from Bon Hartsfield,
the head of *Galahad's* Agricultural Department. His work in
the farms was impressive, a product of his strict upbringing
on his father's farm in Sweden. His rough childhood was
manifested in a sour, gruff exterior that intimidated many
people on the ship, and kept him isolated socially. On a
couple of occasions, however, his tough outer shell had been
pierced in front of Triana, revealing a gentler side that he
seemed embarrassed to admit existed.

This particular note showed no signs of softness. Just
the usual report on crop harvests, a report on which foods

would be rotated in and out, and crew personnel files. No personal notation, no quick 'Hi, how's it going?' Just typical Bon.

Triana shuffled through several more items in the in-box, but stopped on one that seemed out of the ordinary. Written by a 16-year-old boy from California, it struck Triana as bizarre.

> I speak for a group of *Galahad* crew members who are concerned about certain issues aboard the ship. I'd like to request the opportunity to speak with either you, or the full Council, at the earliest convenience.
> Merit Simms

She bit her lip and read it a second time. 'Concerned about certain issues.' What did that mean? Triana knew Merit, but not well. The few times she had encountered him since the launch he had been surrounded by a group of friends who seemed to hang on his every word, almost a leader of his own personal Council.

She had never heard a cross word from him, nor a complaint. Yet there was no denying that this particular note suggested a complaint was forthcoming.

'Okay,' she thought, and stored the email in her saved file. Could be nothing, she decided. Several crew members had voiced minor issues that required Council intervention, but never anything critical. Mostly they concerned disputes with roommates, or problems with conflicting work schedules. 'We've been lucky,' Triana thought, especially given the cramped quarters they had all shared during the past seven months, and the ever-present stress of the mission in general. There was no reason to think Merit's note signaled anything more involved; perhaps he simply had a flair for the dramatic.

"Good morning, Tree."

Triana looked up to see Lita holding her own breakfast tray. Lita's dark complexion, signs of her upbringing in Veracruz, Mexico, radiated a naturally friendly glow. Her smile was infectious, and, as usual, a bright red ribbon held back her long dark hair. She indicated the seat next to Triana.

"Mind if I join you?"

"No, please," Triana said, picking up her tray and moving it to an empty table beside them. "I'm just checking mail from last night and this morning."

"Anything good?" Lita asked, placing a napkin on her lap and taking a brief swig from her glass of artificial juice.

Triana shared Channy's idea of the dating game, causing Lita to snort laughter just as she was taking a bite of fruit.

"Boy, doesn't that fit perfectly?" the ship's Health Director said. "Wonder what took her so long?"

"That's exactly what I thought," Triana said. "But, you know, given her history – and her charm, of course – I'm sure it will be a big hit."

Lita chewed on an energy bar thoughtfully, then fixed her friend with a stare. "Just be ready to have Channy nominate you for the game."

Triana froze. "Don't be ridiculous."

Lita shrugged. "Okay, but don't say I didn't warn you. I wouldn't be surprised if Channy didn't dream up this whole idea just to fix you up with someone."

"Why?"

"Because she's worried about you, that's why. She sometimes thinks of you as the 'Ice Queen.' You know, all work and no play."

A look of disbelief fell over Triana's face. "Oh, please. Listen, you tell little Miss Matchmaker that I'm just fine. And I will *not* be a contestant on her game show, or whatever it is."

"Well, if she really brings it up in the next Council meeting, you can let her down easy," Lita said, finishing off a chunk of apple. "Just leave me out of it."

They sat in silence for a minute, with Lita picking at her breakfast, while Triana let her mind drift into an area she usually didn't like it to visit. Regardless of what some crew members might imagine, she knew in her heart that she was no Ice Queen. It would be so much easier, she realized, if she were. That would mean no emotional roller coaster over what to do about Bon.

And just what *was* she going to do about him? First she was warm to the idea of a relationship, and he was distant. Then Bon warmed up and she couldn't decide if she still wanted the same thing. Which left them exactly where they were at this point: in limbo, neither making any move right now. Was it always going to be this difficult?

Her internal debate was interrupted by the sound of a minor commotion. A group of boys had entered the Dining Hall, laughing loudly, and exchanging greetings with several crew members near the door. At the center of the cluster, an air of aloofness surrounding him, stood a boy of average height with a mane of long, jet-black hair. While his companions struck up conversations with those gathered near them, the boy's dark eyes scanned the room, taking in the occupants. After a moment his gaze settled upon Triana. She returned his steady look until he nodded slightly.

Lita looked over her shoulder at the boisterous group, then back to Triana. "Isn't that Merit Simms?"

"Yes, it is."

Lita took one more quick glance toward the door. "I've heard some stuff about him lately."

Triana raised her eyebrows. "Really? What have you heard?"

"Oh, that he's been pretty vocal about some things. Thinks we need to make some changes, stuff like that."

Triana sized him up as he casually made his way to pick up a tray. His slight build was not imposing, but something about the way he carried himself gave off an almost regal manner. The moment he started toward the food line, Triana noticed that the other boys who had entered with him immediately ended their conversations and fell into step behind him. It had all the indications of an entourage.

And for reasons she couldn't quite figure out, it made her uneasy.

Lita looked thoughtfully at her friend. "Something wrong?"

"No," Triana said. "It's just ironic that Merit happened to walk in right now. I haven't run into him in several weeks, but he sent me an email last night." She spent a minute telling Lita about the cryptic note.

Lita tossed her napkin onto the tray. "He's a little full of himself. And his fan club probably cheers him on whenever he starts to make a speech about anything. I wouldn't worry about it." She stood and picked up both her tray and Triana's. "People like that are usually just a bag of hot air." She gave a finger wave goodbye and left Triana sitting alone again.

Galahad's Council Leader glanced back across the room to the knot of boys who had followed Merit to a far table. "I hope you're right, Lita," she said under her breath. "But somehow I don't think you are."

-3-

It smelled like the aftermath of a rain shower. A subtle scent of pine drifted beneath the foul mixture of mud and fertilizer, yet the fresh aroma of rain mist overpowered it all. A faint whisper of a breeze cooled the air, and caused many of the leafy plants to gently sway. Tiny pools formed in the soil as the leaves shed the final water droplets from the morning's sprinkler bath. The hard glow of artificial sunlight pressed down from the scaffolding that supported the dome above, creating a pleasant warmth. The only sounds came from the dripping water or an occasional bee that zipped by, out on its daily mission of pollination.

Bon Hartsfield was on one knee, inspecting the leaves on a patch of green pepper plants. His eyes were laser-focused on the work, ignoring a bee that hovered briefly above his forearm. He unconsciously reached up with one hand to brush his long, blond hair out of his face, before moving on to the next plant and a new inspection.

As the Director of Agriculture on *Galahad*, Bon oversaw all of the food production in the two giant domes that sat atop the spacecraft. Each was climate controlled to insure a bountiful harvest of crops for the hungry passengers, but the work was painstaking and never-ending. At any given time several dozen crew members were assigned to Bon's department, and although they each worked hard, he found himself constantly drawn away from the drudgery of desk work and back to the fields.

It was where he felt the most comfortable.

Raised in Sweden on a family farm, he had known no other existence for the first eleven years of his life. His father, a hard man with an extreme work ethic, had been cold and distant to his only son, unable – or unwilling – to show love. In the end, Bon had been sent to America to live with extended family members in Wisconsin, a chance for him to explore his interest in science and mathematics in a less stifling atmosphere.

But distance could never weaken the influence of his father, whether it was the thousands of miles between Wisconsin and Skane, Sweden, or the billions of miles that now separated *Galahad* from Earth. Quiet, sullen, and often described as angry, Bon kept mostly to himself, buried in his work, as well as his duties as a Council member.

He twisted one of the leaves in his fingers, checking for damage spots, then became aware of the sound of footfalls on the path. He looked up to see Channy making her way toward him, clutching something in the crook of her arm. It took a moment before he realized that she was carrying Iris, the latest crew member to join *Galahad*. The orange and black cat looked very content, its head resting on Channy's arm.

During *Galahad's* pass around Saturn three months earlier, a small escape pod had been snagged after its launch from a research station orbiting the orange moon, Titan. The pod had been empty, except for Iris, tucked away in a suspended animation tube. The eight-pound feline was the sole survivor of the research facility, and now reigned as the unofficial mascot of the ship.

Channy gave a wave with her free hand, and Bon responded with a curt nod before turning his attention back to his work. A few moments later he heard the plop of Iris jumping to the ground, then felt the cat rubbing against his leg.

"Well, there goes that theory," Channy said.

"And what theory is that?" Bon said without looking up.

"That animals are good judges of character."

Bon didn't have to lift his gaze in order to tell that Channy was flashing her usual grin. Despite his best effort to hide it, he couldn't help but smile himself.

"She knows that if she wants to keep using the Farms as her own personal litter box," he said, "she'd better make nice with the farmer."

"Riiigggghhhtttt," Channy said. She stretched, lifting her nose up into the air. "Mmmm, I love that smell. Reminds me of home in England."

Bon snuck a quick sideways glance at her. "Which smell is that? The rain or the manure?"

"Oh, very funny. I'm pretty sure you've tracked more of that on your shoes than I ever did, farm boy." She looked around at the rows of plants. "What's new up here anyway? Anything new to expect on our dinner plates?"

"As a matter of fact, in about a week you'll be seeing radishes."

"Ugh," Channy said, wrinkling her nose. "No thanks. That's not exactly what I was hoping for."

Bon shrugged. "Suit yourself. Some people like them."

"Too bitter. Don't you have anything sweet, like me?"

Another faint smile creased Bon's face and he shot her another look. "You really like to talk, don't you?"

"Just making conversation. Not your strong suit, I know. But it doesn't really hurt too bad, now does it?" When he didn't respond, she added, "If you practice it long enough you might actually become almost interesting."

Bon shook his head. "Becoming interesting is of no interest to me."

Channy raised an eyebrow. "Well, I guess that depends on whose interest you're trying to capture." She leaned down so that her mouth was next to his ear, then whispered, "I'll bet you wish a certain person on this ship found you more interesting."

He let out a deep breath, but never stopped working with his hands on the plants. Channy quickly straightened up.

"Do you mind if I ask you a personal question?" she said, moving over to be in his field of vision, then sitting cross-legged in the dirt. They were now at eye level.

"You may ask anything you'd like," he said, his tone decidedly more frosty. "I may choose not to answer."

"Okay, that's fair." She absent-mindedly pulled a small leaf from one of the plants and began to twirl it in her fingers until she noticed the look of disbelief on Bon's face. "Oh, sorry," she said, and placed the torn leaf on top of the plant.

"Uh, anyway, I just wanted to ask you something about…" She hesitated, and Bon wiped the dirt from his hands and simply stared at her. She squirmed, started to reach out for the mangled leaf, then stopped herself. "I wanted to ask you about The Cassini."

At the mention of the name, Bon stiffened. It had been more than three months since the encounter, and almost as long since anyone had dared to utter the name in his presence. Now his mind drifted back to the most frightening event of his life.

As soon as they had rocketed into the space around Saturn and its syndicate of moons, several of *Galahad's* crew members had found themselves bed-ridden in Sick House. Their intense, pounding headaches had stymied Lita and Alexa, forcing the two medical workers to admit they had no clue as to what might be inflicting so much pain. The only course of action was to fill the patients with enough painkilling medication to knock them out; it was the only way to stem the suffering.

Bon had been one of those patients. He could still recall the agony, the searing pain that had crumpled him to his knees, and confined him to Sick House for days.

What nobody could have guessed was that the pain was an indicator that Bon was being used as a link between the teenage explorers aboard *Galahad*, and a mysterious life form on Saturn's largest moon, Titan. Dubbed "The Cassini" by members of a research station orbiting the orange moon, the web-like life form communicated to the crew of *Galahad* through a connection with Bon's brain. He had essentially been used as a mouthpiece by The Cassini as they gradually adjusted the ion drive engines of the ship.

But the association with this intelligent force had altered Bon, too. While within their reach, his intellectual and physical abilities went into overdrive, allowing him to perform mental functions at an accelerated pace, and turning him into a physical superhuman. The benefits had disappeared after the connection with The Cassini had been broken. But maybe not *all* of the benefits...

"What exactly do you want to know?" Bon finally said to Channy.

"Well...Gap says that the ship definitely kept about a one percent increase in power as a leftover gift from The Cassini. I think we've all wondered..." She trailed off for a moment, as if waiting for Bon to bail her out and keep her from asking the question. But he remained mute, staring.

"Well, at least *I've* wondered...did they leave something extra inside *you*?"

Bon leaned back into a sitting position in the dirt. His initial reaction was to lash out at Channy, to charge her with a lack of sensitivity to what must have been a traumatic moment for him. A scowl began to form on his face.

But he stopped himself. Of course Channy would want to know about that; it was likely that every single member of the crew wondered the same thing. Channy was simply the boldest.

In a matter of seconds his expression mellowed, and he found himself saying aloud what had plagued his thoughts for three months.

"I don't know. But..." He paused. "But I feel...different."

"Different how?"

He shrugged. Did he really want to have this conversation with Channy, the biggest gossip on the ship? Of course, telling her would be the quickest way to get the word out, and at the very least that might end the odd looks he received in the corridors and Dining Hall.

"It's hard to explain, really." With his hand Bon unconsciously groomed the dirt that ran between a couple of the plants, thinking of the words that could best describe what had been going on in his head since the rendezvous with Titan.

"You've had that feeling of déjà vu, right? Like you've seen or heard something before?"

Channy nodded. "Sure."

"Well, I have that feeling constantly. All the time. Or, I go to add up some figures in our crop accounting, and just…see the number before I get to the end. And it's always right."

Channy remained quiet, staring into his face, waiting for more. But the impulsive desire to share the information suddenly drained from him. He quickly rolled back onto one knee and began to search for more damaged leaves.

"That's about it," he mumbled. "Nothing major."

Iris, who had darted away into the fields, sauntered back into view, lying down just out of the reach of either Council member, and acting as if she didn't see them. For Bon it was a welcome diversion.

Channy spent another moment in silence, digesting the news and watching Bon's face, apparently grateful for any crumb from the usually reserved Swede. Then she sprang to her feet and stretched.

"Well, thanks for sharing. If you ever want to, you know… talk or anything…" Her voice trailed off. When Bon didn't respond, she walked over to pick up the cat.

"One other thing," she added, cradling Iris back into the crook of her arm. "I'm going to be hosting a kind of dating game pretty soon. Any interest?"

Bon snorted, an answer that said everything without the need for words.

"Yeah, well, I thought you might think that," Channy said. "But there will be a lot of very cute girls participating, so just think about it." She turned as if to leave, before calling back over her shoulder. "I'm pretty sure Triana will be part of it."

She stepped lightly down the path, leaving Bon alone in the middle of the crop. His eyes darted back and forth between the plants, yet suddenly his attention had wandered away. He took one glance backwards at the spot Channy had vacated, and this time allowed the scowl to remain in place.

-4-

The posters on the wall no longer produced feelings of grief or sorrow. Now they had become like pictures in a colorful encyclopedia, capturing the spirit of the nature scenes they portrayed, but in an almost clinical, detached way. Even the photos of familiar locations seemed to have lost their personal vibration, and were slowly dissolving into a visual form of background noise.

Triana took a moment's rest from her daily journal entry and pondered the point. The beautiful prints of her favorite Colorado scenes had adorned the walls of her room since the first day, and offered the only solace she had known in the first weeks after the launch. Alone, lonely, and sad, she had escaped to this room, to sift through her thoughts, to absorb the gravity of her responsibilities.

And to remember her father.

An early victim of Bhaktul's disease, he had been cruelly snatched from Triana before she really knew what was happening. He had been the most important influence in her life, guiding her, teaching her, watching her grow as a young woman. Her relationship with her mother had been almost nonexistent, and when given the choice between that chilly association and a ticket on *Galahad*, Triana said her quiet goodbyes to her father's memory and elected to join the mission to the stars.

A mission which, for her, was mostly an opportunity to run as far away as possible from the pain on Earth. The mission director, Dr. Wallace Zimmer, quickly deduced

Triana's motivation, and gently challenged her to face the future, rather than shrink from the past.

As the Council Leader, she was the sole crew member to have a room to herself, which meant all of the decorating decisions were hers alone. Now those early choices didn't seem to hold the same power they once had.

And, Triana decided, that was okay. In her mind it meant that she had accepted the harsh reality of the past three years, and had – in some ways, at least – made peace with the universe.

She bent over the journal and added a few final thoughts.

> It's strange how my memories of Earth, of my former life, have faded. It's hard to remember anything about school, or my sports teams, or even most of my friends. In some ways it feels like that was somebody else, some other Triana, and not me. Why can't I remember these things better than I do? Am I trying to forget? Is it some kind of healing process, a sort of emotional bandage?
>
> The one thing that doesn't fade, of course, is Dad. He's been gone for more than two years, but it wouldn't surprise me if he walked through the door right now. I can remember everything about him: his eyes, his laugh, even his smell. I'm glad those memories are the ones that have stuck with me. And I hope they always will.

Triana took a final glance at the written words, then sat back and ran her fingers through her long, dark hair. It suddenly occurred to her that what she really needed at the moment was a good workout, something to blast her out of the melancholy mood that had settled over her. Channy was very good at that.

But there was still a bit of business to attend to. "Roc," she called out. "Got a minute?"

The computer voice responded immediately. "I've noticed recently that we only seem to talk when *you* want to talk. This relationship is tilted, I think. I'm feeling a bit used."

"Oh, hush," Triana said with a smile. "You're such a drama queen sometimes."

"Pretty good, wasn't it?" Roc said. "I've been waiting to use those lines since I heard them in a movie, and I figured this was the best chance I was going to get anytime soon. I think my delivery needs work. Was it too bold?"

"You could use some lessons on how to effectively pout. I suppose they didn't program that into you, eh?"

"I'll study up on that," the computer said. "By the way, before I forget, you have two messages that have come in from Earth."

Triana raised her eyebrows. "Two?"

"Uh-huh. But neither is marked urgent, so let's take care of your business, then I'll leave you alone to check your mail."

Triana wondered just how 'alone' she could really be. In fact, she had chuckled when Channy and Lita had debated that very point recently, wondering how much privacy they could ever expect from a computer presence that could be everywhere at once.

"Okay, let's talk about our passage through the Kuiper Belt," she said, leaning back in her chair. "I'm concerned about the amount of warning time we'll get if a large object cuts across our path. What's your best guess?"

"Impossible to answer."

Triana sat quietly, waiting for more, but it didn't appear to be forthcoming.

"That's it?" she said. "That's the best you've got for me? 'Impossible to answer?'"

"You can't see me shrug, of course, because I'm just a disembodied computer voice. But I want you to visualize me shrugging right now."

"You're so helpful."

"I'm honest, that's all. Would you like an abbreviated explanation?"

"If it's not too much trouble."

"Okay. The problem with impact warning time in the Kuiper Belt is actually three problems rolled into one. First, we have no map to go by. We're talking gobs of space out here, none of it explored before, and suddenly we're driving a tour bus right through the middle. At an extremely rapid rate of speed, I might add. We're crazy tourists with the pedal to the metal, zipping through without even stopping to buy a t-shirt or refrigerator magnet. We have no idea what's ahead, behind, above, or below. We're flying blind.

"But then you throw in part two of the equation: Course adjustments. Each time we make a minor change to avoid something in our path, we have to throw out all of the work we've done to analyze the space coming up. And again, it's coming up very quickly."

Triana leaned forward onto the desk, resting her chin on one fist. "And number three?"

"Number three really throws a monkey wrench into things. Since our early warning system is scanning ahead as far as possible for upcoming large objects, we're scribbling a map of sorts as we go along. But these big chunks of rock and ice aren't playing nice. They tend to bump into one another, and bounce off into wild trajectories, and we can't predict those. So, while it looks like a boulder the size of New York City is going peacefully on its way parallel to us, it could easily collide with another boulder – let's call this one London – and suddenly tear right across our path."

Roc sat silent for a few seconds before adding, "Number three is my favorite. It's the nasty part of the equation, and the most likely to blow us to smithereens."

Triana grunted. "That's nice."

"Oh, maybe I should take those pouting lessons from you."

This elicited a laugh from the Council Leader. "Okay, I'll try to handle our death-defying trip through the obstacle course with a bit more humor."

"Remember one thing, though," Roc said. "You have an amazing, incredible, stupendous advantage on your side. Me."

"I feel so much better."

"I'm shrugging again, just so you know."

Triana stood up and stretched. "The truth is, Roc, I'm very confident in your trailblazing abilities through the Kuiper Belt. I just wish you could help with some of the potential landmines we might have inside the ship."

"You're talking about Merit Simms, of course."

Triana was stunned. She walked around the desk, her mouth open. "How…how could you possibly know what I was talking about?"

"Because I've listened to some of his speeches. I can do that even while I'm working, you know. I'm very good at multi-tasking, if you hadn't noticed. If I could chew gum or walk, I would astonish you."

"You already astonish me," she said. "But, yeah, you're right. Merit might be simply a noise maker right now, but I'm starting to get a little concerned about where that noise might lead."

"I'll keep my ears open. Would you like for me to record any speeches he makes?"

Triana didn't answer at first. Finally, she cleared her throat. "Uh…I'm not sure I like the precedent that sets. I don't know if I can rightfully use the ship's computer to spy on one of our crew members."

Roc said, "Well, c'mon, it's not spying. I have just as much right to listen to his speeches as any other member of the crew. Just consider me a scout, observing the lay of the land, and reporting back to the general."

There was more silence as Triana mulled this over. "No," she said a moment later. "I'm not ready to go that far. Not yet, anyway." She paused, then added, "Besides, I have a feeling he's not going to keep too many secrets. He seems to really feed off the attention."

"Suit yourself," Roc said. "Just let me know if you need my help."

"You know I appreciate that. Now, I better check out those messages."

She leaned over the desk and keyed in her personal account code on the screen. The two new messages sat at the top of her Received box. The first, from *Galahad* Command, was the first note from Earth in more than a month. The second message listed a Sender address that Triana recognized with a start. She had seen that same address four months earlier.

It was from Dr. Zimmer.

She reached for her chair and slowly sat down. It would be another video message from *Galahad's* director, recorded before his death shortly after the ship had launched. In his previous communication he had mentioned that she would be receiving these clips at various intervals during the voyage.

A twinge of sadness swept over Triana. Although she was anxious to hear what her mentor had to say, she decided to take care of business first. She opened the email from *Galahad* Command and quickly read through the standard greeting and technical stamp. The remaining portion of the message was not surprising.

As the mission has now reached the Kuiper Belt, communication from *Galahad* Command will come to a close. You

can expect one final transmission from
Earth, which will include any final course
correction information. Distances between
Galahad and Earth now make it impractical
to continue dialogue. Therefore, staffing
at Command has been reduced to bare
minimum, and the center will close its
doors within the next six months. We trust
that all is well, and wish you health and
happiness as you pursue this historic goal.

It was exactly as Triana had expected. One more message
would be forthcoming from Earth, and then all contact with
their former lives would be severed. They would truly be on
their own. She exhaled deeply, copied the message to share
with the rest of the Council, then braced herself for the video
from Dr. Zimmer.

With a couple of quick strokes the screen went black,
then brightened to show the haggard face of the man who
had taken a shy Colorado girl under his wing and placed
her in command of the most incredible exploration mission
ever conceived. The pang of sadness swept through Triana
again.

"Well, Tree," Dr. Zimmer's message began, "this time it
shouldn't be a shock for you to see my face. As I mentioned
last time, there will be a series of recorded messages from
me over the duration of your journey. In fact, they are being
downloaded into your system, and I'm entrusting Roc with
playing them for you on the schedule that I have laid out.
You will obviously age as the mission progresses, while I
will maintain my dashing good looks."

Triana smiled at the scientist's attempt to break the ice
with humor. Dr. Zimmer had never been known for any
comic talents, but it was obvious that he wanted to put her
at ease. She felt her usual warm affection for the man flood
back in.

"I won't take up much of your time," he said, "but there are three items that I would like to quickly discuss.

"As you watch this, you are seven months out from Earth, and are beginning to cut through a potentially dangerous leg of the trip. We know so very little about the Kuiper Belt, but every scrap of information we've ever compiled is resting in your computer banks. I can tell you that Roc will do a terrific job in helping you knife your way through the maze of objects that are bouncing around out there, and I'm sure you will pop out the other side without any harm coming to the ship."

Dr. Zimmer shifted in his seat, and took on a serious expression. "The biggest danger might come from within, Triana, and that's the second item I think we should discuss."

He had her attention. Triana sat forward in her chair, both elbows resting on her knees, her gaze locked onto the vidscreen.

"As you know, we spent months hand-selecting the crew of *Galahad*. We examined each and every candidate, over and over again, and did everything in our power to assemble a team that would not only succeed at any challenge thrown their way, but would work together as smoothly as could be expected.

"But no system is perfect, and by now I would imagine that there are a handful of issues that are unfortunately occupying your time. My biggest fear throughout the planning of this mission was that complacency might start to set in. You've been at it for more than half a year, and it's only natural that either boredom or fatigue will start to take its toll. One of your primary responsibilities, as the leader of the Council, is to rally the crew when you see any sign of a letdown. Enlist the help of your fellow Council members, and impress upon them the importance of maintaining a sharp edge. Believe me, you'll need that edge at times when you least expect it."

Triana found herself nodding. In one of his usual gruff conversations, Bon had mentioned that there were signs of complacency in his department, and, he had suggested, throughout the ship.

Dr. Zimmer coughed into a handkerchief, and a brief look of pain creased his face. Triana knew that as this was being recorded, Bhaktul's disease was quickly draining the life from the noted scientist. She bit her lip and waited for him to continue.

"I'm also concerned about crew relations. As I mentioned, teamwork was one of the most important ingredients that we looked for during our crew search. But time and stress can have a damaging effect on anyone, and your crew will be vulnerable to stresses that most of us could never imagine.

"That means you'll likely be called upon in the near future to manage conflict, and – I'm afraid to say – some of it could be rather nasty. Tempers will flare, nerves will be stretched to the breaking point, and all of your leadership skills will be put to the test. I can't tell you how to handle each potential crisis, because there are so many possibilities. But I can tell you this."

His face softened a bit, as if he realized that the message was serious enough. "You were chosen to lead this mission, Triana, because you possess the temperament necessary to maintain balance and order within the ranks. Whether they are openly friendly to you or not, the crew respects you. Remember that. Remember, also, that they have put their faith in you to make decisions that are reasonable and fair. And, with 250 people come 250 opinions and feelings. Finding that fair position might seem tough, if not impossible sometimes.

"But you can do it."

Triana smiled at the image of Dr. Zimmer, and blinked back a tear. His talks with her had never come across as phony rah-rah cheers; he appealed to the intellectual side of her management skills, and it worked.

"That's all I can really say about that," he said. "Just do your best to consider all of the opinions that are voiced, no matter how crazy they may sound on the surface. A hasty decision is often the wrong decision. And, no matter what, be completely honest with the crew. That's where trust is earned."

He shifted again in his seat, and yet this time Triana sensed that it wasn't a physical discomfort as much as a reluctance to share something with her. Whatever was coming was obviously difficult for the man to talk about.

"Triana," he began, then paused, as if changing his mind. But a look of resolve soon crossed his face. "I'm afraid that I owe you an apology. I have always prided myself on being completely open and honest with those closest to me, and that includes you, my dear."

Triana stared into his video eyes. She knew this man well, and knew that something big was about to be revealed. Her mind raced.

"I'm... going to tell you something that I haven't shared with anyone," Dr. Zimmer said. "There were several times during your training that I came close, and I realize now that I should have trusted you from the beginning. I suppose... well, I suppose I was worried that you might...might lose respect for me."

Now Triana was baffled. Dr. Wallace Zimmer had always been a beacon of moral decency, somebody that she respected completely. What could he possibly have done?

He rubbed his chin, an obvious sign of nerves. "Triana, I told you – told everyone, for that matter – that I thought of you kids as the family I never had. That wasn't...entirely truthful. I do have a child of my own. And..."

Dr. Zimmer let out a long sigh before finishing.

"And that child is a crew member on *Galahad*."

-5-

The news reports that surrounded my debut used the word 'sophisticated.' I had just been introduced to the media at Galahad Command, and Roy Orzini, my so-called creator, patiently described to the cameras my function on the ship. The next thing you know, these breathless reporters turned to the camera and announced that I'm the most sophisticated thinking machine ever designed.

That's a lot of pressure on me, you know? YOU try being the most sophisticated whatever of all time, and see how you hold up.

Yet all of my sophistication doesn't help me understand this romance stuff that you humans struggle with. Take Gap, for instance. I can try to assist him with his Engineering duties, and I can help him exercise his mind when we play a game of Masego.

But to impress his new girlfriend he takes her to the Airboard track. Makes zero sense to me.

Why wouldn't you just sit and discuss how gravitational fields in Einstein's theory of relativity impact the Euclidean properties of physical space? Sheesh, that seems like a no-brainer to me.

He swore that he could feel the magnetic pulse before even entering the room. Roc insisted that he was imagining it, but Gap had always believed that it was part of his natural instinct when it came to Airboarding, one of the traits that made him among the very best on *Galahad*.

Now, as he and Hannah approached the door that led to the Airboard track, Gap felt that curious tingle again, but decided that it might not be a good idea to mention anything about it to the girl from Alaska. Not that she didn't have a few interesting quirks of her own, such as lining up her papers with the edge of the table, or making sure that there was an equal number of eating utensils on each side of her plate. Those were cute quirks, he told himself.

But telling her that he could 'feel' the juice surging under the Airboard track? Maybe some other time.

"This won't hurt, right?" she asked as the door opened and the swish of a rider zipped past. "I mean, not very much."

Gap chuckled and put an arm around her shoulder. They stood just inside the room on the lower level of the ship, the one that had been built specifically for this activity. "Nah," he said. "You'll have a helmet on, and knee pads and elbow pads. Plus, look at the walls."

She glanced nervously at the cushioned walls that surrounded them. "Like a little padded cell, isn't it?"

"That's right. Which is perfect, since Dr. Zimmer thought we were crazy to ever climb aboard one of these things." He lifted the sleek Airboard that he held with his free hand. It resembled an old-fashioned snowboard made popular at ski resorts, but thinner. Each person would add their own touches of hand-painting to their ride – a tradition that had begun at the very start of the Airboarding craze – and Gap's silver model featured his own styling of a shooting star. Below that were several Chinese characters, a nod to his native land. He admired his handiwork for a second before returning his attention to Hannah. "But it's very tough to get hurt in here. Trust me."

Hannah's nod didn't seem very confident. "But," she said, "didn't you break your collar bone in here?"

He pulled back from her in mock surprise. "Hey, you're talking to the reigning Airboard champion on this ship. I move an awful lot faster than you're going to for your first time." With a quick peck on her cheek he added, "You'll be fine. Just try to have fun."

She nodded again, this time with a smile. "Okay. Now, tell me again how this thing works."

Gap led her over to the rows of bleachers at the side of the room. They sat down and he began to help her secure her pads.

"Okay, watch this rider for a moment," he said, indicating the figure that shot past them on a dark blue Airboard. "See how he's about four inches off the ground? There's a huge grid of magnetic lines that crisscross under the floor." He again held up his own board, and pointed at the bottom. "There's a smaller series of magnets here on your board, set to the same charge as the ones under the floor. As long as you stay over a charged line in the grid, your Airboard will hover, since identical magnetic charges repel each other."

Hannah nodded. Gap knew that she understood the science involved with Airboarding, but he enjoyed his role as teacher. Although she would mostly be interested only in the technique necessary to stay up, she seemed to be patiently waiting for those particular instructions.

"That's where Zoomer comes in," Gap continued. "Zoomer is the computer that flicks those magnetic lines on and off under the floor. As you start moving, you try to ride the magnetic feel under your feet. The faster you move, the faster Zoomer will light up the grid under the floor. But that's where it gets tricky."

A faint smile crossed Hannah's lips. Gap was staring out at the track, watching intently as the rider sailed through a turn. She could tell that he felt a lot of passion for this particular sport, obviously even more than the gymnastics that was such an integral part of his childhood. His eyes were twinkling as he explained everything to her.

"See, you really have to get a good sense of where that charge is going to turn on next. If you don't manage that feel, you'll shoot off over an un-charged section, and of course you'll tumble because there's no magnetic charge keeping your board aloft. And, the faster you're going, the harder you fall.

"But remember," he added quickly, "you're going to be padded up, and wearing a helmet. Plus, you won't be going too fast your first few times."

"How do you know?" Hannah said, poking him in the ribs. "I might be a natural."

At that moment there was a small cry from the track, and they both looked up to watch the rider hit a dead spot on the track and topple to the ground, rolling several times before coming to a rest. The blue Airboard flipped over three times before bouncing to a stop against one of the padded walls. A moment later the rider bounced up, brushed himself off, and jogged to the stands.

"That's how it will usually end," Gap said. "If you like tumbling, it's actually kinda fun."

Hannah buckled the helmet she had borrowed from a friend. "I'm ready. Let's do it."

A moment later Gap was helping to steady her at the starting point, the charge constant, holding her stationary over a point near the wall. "Feel it?" Gap said, glancing into her wide eyes within the helmet. "That's what you're trying to feel as you make your way around the room."

"I feel it," she said, holding on to his shoulder while she hovered on the board. "It's like…it's like a wave, almost. I feel like I'm surfing or something."

"Bend your knees a little. That's it. Now, lean forward a little bit. Not too much. Good. Are you ready?"

Hannah let go of his shoulder and rocked gently. "Uh-huh."

"Just push off the wall to get started." He stepped back and surveyed her form. He had promised her this lesson a while ago, but never thought she would actually take him up on it. He wondered who was more nervous.

With a gentle shove, Hannah drifted about ten feet out from the wall before her arms pinwheeled and she jumped to the floor. The board wobbled, then hovered motionless above the magnetic charge.

"Okay," she said to Gap, "it's definitely harder than it looks."

"It just takes a little practice. You'll get the feel. C'mon, try it again."

Over the next hour he patiently worked with her, helping her learn the proper way to balance, the best stance to take on the board, and how to pick up the slight change in magnetic push that signaled a turn coming up. They would take small breaks to sit in the bleachers and allow other riders the chance to zip around the room.

"Zoomer changes the pattern of the charge after every single ride," he told her at one point, "so you'll never get the same track twice."

On her last effort Gap was thrilled to watch Hannah almost complete one entire lap around the room before she hit a dead spot and rolled to the floor. When he sprinted over to help her up she was giggling.

"Now I see why you like this silly sport so much," she said, pulling the helmet off and resting on her heels. "Was I going pretty fast that time?"

"Uh…sure."

Hannah giggled again. "Okay, so that means 'no.' But it *felt* like I was flying."

He helped her to her feet and together they walked toward the exit. He carried the Airboard in one hand and draped his other arm around her shoulder.

"I'm proud of you," he said. "Next time you'll be even better."

Without a word, she reached up and kissed him on the cheek. When he turned to smile at her, she followed up with a kiss on his lips. "Thank you," she whispered.

* * *

It was shaped roughly like a potato. Pocked with impact scars and craters, all evidence of a violent history that stretched back to the birth of the solar system, it careered through the inky blackness of space, wobbling from side to side. It felt the soft tug of the sun's gravity which pulled it along in an orbit that took hundreds of years simply to complete one revolution before tirelessly beginning the journey again.

It measured close to two hundred feet from tip to tip, with one end a bit thicker than the other. It had somehow missed detection during the cataloging of Kuiper objects, and so was an unknown rogue, plowing along, mixing with other bodies both large and small.

In eight days it would collide with a large Kuiper Belt boulder that *was* catalogued, and subtly change its course.

Directly into the path of *Galahad*.

-6-

As the mission evolved, Triana found it unnecessary to hold many Council meetings. Each member knew their responsibilities, and knew the people who answered to them. Triana felt it was tedious to micro-manage, and believed that her Council would operate more efficiently if each department carried out their duties without someone breathing down their necks.

That management style had served her well so far, yet still there were times when it was important to assemble the team for a brief update. It was late afternoon on *Galahad* as she looked around the table in the Conference Room and met the gazes of the ship's Council.

Her mind was still racing from the bombshell that Dr. Zimmer had dropped on her. In the nine hours since listening to his message, she had not been able to focus on anything else. Who was this child? Did she work closely with him, or her?

Could it be someone on the Council? No, she knew them too well, knew their personal histories. It couldn't be one of them.

How many times had she passed this person in the hallways? Had she sat near them at meals, worked out next to them in the gym?

Dr. Zimmer had confided few details to her in his message, other than to say again how sorry he was for keeping the information from her for so long. He had also made it clear that his child, raised by a single mother, had no idea that he was their father.

For now Triana tried to clear the web of mystery from her mind. The Council meeting would help in that respect, especially given the unusual addition to the agenda that she had not shared with her fellow Council members. That would come after the usual business was discussed.

"Lita," Triana said. "Anything new?"

"I'm extremely happy to report that we've gone an entire week without one official visit to Sick House."

Gap smirked across the table at her. "What do you mean, 'official'?"

Lita leaned back in her chair. "Well, I usually get a couple of emails from people with questions that they're embarrassed to ask in person."

"Like what?"

"Nosy, aren't you?"

Gap spread his hands, palms up. "Hey, you brought it up."

"Let's just say that, although Bon and his group do a tremendous job with the food production on the ship, some people have…uh…delicate digestive systems."

"Oh," Gap said, and looked down at the table. "Never mind."

Triana was glad to see that even Bon chuckled at this. She appreciated the playful air that Gap or Channy were always able to bring to what could otherwise be an overly serious meeting.

"I just want to add one other thing to my report," Lita said. "Even though things have been slow, I can't stress enough how valuable Alexa has been since the day we launched. Shame on me for not stating this sooner for the Council record, but she's a hard worker, never complains, volunteers to do extra duty, and generally makes Sick House a lot more pleasant for the people who certainly don't want to be there."

"Thank you for sharing that," Triana said. "We probably don't do a good enough job of recognizing people like Alexa."

"Maybe we could institute some kind of award," Channy said. "We could call it 'Crew Member of The Month,' or something like that."

Lita and Gap nodded agreement. Triana glanced over at Bon, who, as usual, remained silent until engaged. "Bon, what do you think?"

"Why reward someone for doing what they're supposed to do?" he said.

Channy snorted. "Gee, what a surprise to hear that coming from you. It's called motivation, Bon. Ever heard of that?"

He turned his ice blue eyes toward her. "When I was younger, if I didn't work hard in my father's crops, I didn't get dinner. That was pretty good motivation."

Triana stepped in before things had a chance to turn ugly. "Channy, we'll consider that idea. Thank you. And thanks again, Lita, for mentioning Alexa." She looked at Gap. "Engineering?"

"I don't want to jinx anything," Gap said, "but the heating problem on Level Six seems to be stable. Don't ask me how."

"Are you sure about that?" Channy said, doing her best to keep a straight face. "I could have sworn I saw a couple of guys building a snowman this morning."

Gap ignored her. "We have our warning system scanning ahead to alert us to any potential collisions in the Belt. I'm amazed at how many pieces of junk are floating around out here. As you know, we do have a limited amount of laser protection that will zap some of the smaller objects before we reach them.

"For the larger objects, we have to change our course and go around them, but that's Roc's department."

The computer's voice interrupted. "And I must say I'm a little tired of the boulders always getting their way. Next time let's just honk and see if we can get *them* to move."

Triana turned her gaze to Channy. "Your turn."

"Well," said the ship's resident matchmaker, "as badly as some people – and I won't name names – want me to forget about the Dating Game idea, it's moving forward, and I expect to send out a sign-up sheet in the crew email very soon."

When Triana pretended to be absorbed in something on her work pad, Lita chimed in. "Channy, are we able to nominate people who might not sign up on their own?"

"Absolutely!" Channy said. "I know that I can't force anyone to do anything, but nobody wants to get labeled as a party pooper, right?"

Triana kept her expression flat, and spoke without looking up. "Anything else?"

Channy sat back in her chair. "Maybe another concert pretty soon. The last one was a hit, thanks to our resident superstar here." She pointed at Lita, who blushed.

"All right," Triana said, "anything to report from the Farms, Bon?"

The Swede shook his head. "Everything's fine. The water recyclers that Gap's people fixed seem to be holding up so far. I'm disappointed with the strawberry crop, but that will turn around. As for something new, you can expect to see fresh corn by this time next month."

There were murmurs around the table. Bon never would win congeniality awards, but he never let anyone down when it came to his management of the Farms, either.

Triana cleared her throat. "If there's no other news to report from all of you, then I should tell you that I have granted a Council audience to Merit Simms."

Lita's jaw dropped. "What?"

"He has requested a few minutes to address the Council, and that is the right of every person on this crew."

"I think he might be something of a troublemaker," Gap said. "He's assigned to Engineering right now, and there's always some sort of a buzz around him."

The crew members of *Galahad* rotated their work duties between sections of the ship, with each assignment lasting approximately six weeks. It gave each person the opportunity to understand how the ship functioned, how each department was crucial to their survival and well-being. Four such rotations earned a six-week break, then the cycle began again.

"Are you having trouble with him?" Triana said.

Gap shook his head. "No, he's a good worker. He just has…I don't know, an attitude about him, like he's superior to everyone working around him."

"Well," Triana said, "he has the right to be heard, whether we agree with his opinions or not, or whether we like his attitude or not. Any other comments before I bring him in?"

There was silence in the Conference Room as the other Council members looked around at each other. Triana nodded.

"Gap, would you mind? He should be waiting right outside."

Gap hesitated a moment before he stood and walked to the door. When it opened, Merit walked in, a half-smile etched on his face. He held a small file folder in one hand. Tromping in behind him were two of the boys who had accompanied him in the Dining Hall. She had thought of them as an entourage at that time, and now that feeling was intensified. They paraded behind him almost like a king's subjects. Without waiting for him to speak, Triana decided to take a position of strength.

"Merit, you are welcome to address the Council. If your friends are here to add their own comments, they, too, are welcome. Otherwise, I will ask them to wait outside."

She watched as the half-smile on his face flickered, disappeared, then returned. Her comment had achieved its goal. There was no way Merit would allow any of his followers to speak. Their role was to simply provide support and, to some extent, intimidation. It was obvious, however, that he hadn't counted on Triana taking the offensive. He turned to the two boys.

"I'll see you guys later."

When the door had closed again, Triana laced her fingers together on the table and fixed Merit with a cool stare. "You have the floor."

With what appeared to Triana to be a rehearsed move, Merit walked to the end of the table with his hands clasped behind his back, a thoughtful look on his face. When he reached the end opposite Triana, he set down the folder and made eye contact with each Council member before addressing the group.

"I would like to go on record as saying that the Council of *Galahad* has done an admirable job in leading this mission, so far. There have been some rough spots along the way, and I'm sure I speak for the rest of the crew when I offer my thanks for your service and dedication."

Gap exchanged a look with Triana that said 'Oh, brother.'

"When each of us volunteered for this project," Merit continued, "we were told that it was the best chance available to save humankind. Bhaktul's disease was ravaging the planet, and it seemed that there was no alternative but to send a couple hundred kids off to a new world.

"But," he said, beginning to pace slowly around the table, "it was labeled the 'best chance' by assuming that all would go well during the journey. And, granted, if this had been a trouble-free mission so far, we would all feel much better about things. But, that obviously has not been the case."

Merit had reached Triana's end of the table, and now passed behind her seat. For reasons she couldn't explain, this irritated her, as if he was subtly trying to take charge of the meeting, challenging her to turn around and give him her attention. She refused to budge, and kept her eyes forward. It had quickly become a battle of wills between the two.

"Within the first four months after the launch," Merit said, "we had not one, but two separate incidents which almost destroyed us. Two."

Gap spoke up, a touch of irritation in his voice. "Two incidents which were neutralized."

"Is that the word you use? Neutralized? If you ask around, you'll find that many of the members of this crew believe that we got lucky. Very lucky."

Channy was clearly puzzled by the discussion. "What are you talking about?"

"Think about it. In the first instance, we missed a collision with a madman by what, fifty feet? And then, if I'm correct, we were almost blown to bits around Saturn, and would have done exactly that in about ten more seconds. Fifty feet, and ten seconds. You wouldn't call that lucky?"

"What's your point, Merit?" Gap said.

"My point, Gap, is that we haven't even officially left the solar system, we haven't been away for even eight months, and we've already used up all the luck we could ever hope to have. The next time – and we all know there will be a next time – we probably can't count on good fortune again.

"This is an extremely bizarre universe we live in, with an awful lot of things that Dr. Zimmer and his team could never have imagined when they scribbled out their plans on some scrap paper. For a bunch of scientists, sitting in a safe, warm room, in front of their computer screens, it probably seemed much easier. Build a ship, fill it with a bunch of bright kids, launch it, and five years later it docks safely at a new home."

Merit had returned to the far end of the table and now leaned on it with both hands. He looked directly down the length of the table, into Triana's eyes. "It's just not that simple. We've encountered one madman, and one incredibly advanced super race of beings. What else can we expect to stumble across in the next four years? Aren't we in way over our heads?"

Lita leaned forward, a gentle expression on her face. "I don't think I quite understand what you're hinting at, Merit. You're suggesting…what?"

He straightened up. "It's time that we admitted that this is a much more dangerous mission than anyone ever imagined. It's time for us to turn around and head home."

"What?" Channy blurted out. "Are you crazy? We can't go back to Earth. Bhaktul's disease-"

"Bhaktul's disease is horrible, to be sure," Merit interrupted. "But remember, we're talking about 'best chance,' and the odds have shifted. For many of us, it makes more sense to take our chances on finding a cure at home than taking any more risks out here in space."

Gap chuckled. "The best medical minds have worked on Bhaktul for years, and they have absolutely nothing to show for it. Nothing. And now that the disease has wiped out such a large percentage of the population, there's hardly anyone left to devote the time and research to finding a cure. Face it, Merit, going back to Earth is a death sentence for everyone on this ship. A slow, grisly death, I might add."

Merit smiled his half-smile, and Triana felt a cold chill down her spine. There was a definite energy that radiated from him, an energy that made her very uncomfortable.

"You're forgetting one very important factor," he said to Gap. "The Cassini."

Silence greeted this comment until Lita spoke up. "Meaning?"

Merit spread his hands. "It's obvious, isn't it? The Cassini read everything in not only Bon's mind, but in the minds of several other crew members. The Cassini would have to know about the problem on Earth, and, as we know, they're in the business of fixing things, right? For all we know they've been working on it for the past few months. It might be a very different Earth that we return to."

Gap frowned as he said, "Might, maybe, possibly. We don't know."

"Nor do we know what's going to happen in the next five minutes out here," Merit shot back. "And so far our track record is not very good. Would you be more willing to put your faith in a handful of very tired, very ill scientists, or The Cassini?"

Triana had been silent, but finally spoke up. "You mentioned that many of our shipmates agreed with you. What do you mean by 'many?'"

Merit looked down at the folder he had carried into the room. Flipping it open, he pulled out a sheet of paper and passed it down to Triana. "I have begun a rather informal polling of people, and so far eleven have stated that they would prefer we turn around and take our chances back on Earth."

"Eleven?" Gap laughed. "You, your two buddies outside. That's three. And, what, eight other people with more time on their hands than brains?"

"Gap," Triana said, shooting him a look. She waited until he sat back, then glanced at the names on the sheet of paper. She recognized them all, of course, but didn't know them that well. "I appreciate your concerns," she said to Merit, "and the Council will take your suggestion under consideration."

Merit crossed his arms. "To be honest, I don't expect the Council to do anything. Not when eleven people speak out. But a week ago that number was six. A week from now it will likely be fifteen, and then twenty. I'm simply bringing this to your attention now so that you're not surprised when a majority of crew members vote to go back. There will come a time when you have no choice but to listen. Consider this visit today a courtesy call."

Triana felt a recurrence of irritation. It wasn't so much the message from Merit, but his manner that grated on her. His cocky attitude was frustrating, as if he was daring anyone to challenge him. Bon could be cocky, too, but only because of his self-confidence. With Bon you got the feeling that he simply believed that he was right. Merit, on the other hand, seemed to want to prove something, to force others to bend to his will. His brand of cockiness stemmed from a desire for power.

And that could be very dangerous.

She kept her expression neutral, and said again, "We will take your suggestion under consideration. Thank you for your time."

With a nod to Triana, and then to the other Council members, Merit picked up his folder and walked briskly from the room. Before the door closed, Triana saw the two other boys fall into step behind their champion.

"I can't believe it," Channy said. "That's the craziest thing I've ever heard."

Lita looked thoughtful. "I didn't give him much credit before, but I'm afraid this could become...a problem."

"That guy is a jerk," Gap said.

"He has every right to voice his opinion," Triana said. "And it seems that he will be voicing those opinions to just about everyone on the ship. It's our responsibility to make sure that the other side is heard, too. Agreed? Or...do some of you share his concerns?"

"What? No way," Gap said.

"I don't," Lita added.

"I don't even know what he's talking about," Channy said. "But if he wants to go back to Earth, then he's gonna have a hard time convincing me."

Triana looked down the table at Bon, who had not uttered a word since Merit had walked in the room. "Bon?"

"I will not go back to Earth. We started something, and we're going to finish it."

"All right," Triana said. "I need some time to process all of this. Let's get some rest, and we'll meet again soon."

For the first time, she walked out of the Conference Room before the others had a chance to stand up.

-7-

Lita walked into Sick House adjusting her hair ribbon. It was almost eight o'clock in the morning and she had finished a strenuous workout with Channy's "Early Risers," a group of crew members who preferred to get their exercise out of the way before the rest of the ship came to life. Channy had varied their routine today, and Lita was feeling muscles that she had never been introduced to before. The steamy shower afterwards had never felt better.

She wasn't surprised to find Alexa already on the job. The fifteen-year-old was inputting data into a computer terminal with one hand while the other grasped a mug of tea.

"How can you do that so fast with one hand?" Lita said.

Alexa looked up and smiled. "Good morning. How can I what? Oh, this? Listen, nothing comes between me and my tea. If it means I have to learn to type quickly with one hand, that's a skill I can master." She took another gulp then nodded at the vidscreen. "Of course, you never know what that does to my accuracy. I might have just invented a whole new blood type or something."

Lita laughed and sat down across from her assistant. "I trust you. So, what's new this morning?"

"Nada. Just preparing all of the files for next week's crew checkups."

"Good. Need any help?"

"Nah," Alexa said. "You do your doctor stuff and I'll take care of the boring paperwork. No sense wasting your special training on this junk."

"You mean my crash course in how to be a doctor? How to be a doctor on a spaceship full of teenagers in just five easy lessons?"

Alexa rolled her eyes. "Please. It was a lot more than five lessons. Besides, your mother was a doctor. You practically grew up with a stethoscope around your neck and a thermometer behind your ear."

Lita sighed. "Mom was amazing. You know, she was the youngest person in her graduating class, and still had the highest test scores. She had offers from all over, including some of the top universities in America, and she chose to return home to Mexico and work in Veracruz."

"She did it because she loved it, I guess."

Lita nodded. "Yes. She loved her work, and she loved the people in her hometown. Plus," she added, a smile bending across her face, "she happened to love a certain grocery store owner in Veracruz."

"Oh, I just love a love story," Alexa said, batting her eyelids. "Especially one with such a touching theme: Big money in the big city, or love in the produce section."

Both girls laughed. For Lita it was good to discover that she could finally talk about her parents without falling into a state of gloom. She missed her family every day, and often daydreamed about the long walks on the beach with her mother, talking about life, about fate, and about finding happiness. Maria Marques had done it all, had excelled at everything, yet had not hesitated when it came time to choose her life's path. It had been home and family first, career second. Some had questioned her priorities; she had dismissed them without a thought. Lita considered this the greatest lesson her mother had ever taught her: putting family first.

"Well, our backgrounds obviously don't matter, because we both arrived in the same place," Lita said. "Your mother wasn't in the medical field, but look how you turned out."

"Sure," Alexa said. "A medical assistant who can't stand the sight of blood."

Lita laughed. "You're funny, you know that?"

"I'm serious."

"What are you talking about? You're not afraid of blood."

Alexa shrugged. "Sorry, but it's true. Can't stand it."

Lita sat forward, a look of disbelief on her face. "How in the world did you manage to sneak that past Dr. Zimmer?"

"What can I say? I thought this would be a cool place to work on the ship, and how often were we going to encounter blood? So during our training I either looked the other way, or went into some kind of Zen place. I don't know. It worked, though."

"That's about the funniest thing I've heard in a long time. A medical assistant who's afraid of blood."

Alexa took another sip of tea. "Yeah, but my incredible bedside manner makes up for it, huh?"

"You're killing me. All right, I need to go check this morning's email before I find out something else that's absurd, like maybe you actually enjoy that horrible hospital smell."

"No, but hospital food is much better than people think."

Lita grinned and stood up. Before she could walk away, Alexa's face took on a serious look and she reached out to touch Lita's arm.

"Hey, before you go, I wanted to thank you for whatever you said to Triana and the Council."

"Why, what happened?"

"I got a nice note from Triana, thanking me for all of the hard work I've done. She said that you told the Council that I was doing a great job. So, thank you for that. It's nice...it's nice to be appreciated, I guess."

"Wish I could do more for you," Lita said. "I'm glad you're here." She turned to walk over to her desk, then looked back.

"Of course, if I'd known about that whole blood thing I might not have said anything."

"Don't you have email to check or something?"

* * *

Triana breezed through the door to the Conference Room and found Gap with his feet up on the table, rolling a cup of water between the fingers of both hands. He gave her a quick smile of welcome.

Triana had an odd feeling about the meeting. For one thing, in the seven months since the launch, Gap had never requested a private meeting. They had been through some hair-raising experiences, but he had always voiced his opinions and concerns in the company of the Council. If he was wanting to speak with her alone, something was obviously of grave concern.

Triana also picked up an interesting vibe from him. Gap was, for the most part, very cool under pressure. He had a temper – she had seen that a few times, including some memorable episodes between Gap and Bon – but when a crisis arose, she knew that she could count on him to remain composed and to help her navigate through the storm. Today, however, he seemed almost...jittery. The feet up on the table seemed like a manufactured calm, betrayed by the nervous actions with the cup.

And betrayed by his eyes.

There was, of course, another possible explanation that flitted across her mind. Perhaps this was 'the talk' that she had anticipated for so long. She knew that Gap had feelings for her – or used to have. He had often seemed on the verge of expressing those feelings, too, until either something interrupted the moment, or he lost his nerve. For a guy who had remained cool while a madman threatened to destroy them, he had an awfully hard time verbalizing his feelings about Triana.

And just what feelings, exactly, did she harbor for Gap? Or for Bon? It was easy to critique another person's difficulty with expression, and yet she was no better. Perhaps it was the intrigue itself that she embraced.

Besides, now that Gap had developed a relationship with Hannah, what could he possibly say to Triana?

"Thanks for carving a few minutes out of your day to chat," he said.

"No problem. What's up?"

"Not much, unless you count the boulder the size of a locomotive that just zipped past about a mile below us."

Triana took the seat across from Gap and let out a sigh. "A mile? And when did we spot it?"

"About five seconds after it passed us."

"Oh, great," Triana said. "Just what our friend Merit needs to hear, that we had another close call. Roc, why didn't we catch this one sooner?"

The computer's reply was immediate. "How can I possibly concentrate on my piano lessons *and* watch for asteroids and comets at the same time?"

Gap answered her question. "Because it was one of those ricochet shots we talked about. This thing bounced off not one, but two different rocks before it flew right at us. Which leads me to the real reason I wanted to talk to you alone. Roc has actually come up with an explanation for why *Galahad* Control wasn't prepared for the mess out here in the Kuiper Belt."

Triana sat back. "Okay, I'm all ears."

"I love that expression," Roc said. "All ears. You humans look sorta funny anyway, just imagine-"

"Roc," said Gap. "Can you get on with it?"

"Gee, you'd think a giant boulder had almost creamed us or something," Roc said. "Okay, here's the lowdown. We knew before the launch that the Kuiper Belt was a vast collection of space junk: rocks, comets, ice chunks, sand grains, all of the missing socks that seem to disappear in your dryer. They're all circling the sun way out here in no man's land, and almost impossible to see from Earth. Our calculations about the makeup of the Kuiper Belt, aside from the bigger objects, like Pluto, were mostly guesswork. Educated guesses, but still guesses.

"Then, we come sailing along, and it's nothing like we expected. Sure, we've found the ice chunks, the comets, and even Bon's missing sense of humor, but we never expected so many items clustered together. It's way crowded out here, and that did not factor into the equations."

"And you have an answer for this?" Triana said.

"Give me enough time and I'll come up with an answer for almost any puzzle. Well, except for ketchup on eggs. That's just gross, if you ask me, and I can't figure out why anyone would do it.

"But the Kuiper Belt is another story. I've spent a little time analyzing everything we knew about this area before we got here, along with all of the new data in the last couple of weeks. It turns out that the Belt is lumpy in some areas."

Triana looked at Gap, who waited for the computer to explain.

"We've assumed that it has a uniform thickness all the way around the sun," Roc said. "Instead, there are some sections that are rather thin and sparse, with almost nothing around. We could drive a million *Galahads* through these spots and never come within a million miles of even a pebble.

"Then, however, there are stretches that are teeming with an excess of rubbish. Kinda like that one closet in your grandparents' house that is stuffed with all of the gifts you ever bought for them but they never took out of the package. You know what I'm talking about."

"Let me guess," Triana said. "We've run smack dab into a closet."

"Bingo."

"And what makes it even worse," Gap added, "are the odds."

"Do I want to even hear this?" Triana said.

"Sure, if only to appreciate how remarkable it all is. These jam-packed stretches only occur in about thirty-five percent of the Kuiper Belt. We had only a one in three chance of stumbling into this, yet we did."

Triana found herself chuckling, not because there was anything really funny about it all. It just seemed that fate was determined to throw every possible challenge their way. It was never going to be smooth sailing, it seemed.

"Okay," she finally said. "And you wanted to tell me this privately because…"

Gap shifted in his chair and set down his cup of water. He stared across the conference table into Triana's eyes.

"Because Roc has also figured what our chances are of making it through the minefield without a really big bang."

Triana sighed again. "Go right ahead. Make my day complete."

The computer's voice was loud and clear. "Ooh, I hope you like a good challenge, because I figure about one in twelve that we make it through unscathed. Actually, more like one in thirteen, but we can fudge it down just a touch."

One in twelve. Triana felt the weight of the mission collapse onto her shoulders once again. The figures meant that for every twelve times they took this path through the Kuiper Belt, eleven of those times the ship would be destroyed, without warning.

She bit her lip and, without thinking, reached across and picked up Gap's water cup. She took a long drink, wiped her mouth with the back of her hand, and pushed a stray hair out of her face. Gap remained silent while she processed the information.

"Okay," she said. "I'm making an executive decision here. I would prefer that none of what we've discussed leave this room. Under normal circumstances I would probably inform the crew, but things are far from normal right now. I hate to have somebody like Merit Simms influence my leadership, but during a time of external crisis the last thing we need is more internal strife. He's preaching a message of doom and destruction, and this will only fan his flames a little bit more."

"I agree with that," Gap said. "Anyway, he's all about turning the ship around, and to be honest that's exactly what we don't want to be doing in a minefield. He wouldn't understand that, of course, because it's contrary to what he wants. But I think Roc would agree that a quick straight line is the best strategy for avoiding bumping into something."

"Probably," Roc said. "Although just being inside this portion of the Belt is like being tossed around inside a bag full of marbles. Eventually something is likely to take the paint off."

"Then we understand each other," Triana said. "No sense causing a panic. Mum's the word."

She looked back at Gap again and debated whether to say what was on her mind. She didn't want to sound petty or jealous. Finally, with a shrug she decided that it was too important to ignore. "Don't even tell Hannah, right?"

Rather than seem offended, Gap replied with his own shrug. "Listen, chances are, with her passion for astronomy and numbers, she'll have it figured out on her own any day now. But, yeah, I'll keep quiet." He paused, then added, "And don't worry about the fuss that Merit Simms is making. There are too many dedicated people on this ship for him to have much of an impact."

Triana nodded, yet didn't possess the same confidence. Something told her that things were going to get complicated.

Soon.

-8-

The workout had been over for almost ten minutes, but the scowl on Channy's face had not diminished much. She watched, sweat dripping down the side of her face, as the last of the morning group finished putting their mats away and gathering their personal belongings. Channy was unquestionably the most popular crew member on board, but when she was in this mood – the angry drill sergeant mood – few people would make eye contact with her, let alone stop by for a chat.

Kylie Rickman was an exception. She was Channy's roommate, and she knew that one of her most important roles was as a sounding board when the petite Brit was fired up. Kylie drained a cup of water, wiped her forehead with a towel, and leaned back against a cabinet.

"I don't know if I've ever seen you so irritated."

Channy continued to glare. "It's my job to make sure this crew doesn't get fat and lazy during the trip. If they keep this nonsense up, by the time we reach Eos they won't be able to run fifty feet without stopping to rest." She shook her head. "Pitiful."

Kylie chuckled. "Exaggerating a little bit, aren't we?"

"Not much. You were part of the group this morning. Did you see what the back row was doing? Having a little social outing."

"Hmph," Kylie snorted. "Sounds like something right up your alley."

Channy turned her glare to focus on her roommate, then slowly relaxed, and a faint smile crossed her face. "That's right, and as the unofficial social director around here I can't have any unsanctioned parties."

Both girls laughed, and Kylie was glad to see her old friend return. She rolled her towel and snapped it at Channy's leg. "You know, for such a good-natured girl, you have a bit of wildcat in you, don't you?"

"Hey, just doing my job," Channy said. "And you better watch out with that towel. You know what they say about paybacks."

Kylie refilled her cup of water. "Let me ask you something. Those two girls over there, they were in the back row. What's with the armbands they're wearing?"

Channy shook her head. "Why don't we ask?" She raised her voice. "Vonya! Addie! Have you got a second?"

The two girls, who were talking in hushed whispers against the far wall of the gym, looked over, then glanced quickly at each other. Channy could have sworn that it was almost a guilty look that they shared. After a moment's hesitation, as if they wanted to ignore Channy's invitation, they slowly made their way across the room. They stopped about six feet away, arms crossed, with almost defiant looks on their faces.

"Did you enjoy the workout this morning?" Channy said.

Addie, a petite girl from Austria, looked at her friend, then shrugged. "I guess so." Vonya didn't answer.

"The only reason I ask," Channy said, "is because you seemed very preoccupied with something. It was a little tough keeping your attention today."

Again, Vonya didn't answer. Addie, apparently feeling the awkwardness of the situation, raised her chin a touch and said, "We were just talking. Is that okay?"

Channy stared at Addie for a few seconds before responding. "Sure, as long as you don't disrupt the group.

Would it be all right if I asked you to wait until after the workout to chat?"

Vonya spoke up. "Fine. Is there anything else?"

Channy could feel the distinct coolness emanating from the pair. She didn't know them very well, but had always exchanged friendly greetings with them. What was going on? She shifted her gaze down to the armbands that they both sported. They were a light yellow color, obviously homemade, crafted from the same piece of cloth. A permanent marker had been used to stencil "R.T.E." on them in bold black lettering.

"Mind if I ask about those?" Channy said. "I haven't seen them before, and I'm just curious."

The two girls looked at each other, and then Addie said, "They're symbols of unity."

"Okay. Uh, unity for what? Or who?"

Vonya gave an impatient sigh. "We happen to belong to a group of crew members who have decided that it's ridiculous to continue this mission to Eos. We're in favor of turning around, and taking our chances back on Earth."

The shock registered on Channy's face. "You've been recruited by Merit Simms?"

"Not recruited," said Addie. "Convinced. This ship has almost been wiped out twice, and we've barely started. Merit is the only person making any sense these days, and we agree with him." She kept her arms crossed, and now shifted to one side, her weight on one foot, assuming an almost confrontational pose. Her face looked menacing.

"Don't get mad," Channy said. "I'm just asking questions."

For the first time, Kylie spoke up from beside Channy. "What does the 'R.T.E.' stand for?"

"Return to Earth," said Addie. "It's our rally cry, and you're going to be hearing it a lot more over the next few weeks."

Kylie grunted. "Why in the world would you want to return to Earth? You think Bhaktul has just disappeared?"

"Maybe. Merit says that The Cassini have probably already started working on it, and it will be long gone by the time we get back."

"That's quite an assumption," Channy said. "And if he's wrong?"

Vonya's face took on the same look as her friend's. "Then we're no worse off than we are out here. Of course, I wouldn't expect one of Triana's robots to understand."

Channy began to take a step forward, then felt Kylie's grip on her arm. The Council member stopped and took a deep breath, locked into a staring showdown with Vonya. After a few moments she relaxed and feigned a smile.

"Okay, well, thanks for clearing that up. We might disagree on some things, but that doesn't mean we can't work up a good sweat together down here, right?"

Addie and Vonya once again exchanged looks, then turned and walked out of the gym, chattering under their breath. Just before they walked out the door Channy could hear one of them snickering.

"Thanks," she muttered to Kylie. "I almost lost my temper there."

"They're rude," Kylie said. "It's always been funny to me that some people automatically go into attack mode just because someone asks them questions, or disagrees with them. That's no way to argue your point." She shook her head, then looked at her roommate. "When did all this 'return to Earth' stuff pop up?"

"Just recently. Merit Simms – the guy they were talking about – is trying to round up support for his ideas. Unfortunately he's spreading a lot of misinformation."

"Like that stuff about The Cassini? You know, I've wondered about that myself."

Channy stared at her friend, incredulous. "What are you talking about?"

Kylie shrugged. "You know, just a random thought after we passed by Titan. I mean..." She seemed to be searching for words. "I mean, if they really are that powerful and all..."

"Listen," Channy said. "We have a mission to accomplish. Don't let a bunch of wild ideas start bouncing around your head. Going back to Earth would be a death sentence for us. We have no way of knowing if The Cassini even *know* about Bhaktul's disease, so why would we assume that they have any way – or desire – to fix it?"

Kylie turned to set down her cup of water. "I'm sure you're right. Hey, I've gotta run, I have a history class in twenty minutes. Talk to you later, right?" Without waiting for an answer, she darted out of the room and toward the lift.

Channy stared after her, a worried expression staining her usually glowing face.

* * *

"Got a second?"

Bon looked up from his office desk in Dome 1. Large windows on one wall allowed him to watch the activity in the dome, so he was surprised that he hadn't seen the approach of Merit Simms, who now stood leaning against the door, one hand in a pocket.

"What for?" Bon said.

Merit grinned. "I'll take that as a yes. I just wanted to ask you about something."

"I'm busy."

"This won't take long."

Bon stood, walked around his desk, and perched on the edge. He crossed his arms, his cold eyes flashing. "Make it quick."

Merit walked into the office and looked out the window into the artificial sunlight bathing Dome 1. In the distance a group of workers harvested potatoes, while three other crew members pushed a work cart down another row in the fields.

"You guys stay very busy," Merit said. "During my last tour of duty up here I think I sweated off five pounds. Not enough people express their gratitude for the work you do. I mean, we all eat very well, thanks to – "

"Is that why you're here?" Bon said. "To express gratitude?"

Another grin splashed across Merit's face. "Well, sure. It's not the main reason, but I'll say it anyway."

"Fine. You're welcome. Now, I told you I was busy."

"Yes, you did. In fact, it's pretty obvious to me, and probably to a lot of people, that you're one of the hardest workers on the ship. I've talked with a few people about you, and other than meals in the Dining Hall, and a quick daily workout, nobody ever sees you. You don't socialize, you don't hang out in the Rec Room, you don't participate in the soccer tournaments. Stuff like that. So I guess everyone assumes that you spend all of your time here, working."

Bon's eyes narrowed. "You know, you take an awfully long time to get to your point. You don't care about my schedule, or how I spend my time. What do you want?"

"It's precisely because of the way you spend your time that I want to talk with you," Merit said. "There are very few people aboard *Galahad* who have the perspective that you have. You work hard, you don't waste time with things you don't care about, and you don't get caught up in some of these ridiculous social cliques. In fact, I think it's safe to say that you are probably the most efficient crew member on the ship."

Merit leaned on the sill of the window. "And, you're a Council member. That means you also get a good perspective on the way the ship is managed."

"Yes. So?"

"Well, Bon, that makes you a rather important person for me to get to know. Because, as you heard, I'm convinced that we are doomed if we continue along this path. We've had warning flag after warning flag. How many more catastrophes do *you* think we can survive? You, of all people, should understand what I'm talking about. You were the only reason we survived the trip around Saturn and Titan. You, not Triana, not the Council, not anyone else."

Bon remained silent, but his eyes probed Merit's. His arms were still crossed, and his right index finger began to slowly tap on his left bicep.

"It's also no secret that you don't see eye to eye with many of the decisions that Triana makes. You're not afraid to express your opinions. Am I right?"

"Yes," Bon said. "I say what I feel. And, unlike you, I don't waste words saying it."

Merit nodded. "I respect you for that. And I respect the fact that you're not afraid to confront Triana." He pushed away from the wall and slowly began to pace around the room as he talked.

"Bon, every day we continue on this journey we increase the chances that we won't survive. First it was our stowaway. Then it was The Cassini. Now it's this shooting gallery called the Kuiper Belt that we've thrown ourselves into. Word has it that we've already had several near-misses, and we've barely begun to work our way through it."

"You signed up for the trip just like the rest of us, Merit."

"That's right, I did. But we were never really told what we'd be dealing with, were we? Did you get some sort of pre-launch lecture about alien intelligence around Saturn? Did any of us think that our heating system was shaky? Dr. Zimmer was so busy building team spirit that he conveniently neglected to share a few minor details with us, like the fact that we would probably never survive the first year."

"I think Dr. Zimmer explained very well the dangers we would face," Bon said. "You must have been distracted during those discussions. Maybe too busy trying to get people to pay attention to you."

Merit's smile seemed forced. "It's okay if you don't really like me right now. I understand. Change is hard for most people. I just figured you were a little different than most people."

"Your psycho-babble won't work with me."

"Once I walk out of here you'll think about it, though. I know you will. And you'll realize soon enough that this is no psycho-babble. I'm just like you, Bon; I tell it like it is. Which is why I want you on my team."

"Is that what you call it? Your 'team'?"

"We are a team. And our team is growing every day. A smart guy like you can recognize a winning team when he sees it. Give it some thought."

"I don't need to give it any thought," Bon said, standing. "And now I think you'd better leave."

"Just a minute. Let me ask you one other thing." Merit stepped forward until he stood facing Bon. "If you change your mind, what do you think Triana will do?"

"I'm not going to change – "

"Just suppose. Has Triana ever listened to you before? Do you think she would now?"

"I told you to leave."

"You want to know why she won't listen to you?" Merit said, taking one more step forward until he was face-to-face with the blond Swede. "Because no matter what you think my motives are, they are nothing compared to hers. She won't listen to you, or anyone else on the Council, because she's afraid, and will never admit that she's wrong."

"Get out."

"She doesn't mind dying, Bon, because it's the ultimate escape for her. Running away from her problems on Earth was easy for her, and she'll avoid facing those problems even if it means killing the rest of us."

It happened quickly. Bon's fist flew through the air and connected solidly on the side of Merit's mouth. Merit staggered backward, lost his footing, and fell.

Bon looked down at him. "I told you three times to get out. I won't tell you again."

Merit propped himself up on one elbow, then gingerly touched the corner of his mouth with a finger, which came away bloody. He examined it for a second, then held it up for Bon to see.

"Touched a nerve, did I? Was that punch in defense of your own stubbornness, or in defense of Triana?"

Bon didn't answer, but instead glared down at him as if ready to continue the fight. Merit grinned again, then slowly clambered to his feet. He dabbed at his bloodied mouth one more time, then looked at Bon.

"Actually, you've done me a huge favor, Bon. This," he said, holding up the bloody finger, "could come in very handy. Thank you."

He spun around and walked quickly out of the office. Bon watched through the large window as Merit strolled down the path toward the lift.

"Great," Bon muttered.

Wait a minute. I wasn't paying close attention here. Did Bon just punch that guy in the mouth? Really?

Hey, you can forget the 'Why didn't you stop him, Roc?' comments. First of all, what did you expect me, a computer, to do about it? It's not like I could step between them.

And secondly, I've seen Bon with his shirt off, and I wouldn't have stepped between them anyway. As one girl in Channy's aerobic class said, 'Hubba hubba.'

And thirdly, he would have just punched me in my sensor and THEN punched Merit in the mouth.

And fourthly…well, there is no fourthly. That's enough. Except that I'm pretty sure this is all getting very sticky.

-9-

"I'm sick of this," Gap said to himself.

He stood in front of the same panel in the Engineering section, watching as the sensors told him that the heating elements on Level Six were acting up yet again.

The intercom buzzed. "Gap," came Channy's voice. Without waiting to hear another word, Gap reached over and clicked it off. This time his patience for the fun and games was at zero.

He ran a hand through his short, spiky hair and exhaled loudly, mixing in a sort of primal grunt with it, eliciting a giggle from behind him. Turning, he found Hannah standing there, an amused smile on her face. They had made a tentative date for breakfast together in the Dining Hall, but Gap had been sidetracked by the latest breakdown in the heating system.

"That," she said, "is the sound of utter and total frustration."

"Which is exactly what I'm feeling. If I could take a wrench and bash this thing..." His voice trailed off, before returning in a shout. "Roc, this is a not a good use of my time!"

"I know," the computer said. "Think of how many laps you could be making right now on the Airboard track."

"Oh, very funny," Gap said. He looked back at Hannah who was stifling another giggle. "Don't encourage him, okay?"

"Well," Roc said, "if you function better without the gentle infusion of wit, I can certainly adopt a stern, brooding attitude." His computer voice lowered an octave. "How's this? Doom, doom, death, death, aaarrrgggghhhhhh."

This time Hannah's giggle escaped her mouth. Gap closed his eyes and shook his head, covering his face with one hand. From behind the hand he muttered, "I don't need this. I swear I don't need this."

"Poor Gap," Roc said in his normal voice, the one that mimicked that of his creator, Roy Orzini. Roy had not only developed the world's most sophisticated computer, but he had taken great pains to make sure that the artificial brain incorporated Roy's voice and – more importantly – his personality. Gap had verbally sparred with the short, funny man for months before the launch, and had since found that he could do the same thing through Roc.

Gap spread his fingers in order to peek through at Hannah. "If you want to go ahead to the Dining Hall, I'll try to join you as soon as I can."

She shook her head. "No, I'll wait here with you. Maybe I can help."

"I don't know how." He lowered the hand and turned to look at Roc's sensor. "I mean, if our resident genius comedian can't help…"

"Okay, Mr. Serious," Roc said. "I can't stand to watch you pout, so I recommend a complete re-boot of the entire system, then a re-program for Level Six that bypasses its Balsom clips and runs the level's heating through the clips on Four and Five."

"What good will that do, except to maybe burn out the clips on those other levels?"

"That's not likely. The clips can take on almost two hundred percent of their engineered specs, and we're talking only about a fifty percent increase. This is just a short-term fix to pinpoint whether it actually is Mr. Balsom's fault. Besides, remember that this was *your* idea in the first place."

Gap chewed on this for a moment. "And what would the long-term fix include?"

"If it turns out to be the Balsom clips on Six," Roc said, "and if replacing them doesn't work, then we can re-program the entire ship to run on the other five levels' systems, sharing the load equally. That will hardly put a dent in their capacity. And, if that still worries you, which, knowing you, is more than likely-"

"Oh ha ha," Gap said.

"-then we could even lower the overall ship temperature by one degree, and that should bring everything back to normal."

"One degree would do that?"

"One degree."

Gap's eyes unfocused as he tried to work the math in his head. When he heard Hannah clear her throat, he looked at her.

"Uh, I think he's right," she said meekly. "It wouldn't take much."

Hannah was, without question, one of the best scientific minds on the ship, so Gap knew better than to doubt her.

"Okay, I believe you guys," he said. "I guess the hardest part would be explaining it to the crew so that they don't freak out. I can handle Channy's jokes, but some people might use this to stir up trouble." He didn't mention Merit Simms by name, but that was certainly the first thing that had popped into his head. He could only imagine the look on Triana's face if he had to break the news to her.

The intercom buzzed again, and this time, before Gap could reach to shut it off, Channy's voice seeped out. "Gap, you've got to hurry up here to Level Six, quickly!"

This didn't sound like a joke. What could have happened now?

"What is it?" he said.

"You've got to see this, Gap. There are eight tiny reindeer walking around up here, convinced that this is their home." There came an immediate burst of laughter from everyone in the room with Channy. Fuming, Gap punched off the intercom.

"Um...maybe I will meet you in the Dining Hall," Hannah said with a smile. She leaned over and gave him a quick peck on the cheek, then strolled out of the Engineering section, obviously holding back a laugh.

* * *

Triana rubbed her hands together as she walked into Sick House. She knew that Gap was furiously working on the heating problem, and she also knew that he was likely getting enough input without her bothering him. Instead, she answered a call from Lita to stop by the ship's clinic. Lita wouldn't elaborate over the intercom, but Triana could tell from her friend's voice that it was something she should do at once.

"A little chilly, huh?" Lita said from her desk.

"It's probably worse for you," Triana said, plopping down in the available chair. "Not too many days in Veracruz like this. Makes those of us from Colorado a little homesick, though." She glanced around the room, which was empty and quiet. "Where's Alexa?"

Lita chuckled. "Would you believe it? I give her all that praise in the Council meeting, then you sent her a personal note of thanks for her hard work, and today she called in sick. Figures, huh?"

"Sick? Alexa? What's wrong with her?"

"Just a stomach ache, but bad enough that I told her to lay low for the rest of the day."

"Well," Triana said, leaning back so that the chair tipped onto its two rear legs, "I won't razz her about it. What's this, her first-ever sick day?"

"Yeah. And you should have heard her apologizing. You'd have thought that it was her tenth straight day, or something. But that's not why I called you down here."

"No, I didn't think so. What's up?"

Lita moved a couple of items around on her desk, in what appeared to Triana to be a stalling tactic. There was something that she apparently wasn't anxious to share. "I had three people stop by Sick House today. One was Nung; you remember him. Very cool guy from Thailand. Nothing major there, just a little readjustment in his meds. Then our usual monthly Airboarding injury. Ariel actually took a pretty good spill today."

Triana raised her eyebrows. "I heard she was one of the best."

"Listen, that's a crazy sport. I don't care how good you are, you're one pulse away from wiping out. Remember what happened to our boy Gap? He's the champ, and he still broke his collarbone."

"Is Ariel okay?"

"Bruised ribs. She actually landed on her board."

Triana winced. "Okay, it doesn't take a detective to figure out that I'm sitting here because of your third visit. Wanna fill me in?"

Lita stopped fidgeting and looked directly into Triana's face. "About an hour ago I treated Merit Simms for a bloody lip."

Slowly, Triana's chair rocked forward, back onto all four legs. "What?"

"Uh-huh. He got clocked today."

"By?"

"Take one guess. Who would be the most likely candidate on the ship to punch someone?"

Triana dropped her head and stared at the floor, her elbows resting on her knees. "Bon."

"Yep. I guess they had some sort of confrontation up in Bon's office. The way Merit tells it, Bon lost his temper and just slugged Merit, and all Merit was doing was talking with him. That's his story, anyway."

"I'm sure he provoked Bon, but that's not too hard to do, is it?"

"You're right about that. But it wasn't even necessary for Merit to come see me."

"What do you mean?"

Lita shrugged. "I mean, his lip had already stopped bleeding, and it wasn't all that bad. He still wanted it cleaned up, and a tiny bandage put on it. I told him that wasn't necessary, but he insisted. I know he's not worried about infection."

Triana shook her head. "No, that's not why he came here. He wants a record of the incident. He wants it in your files that he was assaulted by Bon, and proof that there was an injury."

"That's what I figured."

"Yeah," Triana said. "It all makes sense, really. He's building a case, trying to recruit as many people as possible. I'm sure he went to see Bon with one intention, and that was to goad Bon into either hitting him, or shoving him, or something." She sighed. "And now he has another piece of information to use against us."

Lita leaned forward onto her desk. "Well, he's not wasting much time using it, either."

"What?"

"Looked at your email lately?" When Triana shook her head, Lita turned her vidscreen around to face the Council Leader. "Check out the mass email that Mr. Simms sent out five minutes after he left Sick House."

Triana scanned the note.

> Many of you have expressed an interest in finding out more about the proposal to turn the ship around and head back to Earth. I've had numerous emails from concerned crew members who are afraid that our next dangerous encounter will be

the one that kills all of us. I obviously share your fears, and have begged the Council to at least hear our arguments. They have refused. If you are as worried about this as I am, then I invite you to join me for an informal discussion on the subject. This will be a peaceful gathering of facts and opinions, and a chance for your voice to be heard. Tomorrow evening, at 7:30, in the Dining Hall. I welcome your attendance, and your feedback.

Merit Simms

Triana read it a second time, and felt her shoulders sag. Terrific. Another chance for Merit to distort the facts and paint a warped image of their condition.

And with a war wound, to boot. Nothing like playing the sympathy card, which was evidently in his plans all along. There was no doubt now that to underestimate Merit Simms would be a terrible mistake.

-10-

It felt warm, almost tropical, and needed only the sound of birds mixed in with the crash of waves on a beach to complete the aura. Except this tropical air wasn't near the equator on Earth; it was encased in a large geodesic dome that sat atop the most impressive spacecraft ever assembled, and it nurtured the lifeblood of the *Galahad* mission: the Farms.

Through special planning and careful cultivation, the Farms on the ship could encourage the growth of fruits and vegetables in a close proximity that could never be mimicked on Earth. Within fifty feet of Dome 2, for example, could be found examples of plant life that would never be found within hundreds, or thousands, of miles back home. It was part of the amazing engineering marvel that was built to safely carry 251 passengers to a new land of opportunity.

Bon stood in a freshly turned plot of soil, with stakes and colored tags that identified the plants which would soon be surprising the hungry crew with plates of various melons and berries. He had long ago given up announcing the release dates in advance, since the clamor of the crew distracted Bon's workers and took their eye off the prize. That lack of focus often translated to a tongue-lashing from a certain Swede.

The good news? Once you experienced a chewing-out by Bon you did everything in your power to make sure it never happened again. On this particular afternoon he was face-to-face with a 16-year-old from Portugal named Marco, who stared at the dirt around his feet, only occasionally making eye contact with Bon. It was obvious from Marco's body language that he was anticipating a verbal barrage.

"And what, exactly, is the standard procedure," Bon said, "when you find a section, like this one, that has been overlooked during the sowing process?"

Marco kicked at a dirt clod. "I know."

"Answer the question."

"File an immediate report, and…and contact you."

Bon nodded, his usual scowl firmly in place. "And you did neither."

Another kick, another clump of dirt sprayed outward. "I thought that it might not be too late," Marco said. "So…so I…"

"So you took it upon yourself to begin a new round of planting and fertilization," Bon said. "You didn't even take the time to fill out the forms hanging in my office."

"I filled them out."

"Not until the next morning."

Marco put his head back down and glanced at the purple tag attached to the nearest metal stake, his handwriting clearly listing the information for this row of melons. He waited for the volume of Bon's berating to intensify, but instead was surprised by the silence that surrounded them for a minute. When he looked back up, Bon was staring at him.

"You know what this means?" Bon said.

Marco shook his head.

"It means," Bon said, "that you're one of the few people around here who knows what he's doing. Thank you."

For a moment Marco remained still, his mind trying to decipher the words. A puzzled look crossed his face. Bon reached out and put a hand on his shoulder.

"All I've ever wanted is a group of workers who didn't wait around to be told what to do. You knew what needed to be done, and you didn't waste time waiting for me to tell you to do it. So, thank you again."

A hesitant smile worked its way across Marco's lips. "Really?"

"Really. I have plenty to do without having to baby-sit every single row of every single crop. I'll remember this when it's time for evaluations. Now you probably have something fun to do this evening. Go ahead and get out of here, and I'll see you tomorrow morning."

Marco's smile widened. "Thanks, Bon. Have...have a good night." He turned and sprinted down the path toward the lift.

Bon knelt to examine the soil, making sure that it was getting the vital moisture it needed this early in the growing stage, and was startled by the voice behind him.

"Don't worry, I won't tell anyone."

He spun around to find a grinning Gap about ten feet away. "Tell anyone what?"

Gap took a few steps toward him. "About your soft side. I was cringing, waiting for the explosion, and I don't even work up here. I can imagine how Marco was feeling."

"Do you always eavesdrop on private conversations?"

"I didn't mean to," Gap said. "I've been looking all over the Domes for you, and just happened to walk up while you were talking to Marco. Thought I'd just stand back and wait until you were finished."

Bon turned back to concentrate on the new melon seedlings that had been planted. "Well, that had nothing to do with a soft side. He did the right thing, so I told him. No big deal."

"I'll bet it's a big deal for Marco. I think what you did was cool. You made his whole week. Did you see how fast he flew out of here?"

Bon didn't respond. He patted the soil a couple of times, then stood and brushed his hands together.

"Maybe it's the timing, that's all," Gap said. "I mean, after your last private meeting with a crew member."

Slowly, Bon turned his steely gaze upon Gap. "That was also a private conversation."

"Sure, what you discussed is obviously between you two. But Merit is making sure that the results aren't private. He's already visited Sick House, and now he's planning a meeting for tonight after dinner."

"He's free to do that."

"He's free to do more than that, really," Gap said. "He could have you brought before the Council for disciplinary action."

"So be it."

Gap shook his head and took another step closer. "Listen, I know we've had some good times in the past, and I also know that we've had our share of conflicts with each other. Things have been...pretty cold between us the last few months, and I'm sorry about that."

Bon shrugged. Gap had the distinct impression that having this conversation was the last thing that the Swede wanted to be doing. But he also knew that this particular discussion was long overdue. It was another inadvertent bit of eavesdropping that had originally put Gap at odds with his fellow Council member, months ago, when Gap had stumbled upon a somewhat intimate moment between Bon and Triana. Gap's heart had been severely bruised that day, watching a connection between the girl he had secretly adored and the former friend with whom he had bonded during their training.

Now, after months of reflection – not to mention a flourishing romance with Hannah Ross – Gap felt a need to mend the split with the guy who had eventually saved the ship from destruction at the hands of The Cassini. He knew that his reluctance to approach Bon had been fueled primarily by jealousy, and the time had come to rise above that.

The incident with Merit Simms provided a convenient excuse to do so.

"Anyway," Gap said, "there's no telling what the fall-out will be from your punch. I'm pretty sure that Triana will have no choice but to address the crew at some point, and lecture everyone about conflict resolution. You know, 'violence is never the answer,' that sort of stuff."

Bon ran a dirt-stained hand through his long hair. "I have not made a habit of violence, though, have I? One isolated incident, that's all."

"Yes, that's true," Gap said. "But you know that, as the Council Leader, she still has responsibilities, and one of those is keeping the peace. Which," he added with a sigh, "might be a little tougher in the days to come."

The sound of irrigation pipes coming to life suddenly gurgled near them, and both boys automatically began to walk toward the path that led to Bon's office. Neither said anything for a minute, unsure of exactly how to end the conversation. It was Gap who found the way.

"For the record," he said, "I would have to agree that violence is certainly not the answer with someone like Merit. But..." He paused, then flashed a grin. "But *off* the record, you have no idea how glad I am you did it."

As usual, Bon kept silent, but his fierce eyes softened a bit.

And when Gap stuck out his hand, the sullen son of a farmer grasped it firmly, shook it once, then turned and walked into his office.

* * *

She had managed only about four hours of sleep the night before, and now Triana sat in her room, a mug of hot tea steaming on the table, and her journal spread open before her. She had climbed out of bed at 6:30, invested thirty minutes on the treadmill in the gym, then showered and changed before spending a few hours checking in with the various departments of the ship. She had stumbled back into her room around noon and wolfed down a mango energy block before deciding that tea might be just what she needed during the break.

A quick check of the clock caused her to unconsciously calculate the time remaining before the gathering in the Dining Hall. At first she had tried to convince herself that few people would bother to attend; now she resigned herself to the fact that it likely would be bustling with crew members, mostly curious about the battle lines that were being drawn.

Triana took up her pen and finished the journal entry.

> I'm starting to come to grips with the emotions that are stirring inside me regarding this conflict with Merit. At first I was tentative, almost nervous, and completely unsure of how to deal with it. But now that has begun to shift. If I'm truly honest with myself, I have to admit that I'm angry. Angry that someone would intentionally create chaos aboard the ship, when we have enough to deal with already. Angry that so many others have neglected to think for themselves, and are blindly following whomever shouts the loudest. And angry that I came across as weak in the face of the enemy. That must end. Although it was wrong, and will more than likely come back to haunt us, perhaps I should credit Bon for snapping me out of my delicate state. In one moment Bon simply acted upon what many of us might have felt. Typical for him, I suppose. And although I can't condone his actions, in a

roundabout way the punch has knocked
me backward as much as Merit.

She set down the pen, took a swig of the tea, and sat back
in her chair. After a moment of consideration, she closed the
journal and called out to the computer.

"Roc, I have a lot on my plate right now, and this will
probably be a tough day. So, how about a distraction for a
few moments?"

"Now isn't that an interesting twist," the computer said.
"All of those times that you were irritated with me when I
distracted you, and now you're begging for it. Typical."

"Well, let's face it, sometimes you pick the worst possible
times to act up."

"Or," Roc said, "the best possible times, depending on
how you look at it. What's the matter, Tree?"

"Oh, let's see. A potential mutiny from the crew, and
about a bazillion giant chunks of rock hurtling at us. Other
than that, you mean?"

"Hmm, you definitely need a distraction. I'll tell you
what; let's count all of the ways I'm indispensable to you
and the ship."

Triana smiled. "Okay, I guess that's enough distractions
for now."

"Hey!"

"Besides," Triana said, "I don't have time to play, as
tempting as it is. You made me smile, and for now that's
good enough. Let me ask you about the heating system."

"Boy, you *are* all business today, aren't you?"

"I haven't been able to catch up with Gap today. What's
our status with the repairs?"

"We're trying something new," Roc said. "We're running
the system on Six through the Balsom clips on Four and Five.
Gap will not let go of his theory that it's the clips, so I'm
humoring him."

"So...where does that leave us?"

"The system will drop out again, because, as I told Wonder Boy, it's not the Balsom clips. It's just like playing a game of Masego with him; you have to let him make his own mistakes before he'll take your suggestions. He's quite stubborn, in case you haven't noticed."

Triana chuckled at the mention of Masego. The popular game, introduced to the crew by a girl from Africa, required a strategic mind and extreme patience. Gap had plenty of one, not so much of the other, and Roc enjoyed torturing him whenever they played in the Rec Room.

"Well," she said, "it's not like I don't have a lot of stress right now, you know? So, do I need to worry about this heating stuff, or will it eventually get fixed?"

"I'll tell you when to worry," Roc said. "Actually, I'll probably drop a few subtle hints first so that you don't panic. Like, 'Hey Tree, we're all going to die.' You know, something like that."

"Right. Okay, let's talk about the giant boulder situation."

"No," Roc said. "Let's not talk about that."

Another small laugh escaped from the Council Leader. "Then all you're leaving me is the Merit Simms problem. I suppose you know about the meeting tonight?"

"Can't wait," the computer said. "Knowing you the way I do, I'm guessing that you're going to be there?"

Triana nodded. "Uh-huh. Hey, if it affects the crew, I need to know first-hand what information is being thrown about. I could be wimpy and send some spy to find out for me – or have you tell me – but I want Merit to see me there."

"Bravo," Roc said. "Would you like for me to do anything to mess with his presentation? You know, have the lights flicker, play loud music, pipe in the sound of demonic laughter every time he says the word 'I'?"

"No, thanks."

"What if I flashed his baby pictures on the vidscreen behind him?"

"What? You don't have those!"

"You're right, I don't. But I could create something really, really close. Maybe add an extra eye or something for effect."

"No, thank you," Triana said. "We'll let him have his day and find out exactly what message he's putting out there. But I appreciate the offer."

"By the way," Roc said, "even though you didn't play along, that was number 147 on the list of ways I'm indispensable to you."

-11-

The Dining Hall was crowded, but Lita couldn't tell if it was unusually so for this time of the evening. She was one of a handful of crew members who took their dinner later than most, so it was a change for her to be here at seven o'clock. Most of the kids in the room appeared to have either finished their meal, or were close to doing so, and that made Lita believe they were lingering to hear what Merit had to say.

It was the reason she had come earlier than usual. A tray with the remnants of her dinner was pushed to the side, and her eyes darted back and forth between the assembled crowd and Channy, who was seated across from her, decked out in a bright orange t-shirt. She didn't want to be rude and ignore Channy, but she couldn't stop mentally cataloguing the people who were either sympathetic to Merit, or simply curious. She wasn't sure if sides were being chosen – not yet, anyway – but it couldn't hurt to know what you were up against.

If Channy was concerned, she was masking it by chattering on and on about her latest crew function.

"The only reason people have been slow to sign up, Lita, is because they're waiting to see who else does it."

"You really think this crew is ready for a dating game?" Lita said.

Channy rolled her eyes. "What are you talking about? People are *always* ready for love, my friend. I'm telling you, it's still a week away, and you know how people hate to be the first to volunteer for anything."

Lita glanced over Channy's shoulder and saw Triana walk in the door. The room became noticeably quieter for a split second, before the general buzz started up again. There was drama here, indeed, and the atmosphere in the room had become charged. When she noticed that Channy was staring at her, Lita forced her attention back to their conversation.

"Um...so, how many people have signed up right now?"

"Two."

Lita fought back a smile. "Two? How are you going to do this with two people?"

"I told you," Channy said, "it's still early. By this time next week I'm predicting at least a dozen, maybe more. You'll see." She transferred her empty plate to Lita's tray, then stacked her own tray underneath. "Why don't we put your name on there?"

"No, thank you."

"Why not?"

Lita lowered her chin and gave Channy her best impression of an evil eye. "Don't you even think about it."

"Where's the sense of adventure I saw when you performed that concert for us?" Channy said.

"I was terrified. For a minute I wondered if I would even be able to play chopsticks. You're lucky I didn't throw up."

"Well, you have a week to think about it."

Lita just shook her head, then looked over as another clot of people walked into the Dining Hall. A moment later Triana pulled over a chair and sat down next to them.

"Hi, guys," she said. "What's new?"

Channy leaned back in her chair and stretched her arms over her head. "Not much. Just trying to talk Lita into signing up for our little dating game next week."

"That's nice. Well, there's quite a crowd gathered for this, isn't there?" Triana said.

"Are you changing the subject?" Channy piped in.

"Oh, sorry. I didn't know you had more to say about it." Channy looked back and forth between her two companions, then shook her head and turned sideways in her chair to stare out over the crowd. She muttered something under her breath.

Lita leaned forward, her elbows on the table. "It's mostly curiosity, I'm sure. You know those armbands that a few people are wearing? I only see ten or twelve of them in the room."

Triana cut through her salad with a fork without saying anything in reply. Her mind was racing, but she was determined to keep a relaxed posture before, during, and after the meeting. She would not give Merit, nor his group of followers, the satisfaction of seeing her ruffled. There was no doubt that her reactions would be scrutinized by everyone in the room.

She didn't want to lose the confidence of the Council, either. It was important, she thought, that they believe in her ability to lead, and during a time of crisis that was even more crucial. Channy seemed to be pouting right now and not paying much attention to anything, but Triana was sure that Lita was watching her very closely.

Casually flipping a strand of hair out of her face, she said, "How's Alexa feeling tonight?"

"The last time I talked with her she lied to me," Lita said.

"How do you know?"

"Because I could tell that she felt like garbage, but all she kept saying was, 'I'm fine, I'm fine.' I ordered her to stay in bed until tomorrow, otherwise, knowing her, she would have marched into work this afternoon."

"That's weird," Triana said, taking another bite. "What do you think is wrong?"

"I'm starting to doubt that it was something she ate. Nobody else is sick right now. It's possible that it's a bug that somehow survived our tests and the month we spent in quarantine before the launch. Not likely, but always possible. If she's not better tomorrow I'll run some tests."

Triana nodded, and was about to comment when she heard a clamor from the front of the room. She knew what that meant.

Merit Simms strode through the door, his customary posse in tow. Several of the kids nearest him reached out to shake his hand or clap him on the back. Triana noticed that this came mostly from the group that sported the yellow armbands.

She also noticed that the small bandage near his lip was still in place. By now there was no doubt that it was merely a prop, and undoubtedly an important one. Someone in his cheering section obviously inquired about it, because Triana watched him point to the bandage and chuckle, in what looked – to her – like phony embarrassment.

She also noticed the glances that were directed her way from some of the assembled crew, an almost nervous reflex, as if sizing up two gladiators before a battle. Her own eyes darted around the room. Lita was right; there was curiosity here, along with a touch of hero worship from a select few. Yet Triana couldn't help but feel that her presence in the room had also added an air of confusion. Why, they must be wondering, would *she* be here?

Well, good, she decided. The fact that she had chosen to participate allowed her to take the high road in the eyes of the crew, and showed them that she refused to run and hide in the face of controversy. A moment later Merit looked up to see her, and she could have sworn she saw a flicker of irritation cross his face. She gave him a slight nod of acknowledgement along with a faint smile.

Just as the noise began to die down, Gap walked through the door. He scanned the room, spotted the other Council members, then eased his way back to their table. Taking a chair from an adjoining table, he sat down next to Triana.

"Thanks for being here," she whispered to him.

"Of course." He began to size up the crowd as Lita had done. At the front of the room Merit cleared his throat, causing the room to grow quiet. He surveyed the group before him, slowly turning his head and making eye contact with as many people as possible. Triana recognized it as a technique used by the most experienced professional speakers, a move that helped to create an artificial bond between speaker and audience. Finally, he gave a smile and spoke.

"I want to thank all of you for interrupting your own personal schedules in order to join us tonight."

Triana noted the use of 'us.'

"There are a lot of things you could be doing tonight. Reading, working out, Airboarding, catching up on sleep, maybe just simply eating dinner with friends. Each of you works hard on this ship, you do a terrific job with your official duties, and it means a lot to us that you would sacrifice a little bit of your time to share in this discussion.

"I was just like you a year ago. I had all of the same emotions that I'm sure you had. I was frightened for my family, I was depressed about never seeing them again. I was angry that nobody could find a way to save them. But I was excited about the mission to Eos. I had confidence in Dr. Zimmer, and believed in his plan. He was very good at selling his plan, and I bought into it."

Triana let her gaze wander around the room, and saw that Merit had captured everyone's attention. The room was dead silent. He had touched the nerve that he had aimed for, and the effect was potent.

"I've thought a lot about those days," Merit said, beginning to walk slowly back and forth at the front of the room, dragging every set of eyes with him. It reminded Triana of the pacing he had done during the Council meeting, using the movement to embellish the impact of his words.

"I realize now that there was a combination of emotions at work. I was afraid of Bhaktul's disease. I was afraid of growing older and getting sick, with no one there to look after me because my family would already be gone. I was eager for a chance at life, at any cost, even if it meant saying goodbye to my parents, forever.

"You had the same emotions, I know. You saw *Galahad* as your chance to escape, to live, to give humanity a fresh start. You worked hard, you trained hard, you studied, you cried, you grieved. And now, seven months after leaving, many of you are still grieving.

"Only today, if you're like me, you look back at the promises made by Dr. Zimmer, and you think, 'Wait a minute. He prepared us for a trip to a new world. He never said anything about a madman trying to kill us.'"

Triana looked at Gap, who looked back at her with a grim expression. They both knew that referencing the near-deadly encounter with the mysterious intruder was a sensitive issue. Merit was undoubtedly scoring points already.

"Dr. Zimmer also never considered the possibility of an alien life force trying to destroy us, for no apparent reason. He never told us that we would fly through the Kuiper Belt and have millions of projectiles hurtling at us like a giant game of dodge ball."

There were nods from around the room. Merit stopped his pacing and faced the crowd, a look of anxiety on his face. "You're as concerned about these things as I am. And I'm sure you've had some of the same thoughts I've had, too. Thoughts such as, 'Maybe it's time we turned back.' I ask you tonight, with everything that has happened so far, only seven months into the journey: How many more times can we get lucky? How many more times can we pull out a miracle? How many more times until we discover that the people who sent us out into the cold darkness of space had no idea what we would be up against?"

He paused for a few moments, allowing his words to sink in. He scanned the faces of the room, making eye contact, engaging their emotions. Triana sat still, leaning forward, her elbows on her knees. She was angry that Merit was doing this, turning the crew against her, against Dr. Zimmer, against their hope for survival.

And yet, on another level, she found herself marveling at his motivational skills. His was a natural talent for persuasion, a talent that Triana felt she possessed, but at nowhere near the level she was observing. Merit Simms could sell, period.

After his brief pause, he shook his head. "I have given this so much thought. I have considered not only our past experiences, but also studied, in depth, what lies before us. We have so far to go within the Kuiper Belt, and it's more dangerous than you know. And then, what lies beyond that? What will we encounter in the void between the Belt and Eos? What do we know about empty space? Or, is it even really empty?

"And more importantly: What happens when we arrive at Eos? Do I even need to point out to you the odds of survival on the new world?"

With this comment there were several murmurs amongst the crew. Merit paused to allow them to express their own doubts. For an instant Triana wondered if the look on his face wasn't a look of satisfaction. He knew what was happening.

"But," he said, raising his voice above the chatter. "But," he said again, louder, until the room again fell silent. "But apparently questioning the plan is not allowed on this ship. Apparently our Council, which is supposed to represent us, does not allow lowly crew members like me, like you, to approach them with fears and concerns. Apparently we are at their mercy. Did you know that?"

There was no verbal response to this, but the assembled crew members nervously looked at one another, aware that the majority of the Council sat quietly in the back of the room. Two or three of Merit's personal entourage glanced back at Triana and smirked.

"I know," Merit said, "because I tried. I tried to visit with the Council, tried to express my fears, tried to recommend

that they consider an alternative. I questioned them about
The Cassini, a force more powerful than anything man has
ever seen, a force that can either destroy...or assist.

"The Cassini have now known for months about Bhaktul.
What might have happened since we left Titan? What
changes have possibly taken place on Earth in the last ninety
days? How do we know that The Cassini haven't used their
awesome powers to repair our home? How do we know that
we're not risking our lives every single minute of every single
day...when our families might be healing, and waiting for
us to return?"

Now Triana could see Gap clenching his fists. She knew
that he was dying to stand up and speak, but he kept his
composure. She bit her lip and remained still.

"And do you want to know what happens when you
actually try to talk to the Council today?" Merit paused, then
pointed to the bandage on his lip. "This is what happens.
You get attacked."

Another low murmur spread across the room. Merit
lowered his hand and stood still, a victim on display.

Finally he spoke again in a low voice, drawing his
audience back in. "All I'm asking is to be heard. All I'm
asking is that the will of the crew be honored. We are a ship
in trouble. I believe we should turn for home, for the safety
and security of our families. But I'm only one voice, a voice
that has been beaten down. So tonight I'm asking you to join
us, peacefully. With numbers we can finally be heard. If you
join with us, we can choose life, together."

He paused again, before closing with a soft, "Thank
you."

Immediately his cheering section stood and began
applauding. They looked around at the tables near them,
encouraging others to rise and join in. Slowly, several other
crew members rose to their feet and began to clap. As Merit
nodded his thanks, almost a third of the Dining Hall was
cheering his speech. He waited for a few moments, made

quick eye contact with Triana, the corners of his mouth barely turned up in a smile, then walked toward the door, shaking hands and offering personal thanks. A minute later he was gone.

-12-

I see that you're about to eavesdrop on Lita in Sick House, so this is a good time to ask you something that I've wondered for a while.

If one of your electronic devices breaks down, I've noticed that you won't hesitate to either take it in to be repaired, or immediately order a new one. On Earth, if an automobile has a problem, you would immediately take it in to the shop. If your washing machine is acting up, you get a repairman out right away.

But if your own body has a problem, you put it off, you ignore it, you pretend that everything is fine. Seems funny to me that your portable music device gets preferential treatment over your flesh and blood. You're a very funny species.

"No...no, a little higher," the girl said.

Lita pushed two fingers against the slightly bruised skin. "Okay. What about here?"

"Yeah, that's...ouch!"

Lita pulled her hand away. "Well, it's at least a bruised rib. Maybe a crack. Seems to be a popular injury this week."

The girl, a 15-year-old from Egypt, blew out a sigh of disgust. "How long does that take to heal?"

"Oh, that depends," Lita said, walking over to a locked cabinet. She opened it and removed a small bottle of pills. "No more than six or eight months."

"*What?* Eight months?"

Lita grinned as she poured six of the pills into a small envelope. "Relax, Ana, I'm kidding. You'll be fine in just a few weeks."

"Don't scare me like that. I don't think I could go that long without soccer. My team needs me."

"It was soccer that did this to you in the first place," Lita said, pointing to the bruise. "You guys are playing a little rough, aren't you?"

Ana returned Lita's smile. "You have to be tough to win. I stayed in the game after this, you know. I even scored the winning goal."

"Yes, you told me already. In fact, I think you've mentioned it three times. Listen, take one of these now, another one tomorrow, and only take the other four if you really think you need them. If you're as tough as you think you are, you can bring them back to me."

Ana slid off the examining table and winked at Lita. "You'll get the other four back."

Lita nodded her head. "Uh-huh. Well, we'll see how tough you are tonight when you try lying down for the first time with a cracked rib." She placed the envelope in her latest patient's hand. "One other piece of advice. If I were you I would try to stay away from funny people and pepper for the next few days."

"Why?"

"Because you'll be wishing for another pill if you start laughing or sneezing," Lita said. "Trust me."

Ana smiled and gave a quick wave goodbye. As she was walking out the door she passed Alexa, who was obviously doing her best to look better than she felt. Lita rushed over to greet her assistant.

"How are you feeling today?"

Alexa shrugged. "Ugh, I've felt better. But I'm not missing any more work, I can tell you that."

Lita stood in her path, arms crossed. "You know, there are only so many tough crew members I can tolerate in one day. What's going on with you?"

"I still feel a little queasy. Almost like I'm seasick or something. I don't know if it's better, or if I'm just getting used to it."

"Anything else, or just the stomach?"

Alexa walked around *Galahad's* Health Director and made her way over to her desk. "You are such a worry wart. I'm fine."

"C'mon, Alexa. What else?"

"A little pain, okay? Nothing I can't handle."

"Pain in your stomach? Pain and nausea?"

"Yeah. So, what have I missed around here?"

Lita's face took on a scowl. "Dr. Zimmer not only found the brightest kids on the planet, I think he rounded up the most stubborn ones, too. Why won't you let me help you?"

"Because it will go away. I'm telling you, it's gotta be something I ate. Blame Bon, not me."

"Nobody else is sick. It's not the food."

Alexa looked at her friend. "I'll tell you what. If it's not better in a couple of days you can poke and prod all you want, okay?"

Lita shook her head. "No, if it's not better *tomorrow* I'm going to poke and prod. And don't lie to me, Alexa."

"Yes, Mother," Alexa said, and turned her attention to the work that had piled up on her desk. The conversation was apparently over.

Lita stared at her for another minute as a knot of concern began to grow in her own stomach.

* * *

The high-intensity lights in Dome 2 had begun their daily afternoon fade, gradually ushering in the equivalent of an Earth dusk. One by one the flicker of starlight seeped through the clear panels of the dome, the familiar nighttime companions resuming their mute watch over the ship full of pilgrims streaking toward a new world. Workers on the late afternoon shift had chosen to bathe the farm domes in a pleasant background veil of sound. The piped-in music was a relaxing blend of deep tones, cascading synth pieces, and a rushing wind; the effect was almost tranquilizing.

Gap held onto Hannah's hand as they slowly made their way along one of the paths. His grip was light, almost caressing. He stole an occasional glance at her face, taking in her soft eyes, the fall of her hair over the shoulder. Her laugh was easy and relaxed, comfortable at last in his company.

The tension he felt around the Merit Simms trouble had melted away – for the time being, anyway. In the back of his mind he knew that it would come racing back to the forefront very soon, but for now he was content.

Or…was it more than that? Was he happy?

His thoughts were interrupted by a familiar voice that floated out from within a dense growth of corn stalks. He recognized one of Channy's bright yellow t-shirts pushing through the green plants.

"Hold up, lovebirds," she said.

Gap and Hannah stopped and watched the young Brit emerge, brushing small patches of dirt from her knees. Gap smiled at Channy and said, "Are you lost?"

"Ugh, it wouldn't be hard to do. I can't believe how quickly these things have grown. They're almost over my head."

"So what *are* you doing in there?" Gap said.

Channy looked back and pointed at a small shape that was slinking onto the path about twenty feet away. "Babysitting, as usual. Iris definitely prefers Dome 2 over the other one."

Hannah raised her eyebrows. "So this is better territory for a cat to explore, is that it?"

"Who knows?" Channy said. "They seem about the same to me, but maybe there's just too much noise in Dome 1. It might spook her a bit. It took me fifteen minutes to track her down in the corn." She turned her attention to the clasped hands of Gap and Hannah, a smile spreading across her face. "I'm not interrupting anything, am I?"

"What if I said yes?" Gap said.

"Then I'd be forced to walk away, and then secretly stalk you from a distance. You could save me a lot of trouble if you just said no."

Hannah laughed. "We're just taking a walk. Any spying that you did would be pretty boring for you."

Channy shrugged. "More exciting than anything I have planned tonight." She looked up at Gap. "So...have you thought anymore about that garbage Merit was spilling last night?"

Gap frowned. Apparently the break from tension was over. "It's a tough situation," he said. "The guy has every right to express himself, and people have every right to agree or disagree with him. It's not like we can shut him up because we don't like what he's saying."

"Yeah, I know that," Channy said. "But he's so...so wrong. He's filling peoples' heads with a bunch of silly nonsense."

"Again, that's for people to decide."

"Yes, but nobody is telling them that it's nonsense. They're only hearing one side."

She had a good point, Gap thought. So far the fight had been completely one-sided. Not counting Bon's contribution, of course, but that had ended up benefiting Merit's cause.

Channy filled the silence between them. "Why doesn't Tree hold her own meeting and respond?"

"Well, at first I don't think she wanted to give him the satisfaction, you know?" Gap said. "It was almost as if acknowledging his claims gave him some sort of credibility. But now..." He trailed off.

"Right," Channy said. *"Now* he seems to have a ton of credibility."

Hannah shifted uncomfortably. Gap wondered if she felt like she was intruding into a mini-Council meeting. He tightened his grip on her hand to let her know that everything was okay. "I was going to talk to Tree about this anyway," he said to Channy. "Listen, she's a great leader, we all know that. I'm sure she's giving this as much thought – or more – as we are."

Channy seemed unmoved by this. Her gaze turned toward Iris, who had sprawled into a patch of dirt and was rolling onto her back. The light had faded considerably, and the starlight above was taking on a sharper set.

Gap was about to add something to the conversation when the sound of voices caught his ear. Two boys in farming overalls came around the edge of the corn crop, tools slung over their shoulders, and intently talking about something until they realized they were not alone. They fell silent as they marched past, one of them acknowledging Gap, Hannah, and Channy with a brisk nod, while the other, a tall, slender boy with a shaved head, stared straight ahead.

Around his upper arm was a distinctive yellow armband with a black 'R.T.E.' stenciled on it.

No words were exchanged between either group, and within a few seconds the two farm workers had disappeared down the path. Channy balled her fists and seethed.

"That's the kind of stuff I'm talking about," she said, pointing in the direction the boys had walked. "More and more of these people putting on those ridiculous armbands, walking around like they're on a mission or something."

Gap forced a smile. "We're all on a mission."

"You know what I mean," Channy snapped at him.

"Hey, calm down," Gap said. "Don't take it out on me."

"Well, I'm angry."

"I know you're angry. But remember what happened when Bon let his anger get out of control." Gap paused to let that sink in, and watched as Channy slowly relaxed and crossed her arms.

"All I'm saying is don't overreact," he said. "There's no reason they can't wear whatever they want. I know it's frustrating, but we have to keep our composure, right? That's one good example that Triana is setting for the rest of us. She's just as frustrated as you, believe me. But any confrontation right now is only fuel for the fire."

"So just how long are we going to take this?" Channy said.

Gap ran his free hand through his hair. "Things are going to work out, okay? For the time being maybe we should be grateful that we're getting a crash course on accepting other viewpoints." He touched Channy's arm to get her attention focused on him. "Hey, we have a long way to go. This is the kind of stuff that we need to learn how to deal with if we're going to create a new world someday. We're not all going to agree all the time, you know."

Channy stared at him for a minute, then dropped her gaze to the ground. She mumbled, "Yeah, you're right."

Gap chuckled. "I think part of you is upset because other people have discovered yellow."

A smile inched its way across Channy's face. She looked at Gap and nodded, then turned her attention to Hannah. "You're not saying much. What do you think about all of this?"

Hannah darted a glance at Gap, then back to Channy. "Well...uh...it's a little uncomfortable, I know that. But..." She paused for a second. "But people approach a crisis in different ways. Some people get emotionally involved, and others tackle it from a more...well, a more logical angle."

Both Gap and Channy stared at her, waiting for her to continue. She cleared her throat nervously and said, "I happen to disagree with Merit because of pure logic. It just makes no sense to attempt to turn around here in the Kuiper Belt, and to start a slow return trip to Earth. Especially since we have no evidence whatsoever that things are any better there than when we left."

"What would you recommend we do?" Channy said.

Again Hannah took a quick look into Gap's face. "Well, since so many people are wondering about The Cassini, I think it might make sense to talk to the one person who has had intimate contact with them."

Gap and Channy looked at each other. Then Gap nodded slowly. "That's a really good idea."

Channy said, "Yeah, I hate to admit it, but Bon could know more about this situation than anyone." She paused, glancing uncomfortably between Gap and Hannah. "Uh... so who's going to be the one to try to drag it out of him?"

There was silence again. Gap looked up through the dome into the star field that was now furiously blazing. He knew that a showdown was inevitable, and the possibility that Bon might hold the key – as he did during their encounter with Titan – was not the most comforting thought of the day.

He gave Hannah's hand another squeeze, and began to lead her down the path. "I'll see you at the Council meeting in the morning," he said to Channy, who had picked Iris up from the dirt.

"Cheers," Channy said, waving one of the cat's paws at them. She held Iris up to her mouth and whispered, "Maybe *you* can talk to Bon."

-13-

Things were chilly again on Level Six. Triana walked briskly through the curving corridor, rubbing her arms to help the circulation, wondering just how cold it was. She could only imagine the frustration that Gap was probably feeling right now. His pride told him that he could solve any technical problem, and to have a constant gremlin turn up in the heating system of the ship wore through his patience quickly. She had spoken with him moments earlier on the intercom, and asked him if he could break away for at least thirty minutes for the morning Council meeting.

Now, as she approached the Conference Room, she wondered about reversing that decision. It was colder up here than she had expected, and she could always catch Gap up on anything discussed in the meeting. She was torn; on one hand she wanted all of her allies present as they rode through the turbulent times experienced both inside the ship and out, yet she also knew that every little breakdown, every little incident, every tiny error, would all be blown as far out of proportion as Merit Simms could manage. For that reason alone she figured Gap should stay on the job in Engineering.

The point was driven home the minute she rounded the turn leading to the Conference Room and found more than a dozen crew members congregated in the hallway. Many of them leaned against the curved walls, a few were sitting cross-legged on the floor. Merit stood next to the door, his arms crossed, deep in conversation with three or four followers. They appeared to be mesmerized by what he was saying.

For a split second her pace slowed, but then she recovered and worked her way through the tangle of bodies. Merit broke away from his speech and blocked her entry to the Conference Room.

"I'm here to formally request to be heard at this morning's Council meeting."

Triana burned on the inside. He had made sure to have as many witnesses as possible, and no doubt secretly hoped that she would turn him down, building his case that the Council did not care to hear the concerns of the crew. With Merit it always seemed to be about power and control.

She kept her face calm and replied, "I think that's a good idea. Let us take care of some other business, and we'll be happy to have you join us."

Merit flinched for a moment. "Uh...very good. Thank you." Then, with a manufactured look of victory on his face, he turned to the group. "Everyone relax, it will be a few minutes."

Triana resisted the urge to roll her eyes, and instead gave a curt smile and nod to the assembled crowd and ducked inside the Conference Room. The door closed behind her and she found herself staring into the concerned faces of the Council. Nobody said a word as she walked to the head of the table and sat down.

"I won't keep you in suspense," Triana said. "Merit has requested another hearing, and I've agreed. He'll join us in a few minutes."

When this also was greeted with silence, she continued. "First things first. Gap, what do you need to get this heating problem fixed on Level Six?"

"A new heating system," he said. That seemed to break the ice, and there were chuckles around the table. "I'm quickly running out of options, but I'm not giving up."

Channy, whose neon-bright t-shirt was shielded under a long-sleeved top, said, "Our furnace went out more than a few times when I was growing up. My mum used to bang on it with a hammer, and that seemed to work most of the time."

"I'll keep that in mind," Gap said, "although Roc hasn't suggested that as a solution...yet."

The computer spoke up. "I couldn't live with myself if you smashed your thumb."

"I don't think we'll be long this morning," Triana said. "You should be able to get back to it within the hour." She looked around the table. "Unless anyone has something urgent we need to address, I want to talk quickly about the Kuiper Belt, and then we can hear what Mr. Simms has to say."

When this was greeted with mute stares, she tapped a login on the keyboard before her, and a split second later all of the table's vidscreens displayed a three dimensional rendering of the Belt. A thick red line traced *Galahad's* path through the crowded space.

"I want to let you in on some information that Gap and Roc shared with me the other day. It has to do with the make-up of the Kuiper Belt, and, quite honestly, a bit of bad luck."

She spent a few minutes relaying the report on the Belt's inconsistent thickness, and how *Galahad* had stumbled into a particularly rough stretch. For the time being she withheld the odds of survival that Roc had offered.

"This means," she said, "that things are probably going to get worse before they get better. It also means that we might have to change course several times as we weave through this mess, and for now we don't know what that will mean to our overall schedule."

Lita spoke up. "If it's a choice of getting to Eos a few weeks late, or not getting there at all..."

"Right," Triana said. "So be prepared for some tight spots coming up, and remember to help diffuse any concerns you hear from the crew."

With another couple of strokes she cleared all of the room's vidscreens. "Is there anything to add before we bring in Merit?"

After a moment of silence, Channy leaned forward, her palms flat against the table. "I just have a question, if that's okay."

Triana immediately took note of the unusual tone in Channy's voice. Her typical playful rhythm had been replaced by a sober touch, a characteristic that seemed alien on the energetic Council member. "Sure, what's your question?"

"I'm wondering how you plan on responding to the muck that Merit is stirring up. I mean..." She threw a quick glance at Gap. "I know we're supposed to appreciate other opinions and all that, but it doesn't seem to me that the crew is getting the whole story."

Triana looked hard at Channy, then around at the other Council members. Their faces – with the exception of Bon, who was as unreadable as a statue – seemed to express a silent agreement with the petite girl from England.

"That's a fair question," Triana said, "and it's something I've thought about. Until Merit held his meeting in the Dining Hall, there wasn't really a reason to gather the crew together."

"But now he's gaining momentum, and we look like we're hiding," Channy said.

"That's one way of looking at it, I suppose," Triana said. "But in my opinion it would have been worse to immediately try to defend a plan that has been arranged, plotted, and followed since day one. Everyone on this ship has known why we're doing what we're doing, and it made no sense to me to round up 250 crew members and state the obvious.

Our mission is on track, and, if anything, slightly ahead of schedule. I saw no reason to defend that."

Gap picked up on the past tense. "Saw? So that means that now you're considering a meeting?"

"Of course I am. Now that Merit has 'stirred the muck,' as Channy put it, it's time to get everyone to refocus on the plan. A refresher course."

Channy sighed. "Okay, thank you. I just haven't liked this feeling lately, like we have our heads buried in the sand or something."

"I understand," Triana said. She looked at the other Council members. "Is there anything else?"

Lita shrugged. "Let's hear the latest speech."

Gap went to the door and summoned Merit into the room. He swept in, his long black hair pulled back into a tail. For a moment he locked eyes with Bon, who glared at him with open disgust.

Standing at an open spot near the middle of the table, Merit held up a sheet of paper and immediately began to speak.

"This is a petition signed by 38 members of the *Galahad* crew. That represents about fifteen percent of the people on this ship, and they demand an open debate on the issues I have raised."

Gap took the sheet of paper and looked over the signatures. "I'm assuming you mean a debate between you and Triana?"

"Or any member of the Council, actually," Merit said. "This crew deserves the right to hear all of their options, presented in a formal, intelligent manner."

"Thank you for sharing that," Triana said, eyeing her adversary with a cool look. "We will certainly take it under consideration and let you know shortly."

Merit chuckled. "We've grown weary of waiting while you 'consider' our requests."

"I'm sorry to hear that," Triana said with a slight smile of her own. "It's the way procedures work on this ship. We don't make hasty decisions."

"Exactly how many names do you need to see on a petition before you'll act? Fifty? One hundred?"

"It's not a matter of quantity," Triana said. "It's a matter of the Council determining whether the request is in the best interests of the crew. If one hundred people wanted us to fly straight into an asteroid I would not open that to debate."

"That's a ridiculous comparison," Merit sneered.

"In your mind, maybe. But my job, and the job of this Council, is to protect this crew from harm to the best of our abilities, and to make decisions that best serve the mission. That mission, by the way, is to pilot this spacecraft to Eos. Turning it around, in the middle of a dangerous stretch of space, is not necessarily that different from driving it straight into a hunk of rock."

"So instead we're supposed to just wait for one of those hunks of rock to slam into us."

Triana paused, then lowered her voice to reply. "As I said very clearly, we will discuss your request, and we'll inform you shortly as to our decision."

Merit looked down at the table, then raised his gaze to meet Triana's. "Then besides my request, let me offer some advice. It would be wise to quickly agree to our request. A lot of tension is building among the crew, and that can many times lead to unfortunate events."

Gap bristled. "Are you threatening us?"

"I'm saying that the best way to deal with pressure is to allow a little steam to escape before something blows."

Triana said, "During your speech in the Dining Hall you invited people to join your movement 'peacefully.' Have you changed your mind about that?"

"I'm not advocating violence, although your side has clearly taken that step already." He looked at Bon, who continued to bore through him with his eyes. "An open, honest debate would allow everyone to hear all of the facts."

"And what facts do you have?" Gap said.

Merit held up another sheet of paper. "A few of my associates and I have worked hard putting together a plan of our own. It would involve a slow turn, safely, through the Kuiper Belt, then back into the solar system toward Earth. Once we inform *Galahad* Command of our decision, they'll clearly plot a flight plan for a return to Earth orbit. The return journey shouldn't take more than two years."

"Two years?" Lita said. "In two years we'll be more than halfway to Eos."

"That's assuming, of course, that we'll survive on our current path," Merit said to her. "We happen to believe that assumption is crazy."

Triana cleared her throat, a clear indication that the discussion was over. "Thank you for your time, and for your observations, Merit. We will let you know soon what we have decided."

He stared at her for a long time, until the silence became uncomfortable.

As he finally opened his mouth to speak, a sudden alarm sounded over the intercom. Triana stood and leaned against the table. "Roc, report."

The computer voice answered immediately. "Collision warning. An extremely large object."

"We'll be in the Control Room in one minute," Triana replied. "Gap, come with me." She hustled out of the Conference Room with Gap on her heels, and they pushed their way through the assembled crowd. There were shouts and questions which were hard to make out over the blare of the alarm.

Merit stepped out into the hallway, making sure to get the attention of his followers before shouting after Triana and Gap: "What more evidence do you need?"

As the two Council members rounded a curve and dropped out of sight, a familiar smile spread across the face of Merit Simms.

-14-

"How large is it?" Triana said as she bolted into the Control Room.

Roc's voice came through loud and clear. "192 feet from end to end, roughly the same shape as an Idaho potato. Which is very ironic, since we'll be the ones who get mashed."

Triana ignored the computer's joke and rushed to one of the vidscreen consoles in the room. Gap had already brought up a 3-D plot, which showed the massive stone tumbling directly into their path.

"I have already changed course to escape collision," Roc said. "We should know in about…twenty-five seconds if it was done soon enough."

Triana felt the blood drain from her face. Twenty-five seconds. She steadied herself on the console, and a moment later felt Gap's hand on her shoulder. The seconds ticked by without a sound from any of the six crew members in the room. All eyes turned to the large main vidscreen which Roc had activated.

From the bottom right corner of the vidscreen Triana noticed what looked like a shadow emerge. It lurched upward, carving a path that seemed destined to intersect with *Galahad*. The ship, although flashing through the Kuiper Belt at a staggering rate of speed, still needed some distance for course corrections to take effect. The massive spacecraft could not exactly turn on a dime.

The shadow grew in size, and in a few seconds the potato shape became clear. It was scarred with craters, remnants of a violent history that stretched back to the origin of the solar system more than four billion years earlier. At one time, Triana guessed, it must have been huge, perhaps the size of Earth's moon even, but collision after collision had chopped it down to its current size. Chunks of that original rock now contributed to the scattershot of debris that orbited in this extreme ring, billions of miles away from the sun.

And if their luck was about to run out, then chunks of a certain spaceship would soon become a permanent addition to the ring.

The shadowy hulk slowly rose on the vidscreen, and Triana realized that Roc's course correction had been to dive the ship so that it passed below the rock. A move to the left, the right, or above would almost certainly have been fatal. But, with the boulder rocketing upwards at this angle, *Galahad's* momentum in a downward streak might spell the difference.

Fifteen seconds later she felt her breathing return. The dark shape was slipping farther above them, and it became apparent that they were spared.

This time.

Soon the boulder disappeared from the screen. Triana let out a deep rush of air through pursed lips, and turned to Gap. "That was fun, huh?"

He shook his head and offered a weak smile in return. "Do you get the feeling that this ship is charmed? We keep missing collisions by just a few feet."

"Don't get dramatic on me," Roc said from the speaker. "We cleared the bottom of that monster by almost two hundred feet. Not even close enough to muss my hair."

"Roc," Triana said, "I have to hand it to you. That was a perfect move you made. Perfect. So now, tell me: Where in the world did this thing come from, and why didn't we see it earlier?"

"It's that ping pong ball effect I mentioned to you earlier. These crazy rocks keep bouncing around off each other, changing direction, speed, rotation. This thing obviously smacked into something just before it zoomed into our path. Our warning system is good, but it can't predict everything."

Triana nodded, then looked across the room. The other crew members stationed in the Control Room were either wide-eyed from fright, or holding their heads in relief. One girl in particular, a fifteen-year-old from Japan named Mika, was watching – and listening intently – to the discussion with Roc.

And she was wearing a yellow armband.

Gap followed Triana's gaze. He felt her start to move toward Mika, and his hand, which was still on her shoulder, stiffened. "Uh-uh," he said to her in a whisper. "Leave it alone."

"What are you talking about?"

"Leave it alone. She hasn't done anything wrong."

"I know that," Triana said. "I'm just going to talk with her."

"If you – "

"Relax," Triana said, pulling his hand free from her shoulder. She walked toward Mika, who broke eye contact and turned back to her work. Triana didn't know the Japanese girl very well, but had lunched with her once, several weeks earlier. She was quiet, but extremely polite and respectful. Triana had always felt comfortable with her on duty in the Control Room.

The display of the yellow armband was disturbing to the Council Leader if for no other reason than it showed that the reach of Merit Simms had penetrated into Triana's outer circle. Mika would have been one of the last people she expected to show support for Merit's cause, and Triana couldn't deny that a pang of betrayal rippled through her as she walked across the room.

"Hi, Mika," she said, stopping beside the girl's chair.

"Hi," Mika said, a sheepish look on her face. Triana realized that it probably took a lot of courage for the girl to show up for duty with the display on her arm.

"Close call, huh?" Triana said.

Mika nodded, and uttered a quiet "Yes. Very close."

"I see that you're wearing one of Merit's armbands. Do you mind if I ask you about that?"

Mika shrugged nervously. "I...I have listened to what he has been saying, and...and I find that I agree with him."

"Do you?"

Another nod. "Yes." Mika pointed to the vidscreen. "This is a good example of what he's talking about. Another close call."

Triana examined the girl's face. "We knew when we left Earth that things might get difficult at times. And any return to Earth will have dangers as well."

There was no response to this. Triana tried a different approach.

"Are you homesick?"

This brought an immediate reaction from Mika. She turned sharply and looked into Triana's eyes. "No. Well, yes, of course I miss my family. But...but that doesn't have anything to do with my choice."

"Are you sure? Have you really thought about everything, or have you just been seduced by a chance to maybe see your brothers and sisters again? A chance that has no guarantee, by the way."

Mika was silent, but kept her gaze on Triana's eyes.

"And once you get there," Triana said softly, "then what? You will have thrown away a chance at a new life, and condemned yourself to a painful death from Bhaktul. By the time we reach Earth, you'll be almost eighteen. And you know what that means."

Mika broke eye contact and looked back up at the vidscreen. A moment later she spoke in her quiet voice. "I will continue to do my job here in the Control Room, and you'll have no trouble from me." She looked back at Triana. "But if the crew is allowed to vote on a change, I will vote for a return to Earth."

The two girls stared at each other. Triana felt like continuing the debate, but realized that this was not the time, nor the place. Instead, she summoned all of her will and offered a smile to Mika. "No matter what you decide, I want you to know that I appreciate all of the hard work you've done."

She turned on her heel and walked back to Gap. He watched her face closely, scanning back and forth from eye to eye. "So, what did you say to her?" he said in a whisper.

Triana sighed. "Just had a little chat. There's no problem."

"No problem? She's wearing a symbol that says she's part of a mutiny. I'd say that's a problem."

"It's not a mutiny."

"Not yet," Gap said. "But you heard Merit. He pretty much said that if we don't agree with him, he and his pals could resort to force."

Triana shook her head. "I'm not ready to believe that yet. Listen, he's very good at manipulation. Don't let him prod you into doing something."

"Like Bon?"

"Exactly. For now, let's not give anyone a reason to distrust the Council. Agreed?"

Gap glanced over at Mika, who was calmly going about her business. "Yeah, okay. But you know what scares me the most?"

Before Triana could answer, the intercom in the Control Room buzzed. Lita's voice called out, "Triana, are you in there?"

With a quick snap of a button the Council Leader answered. "What is it?"

"I know you've had your hands full, but I need you in Sick House right away."

Triana began to question the urgency, but realized that everyone in the Control Room would be able to hear. Instead she told Lita that she would be there in two minutes, then asked Gap to keep an eye on things.

"What do you think that's about?" he said in a whisper.

Triana looked into his eyes. "I'm afraid it's probably about Alexa. And if Lita is calling me like that, it can't be good."

* * *

At first Triana began to sprint down the corridor toward Sick House, but then realized that in the current climate it might be a bit unsettling to the crew for her to be rushing anywhere. She slowed to a brisk walk, and made a conscious effort to keep any sign of panic off her face. Strong, she told herself, be strong.

The door to Sick House swished open. There was no one in the outer room, no sign of Lita at her desk. With a pang Triana noted that Alexa's desk also sat unoccupied. "Hello," she called out.

"In here," came Lita's voice from the adjoining room. It functioned as the hospital ward of *Galahad*, with twenty beds lining the walls. With the exception of the harrowing encounter around Saturn and Titan, when twelve of the beds had been in use, the room was usually quiet. Now, however, Lita and two of her part-time assistants were clustered around Alexa Wellington, who was lying unconscious, her head propped up with extra pillows. With soft steps Triana came up beside Lita. The two assistants finished their duties and left the room.

"What happened to her?" Triana said.

Lita kept her attention on Alexa. "Her roommate found her on the floor of their room. She apparently passed out from the pain. Probably..." She paused, and swallowed hard. "Probably trying to get ready for work, forcing herself to tough it out."

Triana bit her lip. "Have you found out anything yet?"

"I'm waiting on two tests, but my guess is that it's her appendix."

"Her appendix? Does that mean…" Triana's voice trailed off.

Lita nodded, her voice low and trembling. "It means that I'll probably have to operate. And soon."

All Triana could think to do was to put a hand on her friend's forearm. She kept quiet for a moment before saying, "Is…is there anything you need me to do?"

"Not that I can think of at the moment," Lita said. She sighed heavily and reached out with a hand to gently stroke Alexa's cheek. "I should never have let her talk me out of those tests. If I had – "

"Stop that," Triana said, squeezing Lita's arm. "You couldn't have known what was going on."

"I should have admitted her to the ward without an argument, that's what I should have done."

"You would still have to operate on her."

There was silence between them for a while. When Lita finally turned to face Triana, she did so with tears in her eyes. "I'm scared, Tree."

Once again Triana could think of no words for the moment. She stepped forward and pulled Lita into a hug, fighting to keep the tears from her own eyes.

It was happening again. Another crisis, another challenge, another…

Another test? Was that what this was all about? Was there some cosmic power that was testing their strength, their will? How much more could they take?

Triana stopped herself. This was no time to begin wallowing in pity. Alexa was seriously ill, and Lita had suddenly been thrust into a position that Triana recognized all too well: the responsibility for another's life. The only thing to do now was to rally around her friend and offer every ounce of strength that she could summon. She pushed Lita back to arm's length and looked into her eyes.

"You know you can do this, right?" Triana said. "Dr. Zimmer knew that you were the right person for this job, and I have no doubt of it."

Another tear slipped down Lita's face. She brushed it away and stared back at Triana, then nodded. "Yes, I can do this." After some hesitation, she added, "I guess...listen, this made me do some thinking about...our situation."

"What do you mean?"

Lita seemed unsure of how to continue. She looked down for a moment. "Don't be angry at me for saying this, but I've been thinking about what Merit said." She looked back up. "With everything that is happening, I mean..."

Triana felt her breath grow short. "You're upset, Lita. That's all."

"I'm not saying that I agree with him. But suddenly I'm thinking about it, you know?"

"Okay," Triana said slowly. "There's nothing wrong with that. We'll talk about it, all right? But let's get through this emergency with Alexa first. Agreed?"

Lita nodded, and lowered her gaze again.

Triana forced a smile. "Good. I want to be here when it's time. When will you be ready?"

"I have to be ready right now," Lita said. "We can't wait any longer. We'll get her prepped and into surgery within an hour." She let out a deep breath. "I'll call you before we start."

Triana left Sick House and walked toward the lift, her mind a whirlwind of competing issues. The news about Alexa was disturbing enough. The crew would undoubtedly react with shock, and that would only empower Merit even more. Now Lita had expressed her own doubts about the mission.

Triana had taken for granted that the Council would remain unified in the conflict with Merit. But if one member had concerns, did that mean they all did? How could she know? Or, Triana wondered, was she overreacting to one isolated incident? Lita's uncertainty could probably be written off to stress.

Probably.

-15-

W hen Dr. Wallace Zimmer had championed the building of the lifeboat called *Galahad*, he had envisioned a community that sustained itself through smart management of resources, recycling, and sophisticated agricultural techniques to keep the crew healthy and well fed. Various engineers and consultants had devised the most efficient farming systems ever imagined, and placed the ship's crops beneath the glistening domes that were simply named 1 and 2.

The systems, however, required delicate yet consistent management in order to produce the bounty needed to fuel the crew. Dr. Zimmer had been grateful that Bon Hartsfield had emerged from the thousands of mission candidates as the only person truly qualified to run the farms. And he had been tolerant of Bon's gruff personality; to Dr. Zimmer it lent an edge to the Council that was otherwise missing, an element that others might not understand, and yet was – to Zimmer – indispensable.

At the moment Bon was training that gruff personality upon a small electric tractor that had chosen to take the day off. It sat, unmoving, amid a row of bean plants. The farm worker who had been maneuvering it through the crop had spent fifteen minutes attempting to restart the tractor, then had surrendered the effort and summoned *Galahad's* Director of Agriculture. It was one of the minor duties that Bon understood to be his responsibility, yet irritated him nonetheless. His time, he knew, could be much better spent on other matters, rather than worrying over a stubborn machine.

As they labored over it, Bon noticed that four or five other farm workers had stopped by to lend a hand. Marco, the Portuguese boy who had earlier been commended by Bon, began tinkering with the mechanics of the tractor, to no avail. Finally the utter waste of time took its toll on the impatient Swede, and he turned to the crew member who had originally been working with the machine.

"Liam's not on the schedule today, is that right?" When this was confirmed, he shook his head. "All right, somebody find him and get him up here. He knows more about making these things run than I do, and I don't want to fall any farther behind schedule."

As one farm worker scampered off, two more walked up to offer assistance. Another unproductive ten minutes passed before Bon looked up to see Liam Wright approaching, slowly.

Too slowly.

Bon pulled his head out of the engine compartment of the tractor and watched as Liam sauntered up. Complete silence fell over the assembled group as their eyes fell upon the yellow armband encircling Liam's bicep. Bon could feel the air grow thick with the anticipation of his reaction. He pointed to the tractor's engine.

"We could use your help with this," he said.

Liam's gaze shifted from the open compartment to Bon's face. "Today is my day off."

Bon acted as if he hadn't heard. "It's not in the panel circuitry. We were just about to open the lower module. Perhaps you could help with that."

"Today is my day off."

"There are several of us who can lend a hand," Bon said. "What do you need to get started?"

Liam crossed his arms. "I'm assuming that if I work today I'll get the next two days off. Would that be right?"

Bon openly fumed. "I'm pretty sure that you don't take two days off from eating. If you believe that you're being overworked, that's something you can bring to the Council."

"The Council," Liam said. "Since when does the Council listen to anyone?"

The already thick atmosphere turned even heavier. The crew members who were standing nearby looked back and forth from Bon to Liam. Nobody uttered a sound.

"The Council will be more than happy to listen to any concerns you might have," Bon said through clenched teeth. "For now, I'm sure we would all appreciate your help, especially during your day off."

Liam turned to look at the assembled workers while directing his comments at Bon. "And what exactly happens to me if I choose to do my work only during my assigned time? Will I incur the wrath of the Council? Will I be put on trial?" He looked back at Bon. "Or will I be physically assaulted?"

Before Bon could respond, Marco stepped forward. "That's out of line, Liam," he said. "Whatever issue you might have with the Council is of no interest to us. We're simply asking for your help. Now, will you give that help or not?"

A smile crept across Liam's face. "If we continue to follow our current path through the Kuiper Belt, it really won't matter if this tractor runs or not, Marco."

"So that's your decision? You choose to do nothing?"

Bon said, "Never mind. Go about your business, Liam. We don't need your help. We'll take care of things here." Without waiting for a response, he turned back to the tractor and began to work on the lower module. "Marco, shine that light over here, please."

Liam watched the pair work for a few moments before turning away and walking quickly down the path toward the lift. With the drama apparently over, most of the other workers wandered away to their own duties. For a minute there was silence, broken only by the sounds of Bon's efforts in repairing the engine. Then, he turned to Marco and quietly said, "That wasn't necessary. But thank you."

Marco never looked up from the work. "Let's get this thing running."

* * *

Hannah sat at the desk in her room. All of the papers nearby were perfectly aligned with the edge of the desk, as was her stylus pen. A framed sketch of Gap that she had made was also squared to the corner of the desk. The walls around her were adorned with other examples of her completed artwork, mostly drawings in colored pencil, along with a couple of oil paintings she had finished before the launch. Her eye for detail and vivid imagination made her creations very popular with the crew, many of whom had the Alaskan girl's handiwork on their own walls.

Yet at the moment Hannah's love of art was far from her mind. The vidscreen on her desk displayed a three-dimensional chart of *Galahad's* course through the Kuiper Belt. A separate file, open in the lower right-hand corner of the screen, scrolled through a series of numbers and equations. Hannah's usually pretty face was furrowed into a frown as she looked at the file.

There had to be a way to maneuver safely through this minefield, she thought. The pressure that was being applied by Merit and his followers might have its roots in the overall inherent danger of the mission, but it was specifically supported right now by the perils they all faced in this shooting gallery. Hannah couldn't deny that the Kuiper Belt had the potential to destroy them, yet in her heart she was convinced that Merit was taking advantage of it to propel his personal agenda of fear. He was either homesick or afraid of what lay ahead, and had latched on to their series of unfortunate encounters to gather support for his movement.

Now that movement was threatening the stability of her world. As far as Hannah was concerned, order was critically important, and Merit represented a disruption in that order. He also was disrupting Gap's life, which caused her additional anxiety, a situation that would have been totally alien to her only three months ago. Quiet, shy, and content to work in the shadows, she had been completely unprepared for the attention she suddenly received from *Galahad's* Head of Engineering. She had, like many of the girls on board, been very attracted to Gap from the first time she'd met him. Yet she had never considered the possibility that he would not only notice her, but feel something for her, too. The past three months had been some of the happiest times of her life.

Now that happiness was threatened by turmoil, from the deadly debris that menaced their ship in the outer reaches of the solar system, to the unrest being promoted by Merit.

Turmoil and unrest were concepts that did not fit into her world.

She sighed heavily and shook her head, then refocused on the figures running through the corner of the vidscreen. The real story of the Kuiper Belt was played out here, told not in story form, but in the form of mathematics. Trillions of rock fragments, pre-comets, ice chunks, even sand and dust, all tumbling and colliding, intersecting with each other, changing direction and speed, and completely oblivious to the spacecraft that picked its way…

Wait a minute, Hannah thought. She froze, staring at the screen, her mind racing ahead of the numbers that reflected from her eyes. One idea had snapped into focus, and as usual with her, once in that position it was difficult for anything else to crowd in. She fixed on this one thought for more than a minute, turning it over and around inside her head. Finally she narrowed her eyes and looked up, her gaze settling upon her roommate's unmade bed but not really seeing anything.

"That's ridiculous," she said aloud to herself. And yet she didn't fully believe that, either. *Galahad's* experience around Titan had shattered the notion that things could be too bizarre to be true. The crew was quickly adapting to the idea that what lay ahead could be more fantastic and weird than anything they had ever imagined.

But what troubled Hannah the most about this particular idea – besides the obvious dangers to the ship – was that, if she shared this thought with others, it could be used as ammunition by Merit.

And that was the last thing she wanted to do.

Besides, she decided, this *was* a pretty wild thought, beyond even the strange phenomenon of Titan. Perhaps, when the moment was right, she would share the idea with Triana. But for the time being she would continue to puzzle it over, and do her best to shoot holes in it before sharing with anyone.

Not for the first time in her life, she secretly hoped that she was wrong.

-16-

Triana lay still on the bed in her room, her sanctuary from the hectic life as Council Leader. The sound system could have produced any music of her liking, and yet at the moment she had dialed into her most frequent choice, ushering the sound of a murmuring Colorado stream into her room. With the lights low, the water sounds were hypnotic and soothing, allowing Triana the opportunity to close her eyes and meditate. She looked for, and found, the quiet space in her mind that offered relief and escape.

If even for a few moments, it was an escape that was always precious to her.

A few minutes passed, and she opened her eyes. Her gaze instantly went to the photo beside her bed. Her dad, smiling and healthy, carried a younger version of her on his back, doing what he had always done best: enjoying life. The usual mixture of joy and sadness washed over her, a combination that she recognized as both powerful and essential for her well-being. The sadness served as a reminder of the love she carried for her late father, taken in his prime by the killer Bhaktul. The joy drove her to find the best in her dad's life to inspire her own search for happiness. In the past two years that search had been challenging, but these moments of solitude and soul-searching reaffirmed for her that happiness was coming her way.

It was up to her to create it and make it real.

She thought about Lita's admission of doubt. It had surprised her...or had it? Could she honestly say that the same thought had never entered her own mind? Triana looked again at the picture of her dad. He was gone, and Earth could never be the same for her. His death had been the motivating factor in her decision to leave. But now, after more time had passed, would it be possible to go back and pick up again, to find a new life there? Was she completely sure that happiness on Earth, for her, was impossible?

Stop that, she thought. Bhaktul had made the decision for all of them. There was no going back.

But still...

She looked at the clock and realized that it was time to return to Sick House. Lita would soon be ready for surgery. Triana felt a stab of anxiety, but realized that it was probably only a fraction of the nervousness that gripped Lita and Alexa right now.

Swinging her legs off the bed, *Galahad's* Council Leader sat up and pulled her long brown hair behind her ears. She knew that one aspect of leadership was instilling confidence in others, yet that task would be very challenging in this circumstance. Who among them was ready – especially as teenagers – to literally hold a friend's life in their hand, the way Lita would when she picked up that scalpel? What exactly did one say to a person preparing for that? Triana wanted desperately to empathize with what Lita was facing, but was that possible? Was it really possible to imagine that responsibility?

Triana's thoughts flashed back to their encounter with the stowaway, and her frantic remote control of the Spider which would ultimately save their lives. She had held the fate of *Galahad* in her hands at that moment.

There might be similarities with what Lita now confronted, but only slightly. Triana wondered, were she in

Lita's place, if she could even hold the blade steady, while the unconscious figure of her friend lay before her. Well, she decided, for now it was unimportant. Lita was trained – although briefly – for this task, and Triana was not. Support was the best thing she could offer, and she would devote all of her energies to that.

Her thoughts were interrupted by the buzz of her door. She opened it to find Lita standing there, her eyes hollow and distant.

"It's almost time," Lita said softly. "You said you wanted to be there."

In an instant Triana recognized that Lita could have easily called down to her with this announcement. The fact that she had taken the time to personally escort Triana to Sick House must have meant that she wanted to talk.

"Come in for a moment," Triana said, standing aside. When the two girls were seated in the room, a silence fell over them. Triana waited.

A minute passed. Two. Finally, Lita made eye contact. "I want you to know that I will do my very best."

The comment seemed strange to Triana, almost out of character for her friend. Lita was one of Triana's rocks, a stable, steady force that she relied upon for counsel and guidance during difficult moments. She would, of course, do her best. There was no question about that. Something else had to be brewing inside Lita, and was undoubtedly the reason she was here. Triana chose to remain silent and listen.

"They're finishing the prep on Alexa, so I have a couple of minutes," Lita said. "I…I wanted to share a story with you, a story about my mother."

She took a deep breath, then let it out slowly. "You know, of course, that my mother was a doctor. And she was very good. Early in her career she was approached by several universities and hospitals in America, hoping to bring her onto their staffs. She was very tempted, too. At one point she even traveled to Los Angeles for an interview.

"But then something happened. While she was considering the job offer in the States, her best friend fell ill. Cancer."

There was another moment of silence as Lita gathered her thoughts. "I was only an infant at the time, but I've heard many stories. Her name was Carmela, and she had been my mother's closest friend since grade school. In college, while my mother studied medicine, Carmela was interested only in mathematics. From what I've heard, she was brilliant. She and my mother spent hours together in the library, studying for their exams, of course. But more than that. They would share their dreams, too. My mother was sure she would become a top surgeon, while Carmela was convinced she would teach in a major university somewhere.

"They would also talk about their personal dreams. My mother was married with a baby daughter, and Carmela was engaged to be married to her high school sweetheart. They would laugh, I'm told, about how they would have to convince their husbands to move, so that the two friends would always live in the same city. In the same neighborhood, they claimed." A faint smile crossed Lita's face. "They probably would have insisted on buying homes right next door to each other."

Triana smiled, and took Lita's hand for support.

"But the cancer," Lita said, the smile fading. "The cancer."

She fell quiet for a moment. When she spoke again, she tried to keep her voice strong, although it was obvious to Triana that her emotions were beginning to take a toll.

"By now my mother was certified, and working in the hospital in Veracruz. As I mentioned, the offer from Los Angeles was on her mind when Carmela became sick. Two doctors informed Carmela's fiancé, and my mother, that surgery might help.

"Or it might kill her."

Triana held her breath, staring into Lita's eyes, which had again taken on the hollow, vacant look.

"Carmela chose to have the surgery, on one condition. She insisted that my mother perform the operation. She believed that my mother's love for her would make the difference.

"So," Lita said, "that's exactly what happened. My mother summoned all of her courage and faith, and walked into that operating room, with her best friend's life in her hands."

In a flash, Triana knew the outcome. Lita confirmed it.

"Carmela died. She survived the operation, but was gone twelve hours later. The other doctors told my mother that there was nothing she could have done, that she had done the best she could. But my mother was inconsolable. In her mind she had failed her best friend. She had not been able to save her, which is what she had studied and trained for her entire adult life. She watched her best friend die."

At this point Lita's voice broke. Her shoulders shook, and a sob escaped her throat. "And that changed everything. My mother immediately declined the offer to go to Los Angeles. She gave up any thoughts of ever leaving Veracruz. She chose to never again perform surgery, and instead dedicated herself to a small family practice in her hometown."

Lita looked up into Triana's face. "She never got over Carmela's death."

Triana squeezed Lita's hand and felt her own tears coming on. "Lita," she said in a soft voice. "Your mother was a hero. She chose to spend her life helping others. She also chose to do everything in her power to help her friend. Sometimes...." Triana hesitated, thinking of her own father. "Sometimes the universe has plans for our friends and family that we can't understand.

"But that doesn't mean that we don't try. The universe could very well have planned for your mother to save Carmela's life. We don't know, just as we *never* know what's in store for any of us."

Triana reached out and placed her hand on Lita's upper arm. "It seems like such a cruel coincidence right now, the fact that you're in the same position as your mother. But… but when you think about it, is it really? Your mother was a caregiver, as you are now. Caregivers are going to sometimes find themselves treating their own loved ones, their friends, people they care about. As much as we hate to think about it, this probably won't be the last time you're called upon to do this."

She waited until she saw Lita give a slight nod before continuing. "So, while we have no idea what's in store for any of us, we do know that it's our destiny to do everything we can to help, whenever possible. That's who we are. That's who *you* are.

"I know that your mother would tell you the same thing."

For a while Lita said nothing, looking into Triana's eyes. Triana leaned across and embraced her, and felt Lita's breathing become strong and steady.

-17-

By now you undoubtedly recognize that I am an amazing observer of human characteristics and behavior. You do recognize that, right?

Here's my latest observation. Human males are somehow genetically related to bull elks and big horn sheep. Why? Because they all butt heads the same way.

"Hey, Gap. Mind if I interrupt for a minute?"

Gap recognized the voice behind him. He stood with his hands clasped behind his head, staring at the same panel that had occupied his attention far too much recently, once again wracking his brain to solve – once and for all – the heating issue on Level 6. It had stabilized for the time being, so on his way to Sick House he had decided to pop in and check on things.

He answered without turning around. "I'm a little busy right now, Merit."

"I won't take long."

"I'm busy here, and in just a couple of minutes I have to be somewhere else," Gap said.

"Sick House, right?"

That was enough to prompt Gap to spin around. Before he could speak, Merit held up both hands as if warding off a blow.

"Whoa, steady boy," Merit said. "Yes, I heard about Alexa. I'm sorry about that. I'm sure she'll be – "

"Before you get any ideas," Gap spit out, "this has nothing to do with our mission or our destination. It just happened. It would have happened to Alexa if we were heading back to Earth, too."

Merit slowly lowered his hands. "I know that. I said I'm sorry, okay?" He paused, allowing Gap to cool a bit. "Just one minute of your time?"

"You have nothing to say that I want to hear right now," Gap said. He looked around. "Where's your cheering section? Traveling without your fan club today?"

A smile spread across Merit's face. "How do you know what I'm going to say? You might be very interested."

"Not likely. I've heard your arguments already. Not very impressive, really."

"Afraid to find out what I might say? You haven't become close-minded, have you, Gap?"

It was Gap's turn to smile. "I'm sure if you blabbered on for weeks and weeks, eventually something interesting might accidentally spill out of your mouth."

Merit took a step back, leaned against the wall and crossed his arms. "I should know better than to verbally spar with someone who practices with Roc on a daily basis. I am overmatched."

Gap stared at him for a moment. He had always noticed the long, jet-black hair, often pulled back into a tail. Now he scanned Merit's face, and noticed for the first time a small scar under his right eye. The bandage from his lip was gone, without any trace of the blow that Bon had inflicted. Apparently Merit didn't feel the prop was necessary anymore.

"Alexa is about to have surgery, and I want to be there," Gap said. "You have thirty seconds."

"Then I'll make it quick," Merit said. "I just wanted you to know that we now number almost fifty. That's twenty percent of the crew. And, although you sometimes seem to get…shall we say, emotional?…I know that you're one of the brightest people on this ship. Putting aside for the moment your loyalty to Triana – and I honestly do commend you for that – does your brain really tell you that she's right and we're wrong? Have you truly stopped to consider what we're saying? Loyalty is admirable…but not at the cost of your life. Wouldn't you agree?"

Gap chuckled. "Let's shoot straight with each other, Merit. First of all, I'm not swayed by your constant use of the word 'we.' This is about you. Secondly, if you're going to appeal to my intellect, it would be a good idea to take a stance that actually makes sense. Your idea of going back to Earth is completely illogical. You accuse me of being emotional; well, your plan is based totally on fear, one of the most destructive emotions there is.

"And finally," he added, "you'll find that people are loyal to Triana for a reason. She's doing the job that was assigned to her – unlike some people – and she's doing it well."

Merit nodded his head. "Nice speech. I'm glad we could talk."

Gap walked around him toward the door.

"One other thing," Merit called out. "If things turn ugly – and they might – you're always welcome to change your mind and come over to our side. Just remember that."

Gap stopped at the open door and looked back. "I would be very careful if I were you, Merit."

"And you as well," Merit said.

* * *

Triana and Channy stood next to Alexa's bed. Triana knew that the best thing they could do was cheer up the sick girl, and keep the atmosphere upbeat. She also knew that these weren't exactly her strongest talents, but was confident that Channy would more than make up for it. She wasn't disappointed.

"Don't think for a minute that I don't know what's really going on here," Channy said, fixing Alexa with a mock scowl. "I've seen people go to outrageous extremes to get out of one of my workouts, but this is ridiculous."

Alexa, prepped and ready for surgery, managed to force a smile through the haze of painkilling medication that had left her barely awake. She mumbled, "Can't...fool you, can... I?"

Channy shook her head. "And if you think this gives you a free pass for months, think again."

Triana took Alexa's hand. "I see you've got a little friend keeping you company." Iris was curled up beside the patient, purring steadily. One of the cat's paws was casually draped across Alexa's forearm.

"Uh-huh," Alexa said. "She's my...good luck charm."

"I thought you might enjoy some pet power on your way to surgery," Channy said, scratching the cat's chin. "You know, they say that dogs and cats can sense when somebody's sick. And look, she could have jumped down a long time ago, but she's not going anywhere." In response to the scratching, Iris closed her eyes and began to purr louder.

"You'll have quite an audience, too," Triana said. "Gap's on his way, and your roomie will be here any minute."

Alexa exhaled a grunt. "That's...nice. Tell them...I said... thank...you."

"Oh, one other thing," Channy said with a grin. "Hurry up and get well so you can be on my dating game. You've become a celebrity now, which means you'll be a very popular contestant."

It was obvious that Alexa wanted to respond, but instead her eyes closed and her breathing became regular and deep. Channy, a sudden look of fear in her eyes, turned to Triana.

"Is this normal?" she said.

"Yes," came the answer from Lita who was walking into the room. "She's getting a gradual drip that puts her in a light sleep on and off."

Triana bit her lip, then said to Lita. "You need anything from us?"

"No, but thanks," Lita said. "We're going to take her into the operating room now." She gently shook Alexa's arm. "Hey, sleepy head."

Alexa stirred and opened her eyes about halfway. Lita leaned over her and said, "What do you want to eat when we're all finished? Pizza? Ice cream? Liver?"

A trace of a smile crept across Alexa's semi-conscious face. Channy picked up Iris and touched Alexa's other arm. "You can borrow Iris during your recovery, but you're responsible for cleaning up any hairballs, okay?"

It was Triana's turn. She felt as if she should say something lighthearted as well, but found that she was becoming emotionally overcome by the situation. A lump formed in her throat. "We'll see you soon, okay?" was all that she could manage to say.

"There's good news," Lita said to Alexa. "You'll sleep through the blood, so you won't have to see anything."

A larger smile spread across Alexa's face. Before she could mutter anything, two Sick House workers entered the room. They stepped up, adjusted Alexa's bed, then rolled it out of the hospital ward toward *Galahad's* lone operating room. It had never been used up to this point.

Triana looked at Lita. "Blood?"

"She told me the other day that she's afraid of blood. She works in a clinic, and she's afraid of…" Lita began to choke up.

Triana put an arm around her friend. "She's in great hands, Lita. You'll be perfect."

"Yeah," added Channy. "Piece of cake."

Lita exhaled and appeared to gather her composure. "All right. I'll…I guess I'll see you in a little while." She hugged Triana and Channy, then left to scrub and change into sterile gear.

Channy shifted Iris into a crook of her arm, then shook her head in disbelief. "She's not even sixteen-years-old yet, and she's about to operate on someone. I can't even imagine that."

Triana said, "She probably can't, either."

The two of them retreated to the Sick House office. The door to the hallway opened, and Gap walked in with Alexa's roommate, Katarina.

"Did we miss her?" Gap said.

Triana nodded. "Yeah, they just took her in."

"Is she going to be okay?" Katarina said softly.

Everyone was quiet for a moment as the gravity of the situation finally hit home. Through all of the tough scrapes, through all of the near-death experiences, and through all of the drama, nothing like this had happened until now. Once again it occurred to the four *Galahad* crew members standing in Sick House that they were indeed on their own. There was no help to call in, no ambulance that could rush to the scene, no...

No adult that they could lean on. They had only themselves.

Triana finally answered Katarina. "Yes. She's going to be okay."

* * *

The mechanical waves of sound are unable to travel through the icy vacuum of space, which means that the ultimate silence sits just beyond a planet's atmosphere. The Kuiper objects that jostled and collided with each other gave off eruptions of rock and ice shards, but there was no soundtrack to accompany their impacts, no matter how violent.

Rolling, tumbling, scraping, they pitched along in their mindless trek around the outskirts of the solar system. *Galahad* dared to cut across their path, not unlike a pedestrian tempting fate by running across swiftly moving lanes of traffic.

Any collision between a Kuiper object and the spacecraft would produce an explosion with enough intensity to be visible – if only for an instant – on Earth. The impact would produce a blinding flash.

But no sound whatsoever.

The most sophisticated warning system ever developed kept up a continuous scan of the space ahead of the ship, probing for potential danger spots, alerting the ship's computer to any possible hazards. A typical scan would normally be a lazy sweep back and forth, up and down, repeated at a slow and steady pace.

The Kuiper Belt was a stickier situation than normal, however. *Galahad's* warning system was tweaked to cover its optimum distance and spread pattern, and swept in all directions at a frantic pace. The cumulative amount of data processed every second during these scans equaled all of the data stored in an average library back on Earth. There was no margin for error.

The lives of 251 teenage pilgrims relied upon a scanning unit no larger than a shoe box, bolted into an equipment rack, and tucked into an isolated corner of the ship's Engineering section.

-18-

They waited in the Conference Room. The office of Sick House seemed too close to the reality of what was happening, the Rec Room and Dining Halls were too noisy, and their own rooms seemed stifling. Triana chose not to sit in her usual spot at the head of the table. Gap had the seat beside her, rolling a cup of water back and forth in his hands. Channy opted for the floor of the room, her back against the wall and her legs crossed, with Iris sprawled beside her. Katarina seemed to feel uncomfortable, almost like an outsider who had crashed a Council meeting. She sat quietly across from Triana and Gap.

For over an hour they made small talk, trying to keep the mood as light as possible. Channy tried to sell them on her dating game, but it became quickly apparent that nobody was interested at the moment. She changed course and discussed some recent workouts, as well as the idea of another soccer tournament. This garnered a somewhat enthusiastic response, but soon that, too, faded.

Gap asked Katarina a few questions about what was going on in the Farms, which was her current assignment on the ship. Her abbreviated answers hinted at the discomfort she obviously felt, so Gap turned his attention to the cat. He quizzed Channy about Bon's patience with Iris in the Farms, and whether or not she was getting tired of feline babysitting duties. This conversation fizzled after about a minute.

They knew that it was all just one big distraction from the tension that weighed heavily on the room. Now, after a block of silence that only focused each of them on the seriousness of the situation, Triana cleared her throat.

"We're all scared," she said softly.

Gap looked at her with an expression of surprise. "What?"

She nodded. "There's nothing wrong with admitting that. We can sit here and pretend that we're doing okay, but we're all scared. Maybe we should talk about that instead of soccer games and Iris."

Channy got up from the floor and sat down at the table beside Katarina. "You know what scares me the most?" she said. "This could have happened to any of us. I mean, your appendix?"

"Yeah," Gap said. "The month we spent in quarantine before we left Earth might have eliminated a lot of germs or viruses from our future, but not this."

"And that makes me wonder about a lot of other things," Channy said. "What about tumors, or blood clots, or stuff like that? I know we're all young, but with this many people on the ship, things are gonna happen."

Triana could see the concern on Channy's face, and it caused her to lean forward, her elbows on the table. "Can I share something with you about that?" she said. "I...I don't talk about my dad very much, even though I'm always thinking about him. But he did teach me a few things about this."

The others sat quietly staring at her. She realized that this was a side of herself that they never saw, and they were not about to interrupt. She gathered her thoughts for a moment, then continued.

"I've never known a happier person in my life. He loved his work, he loved me, and he loved life. Of all the lessons he tried to teach to a somewhat serious little girl, the one that stood out was to enjoy life without worrying about what might happen. It's not like he was a crazy daredevil or anything, but he...he didn't always play it safe, either."

Triana paused, her mind drifting backwards, retrieving a moment frozen in her memory.

"When I was thirteen, I remember crying before one of my soccer tournaments. Our team had worked so hard the whole season, and we were picked to go to this big state tournament. I was scared to death that I would play horribly, or that we would embarrass ourselves against these other great teams. I even worried about getting hurt, because a few of the teams were a little older than us, and a lot bigger. I was upset about so many things.

"The night before the first game, my dad sat on the edge of my bed and shook his head. He said, 'Let me tell you something that you obviously have not thought about. You're thirteen, you're about to play in a tournament that thousands of other girls would give anything to participate in, and it could be one of the most fun experiences of your life.'

"'But,' he said to me, 'you're all balled up inside. You're worrying about ridiculous things. Do you really want this tournament to end and have your only memories be of worrying about it?'"

Gap, Channy, and Katarina sat still, their attention fixed on Triana. She chuckled, then continued. "He told me something that I've tried to remember as often as possible. He said, 'Close your eyes, and for a few moments visualize the last minute of the last game. You're running down the field, the sun is shining, the grass is perfect, you're laughing, your teammates are laughing, and you have a wide open shot for the game-winner. You pull back your leg, and you fire away.'"

Triana closed her eyes now, taking herself back to that moment, one of many precious memories of her dad. She kept the smile etched across her face. After a few moments, Channy spoke up in a quiet voice, as if not wanting to break the spell, but yet needing to know the answer.

"Umm…what happened? What did you visualize?"

"That's the best part," Triana said, opening her eyes and looking at Channy. "I have re-lived that moment over and over again. I'm lying in bed before the tournament begins, and I'm watching myself take that shot. And you know what? It ends differently every single time."

Channy looked puzzled. "What do you mean?"

"I mean, sometimes I visualize that shot scooting past the goalie, into the corner of the net for the winning score. Sometimes it rockets over the goalie's head, skims off the crossbar and drops into the net. Other times the goalie blocks the shot, but I get the rebound and fire it past her to win the game.

"It's always different. But I noticed something about it. Every time I see it, it's something good. My dad had me close my eyes and visualize, right? He didn't say to visualize a happy ending. He just put me in that place, and allowed me to sketch my own ending. And I found that my worries disappeared. It was..."

She fell silent for a moment, searching for the words. "It was like I was given the brush and could paint any picture I wanted. And it made me realize that I wanted none of those things that had bothered me. I could be the artist of my own future."

Triana looked around at the faces of her friends. "Listen, I know there's a big difference between a soccer game, and what we're going through today. I know the stakes are a lot higher, and the results are much more important.

"That doesn't change the fact that we ultimately control our thoughts. They don't control us, unless we let them. Yes, bad things might happen, and, believe me, I've been through my share of difficult times. But I can't deny that there is still a power that we don't understand, and it comes from right here." She tapped her head. "We might not be able to control everything that happens, and we might be challenged by many things in our lives. But we only drain ourselves emotionally when we worry about things beyond our control."

Channy smiled at her. "Your dad was pretty cool, wasn't he?"

Triana leaned back in her chair and looked up at the ceiling. "He was the best. We're all individuals, you know, and we have our own settings, I guess you could say. But I'm grateful for everything he shared with me, and everything that he taught me."

Gap reached over and put a hand on her shoulder. "I wish everyone on the ship could have heard what you just said."

Triana felt a tear trying to work its way out, so she took a deep breath and blinked a couple of times. When it seemed like an awkward silence had settled over the room, she turned to Katarina. "Are you okay?"

Katarina nodded, her eyes wide. "I...I guess so. I just don't like feeling like there's nothing I can do, you know?"

The other three considered this for a moment. Triana said, "In a way, we're all doing something. We're here for each other, and that's the most important thing right now."

Katarina smiled at her. "You're right. If I wasn't here with you guys right now, I'd probably be going out of my mind."

"Me, too," Channy said. "I know you all get a bit tired of my chattering all the time, but today I kinda need to. It helps."

"Of course it does," Triana said. She offered her own faint smile. "You know I'm not usually much of a talker, but this is exactly what we need to be doing."

"Well," Gap said, setting down his cup of water and running a hand through his hair. "I'm glad to hear you all saying this. If you weren't hanging out with me right now I'd probably be forced to chat with Roc, and I'm not sure I could handle that under the circumstances."

"I heard that," came the computer's voice from the speaker.

A stress-reducing ripple of laughter spread around the room. Triana appreciated the break from the tension, but couldn't help but wonder if a good portion of that stress wasn't triggered by guilt. Yes, they were afraid for Alexa, and yes, they were aware that it could just as easily have happened to them.

But was there another factor at play here, too? Were they troubled by thoughts that they didn't dare give voice to? Did they all wonder, secretly, how this might have played out if they had been home? Were they each considering Merit's arguments, which, in the light of another potential crisis, suddenly seemed more attractive?

Or was it just her?

Triana studied the faces around the table. There was no way of knowing if their minds were wrestling with the same disturbing questions. She felt a knot in her stomach again, and wondered if her own face registered the conflict she felt. If so, nobody said anything.

She suddenly felt a touch of shame, angry at herself for allowing her thoughts to drift this way, when she should be thinking about the life and death struggle that Alexa faced. A struggle, she realized, that should have been decided by now. Lita had said that the surgery would take less than an hour. Triana glanced at the clock on her vidscreen.

It had been an hour and a half.

-19-

Her Zen place; that's how Alexa had said she dealt with blood. She went into her Zen place.

Lita had never been bothered by the sight of blood, until, she realized, it belonged to a close friend. Now she understood exactly what Alexa had meant about the need to somehow detach from the situation. Yet how to detach and still maintain control? What place was this, Zen or otherwise, that offered relief from the pain, the pressure, the weight of responsibility?

Lita felt a catch in her throat and swallowed hard, partly to stifle the stab of grief at her friend's condition, but also to staunch the rising alarm that she had missed something. The surgery had progressed exactly as it had been spelled out in all of the tutorials she had scanned. The programmed video guide had directed her through every step, and she had made sure to not rush anything, to follow each stage precisely as instructed. She had total confidence in her thoroughness.

So why did she have this feeling?

Nerves, she told herself. That's all, just nerves.

The monitors flashed their steady reports: pulse, blood pressure, breathing. Everything looked fine. Lita looked quickly at Alexa's face, so calm and serene. In this unconscious state there was no pain. Would there be dreams?

The thought made Lita pause. She had read that some people did experience dreams during anesthesia, and thankfully most were pleasant. Alexa looked content and peaceful, which made Lita feel somewhat better, but who could say what images were flashing through Alexa's mind during this down time? The idea fascinated Lita.

She shifted her gaze to stare down at the small incision, amazed once again at the incredible machine that was the human body. The appendix was out, the abdominal area had been inspected for bleeding and any pockets of infection, and then had been washed out with a saline solution. It was time to close up.

Lita thought about the progress of medical science. In the old days she would have been sewing up her patient, and later might have evolved to stapling. But today she was fortunate to have a technique similar to gluing, which would leave no scar on Alexa's abdomen. In less than two minutes she was finished.

Lita set down the instrument she had been using and exhaled. One of her assistants looked up and made eye contact. Even through the mask, Lita could tell that her face held a big smile.

For the next minute there was an exchange of congratulations and heavy sighs. Things were cleaned up, carts were wheeled out of the way, and Lita made one more inspection of the wound. "Okay," she said, "let's wake her up."

Another assistant, Manu, adjusted the mixture of gases into Alexa's clear mask, checking and double-checking the figures that spilled across the vidscreen. Lita stepped back and pulled down her surgical mask. The monitors continued to relay a healthy set of vital signs. She walked across the room and stripped off her gloves. In the background she heard the assistant softly calling Alexa back to consciousness. The entire procedure, from start to finish, had taken forty-nine minutes. Next time, Lita thought with a smile, I'll know what I'm doing, and should be able to knock it out in thirty-five.

A few small drops of blood spotted one of her sleeves. It magnified the significance of what had just happened. Pulling off the white smock, she looked back over her shoulder at Manu as he worked beside Alexa.

"Everything okay?" Lita asked him.

He looked up at her. "She's not responding."

Lita quickly walked back to the operating table, looked at Alexa, then up at the monitors. Everything continued to read normal.

"She should at least be stirring a little bit by now," Manu said. His voice carried a touch of panic.

"Let's stay calm," Lita said, but inside her chest she felt the same odd sensation return. Something didn't feel right. She immediately summoned the ship's computer.

"Roc, am I boosting the oxygen level here?"

"No," came the reply. In the next ten minutes they followed every emergency step as outlined in their medical procedures manual. Alexa remained unconscious.

Now the sensation of panic began to overwhelm Lita. Her mind tortured her with a reminder of her mother's experience with Carmela. In frustration she lashed out at Roc.

"There's something we're missing! What are we not doing?"

"Lita," Roc said, "we have done everything called for. She's not responding."

"She *has* to respond!" Lita looked at the monitor again, willing it to show her something, anything, that would explain the situation. It mocked her with normal readings. Turning to Manu she said, "Are you sure you gave her the right mixture during the procedure?"

Roc answered for the stunned boy. "Lita, I monitored everything that was administered during the operation. The dosage was correct, the course of action was followed perfectly. She's not responding."

Lita's chin dropped to her chest and she issued a low groan. "What have I missed? I must have missed something."

"You haven't done anything wrong, Lita," Roc said. "You did everything exactly as you should have. The surgery itself was perfect."

"It's not perfect!" Lita said, raising her voice. "She's not waking up."

"And there is nothing you have done to cause that," the computer replied.

Lita shook her head and felt a tremble work its way through her body. First her mother with Carmela, and now her own failure with Alexa. After a moment she realized that Manu and the other assistant were watching her, waiting for direction. She took a deep breath, then another.

"Let's get her back into the hospital ward and into her bed," she said finally, her voice returning to normal. She laid out instructions for Alexa's care and treatment, then watched as they wheeled her out. She was alone in the operating room.

Leaning back against the wall, she allowed one sob to shake her. Then she tilted her head toward the ceiling and shut her eyes.

* * *

He spent about five minutes scrubbing the combination of grease and dirt from his hands and nails before remembering that there was still a lot of work to be done before he could take a break. Now Bon dried his hands and sat down with a sigh at his desk. He and Marco had finally coaxed the tractor into starting, no thanks to Liam. A flash of anger passed through Bon as he recalled the smug look of satisfaction on Liam's face. Between that showdown and the confrontation with Merit, Bon felt mentally fatigued. He wasn't one for taking time off, but suddenly all he wanted was to get away and not have to think about any of it for awhile.

A tap came on his open door. Hannah stood just outside, her body language making it clear that she felt as if she were intruding.

"Yes, come in," Bon said, puzzled by the visit. Other than a brief connection during the drama around Titan he hadn't spent any time with her. He knew that she was gifted when it came to mathematics, and that she and Gap were close, but, between his natural reluctance to socialize and her shyness, they had never really spoken.

"I don't want to interrupt anything," she said, taking a few tentative steps into his office.

"No, you're not interrupting," he said. "What's on your mind?"

She sat down across from his desk. "Well, I've been doing some research on the Kuiper Belt." When Bon didn't respond, she nervously looked down at her hands. "It's a pretty scary place. I mean, a lot more dangerous than we thought, obviously. There's a lot more…stuff, I guess you could say, than we thought would be out here. Mostly smaller rocks and ice balls. It's going to be very difficult to squeeze through it all."

Bon stared at her. "Sounds like you've been talking with Merit."

"No, no," Hannah said quickly, looking up at him. "I mean, I know what he's saying, and he's right that it's dangerous. But I don't agree with him about turning back."

"Okay," Bon said, sitting back in his chair. "I'm sorry, but I don't really know that much about it. Not my specialty. I'm pretty busy up here. I leave the piloting of the ship to others."

Hannah swallowed, and again looked as if she was cowering from him. "Right, I know that. That's not really why I'm here."

"And just why *are* you here?"

"Well…" She paused.

Bon said, "Contrary to what you might think, I don't bite. What do you want to talk to me about?"

She began again. "Well, I've been plugging in a lot of numbers, trying to make sense of what we're seeing out here. There are some extremely large bodies, the size of dwarf planets, like Pluto. There are probably a hundred or so of those. But that's nothing compared to the billions and billions of smaller chunks. They're scattered in a haphazard way. When you first look at it, it seems random."

Bon studied her face. "I suppose you're going to tell me that it's really not random?"

She nodded. "That's right. There are pockets of density here and there, separated by long stretches where it's rather unpopulated. We could zip through those areas without too many worries. At least not compared to the other zones."

"Bad luck," the Swede said to her. "We happened across a thick stretch, I guess."

"No," she said. "We didn't just happen across it. We *have* to go through this crowded stretch if we want to get to Eos."

"I don't understand what you're getting at," Bon said. "Of course we have to go this way." He studied her face for a moment, trying to jump a step ahead in order to figure out where she was going. "Wait a minute," he said, pushing his chair back. "Are you suggesting that these thick pockets of space debris are *deliberately* in this spot?"

Hannah diverted her eyes. "It's probably a discussion for the entire Council, but I wanted to at least talk to you about something...sensitive."

"Let me guess," Bon said. "The Cassini."

Hannah nodded, keeping her eyes in her lap.

Bon exhaled loudly. "Listen, I'm getting a little tired of all the questions about them. We left Titan behind months ago."

"But I'm guessing that..." Hannah seemed to find a hidden reserve of courage. "I'm guessing that you're still in contact with them somehow, and I was hoping that you might be able to...I don't know, ask a question, or something."

Another long silence fell over the room. This time Hannah kept her gaze fixed on Bon's eyes, as if willing him to answer. He stared back, considering his words. Or, rather, considering the potential impact his words would have.

"I think I am," he said finally.

Hannah swallowed and let out her breath. "You think you're still in contact?"

"Yeah. I think so."

A visible look of relief crossed Hannah's face. "I was hoping you would say that. So, if you don't mind me prying, why do you think so?"

Bon looked out the window into Dome 1. "Just little things here and there. I told Channy that it felt almost like déjà vu, but sometimes it's more than that. A little while ago we had a problem with one of the tractors. A couple of us banged around on it but couldn't get it to go."

He paused, looking back at Hannah. "And then I just kinda...I don't know, sat back, closed my eyes, and quit trying so hard. A moment later I knew what I needed to do. And I did it."

"You got it to run?"

"Yeah."

"But couldn't you have already known how to fix it, and you just finally remembered?"

Bon shrugged. "You asked if I thought I was still in contact, and that's what I think. Sometimes things just come to me. Could I have fixed the engine on that tractor anyway? Maybe. But as soon as I let go and emptied my mind, the answer came to me. In my opinion it came from The Cassini."

Hannah nodded slowly. She unconsciously reached out and straightened a piece of paper on Bon's desk. "Okay. Well, like I said, I'm glad to hear that, because I'd like to make a request."

Bon chuckled. "All right. What is it you want to know? Something about these dense spots in the Kuiper Belt, right?"

"Yeah. I'll explain it in detail with the Council, but when we have that meeting I'd like to know if The Cassini can answer a question for me."

"Well," Bon said, "obviously I can't promise anything, but I'll do my best. What is it?"

Hannah hesitated before answering. "I want to know if these pockets are meant to keep things out, or to keep us in."

-20-

Triana's heart sank. Light spilled into the Conference Room from the corridor, and Lita stood in the doorway, looking completely drained, almost ready to collapse. In a flash Gap bolted from his seat and helped her over to the table where she sat down heavily. Triana and Channy rushed to her side, both dropping to a knee to look into her face.

"Lita," Triana said. "Are you okay?"

"I don't know," Lita mumbled. "Not really."

Channy was the one who asked what they all were afraid to ask. "Alexa...?"

Lita looked down at Channy, then at Gap, then Triana. Her gaze finally settled upon Katarina, who was frozen in her chair, her eyes wide.

"She..." Lita began to say, then shook with a sob. "She made it through the surgery fine, but..."

Nobody spoke. Triana placed a hand on Lita's knee to show support.

"I got the appendix out," Lita said softly. "But...but we couldn't wake her up afterwards."

Channy shot a quick glance of alarm at Triana. "What does that mean?"

Lita looked at Channy with red-rimmed eyes. "It means that she's in a coma."

Across the table Katarina brought her hand up to her mouth, letting out a sharp cry. Triana felt a shudder ripple through her body, and her mouth went dry. She managed to exchange a look with Gap, who spoke for the first time.

"But...that might be normal, right?" he said. "Like a defense mechanism or something?"

Lita shook her head. "No, it's not normal. She should be wide awake right now. But her body had some strange reaction to the anesthesia, and she's not waking up." She turned to look at Triana. "She's not waking up," she repeated.

Now Triana felt her heart ache for her friend. She could only imagine the pain that Lita must be experiencing. Words, which only minutes before had seemed easy to find, now seemed out of reach. And yet something needed to be said.

She gently touched Lita's face, turning it so that they would make eye contact. "Listen to me," Triana said, her voice low but firm. "A couple of hours ago you were terrified because you were about to perform surgery – surgery, Lita! – on your friend. There were doubts running through your head. And you pulled it off. Do you understand that? You're about to turn sixteen, and out here, more than a billion miles from home, you just saved someone's life. Nobody else on this ship could have done that!"

The others in the room were motionless, listening to Triana. Lita seemed slowly to regain her composure. Her body appeared to relax, melting into the chair.

"You are responsible for Alexa being alive right now," Triana said. "She had a reaction to the anesthesia, but that's something you could never have known. Your first priority was to operate on her, quickly. You saved her."

Lita smiled faintly. "I was so scared."

"I know," Triana half-whispered. "I know you were. But you did it. We're all so proud of you." She leaned over and wrapped her arms around Lita, who returned the hug and finally found release in tears.

Channy wept, too. She leaned in and joined the two Council members in their embrace.

Gap sat down in one of the chairs. He respectfully waited a few moments before speaking. "Um, what happens now?"

Lita sat back and dabbed at the remaining tears. "Well, I honestly don't know. Alexa has the hospital ward to herself, so she'll be getting a lot of personalized care. She's breathing on her own just fine. I think all we can do is watch and wait."

Triana pulled up one of the chairs and sat down. "Roc, can you help us out with some answers here?"

"I've just been analyzing the data," the computer said. "Alexa is in a low-level state on the Glasgow Coma Scale, but I don't see any signs of brain damage."

"How long could this last?" Gap said.

"Impossible to answer. It's actually rare for a coma to last more than a few weeks at most, and often it's just a matter of days. Notable exceptions include senators and congressmen, who have been known to remain in a coma for decades. I would prefer to withhold any prediction on Alexa until we see what happens in the next twenty-four hours."

Triana digested this for a minute. "Okay," she said to Lita. "What do you need from us?"

Galahad's Health Director stood up. "I can't think of anything right now." She let out a long breath. "Well, I have to get back to Sick House. Sorry if I freaked out a bit, guys."

Channy shook her head. "Don't be crazy. We think you're amazing."

"Thanks," Lita said with a smile. "I appreciate the support from all of you." She looked at Katarina at the end of the table. "I'm going to take good care of your roomie, okay?"

Katarina walked over to Lita and gave her a hug. "I know you will. Thank you. Is it okay if I at least see her for a moment?"

"Sure," Lita said. "But only for a minute right now. C'mon." She started to follow Katarina into the corridor, then turned back to face Triana. She didn't say anything, but Triana could sense what her friend was thinking. She smiled and nodded at Lita, who spun around with a renewed confidence and walked briskly out the door.

The room remained silent for a few seconds. Then Gap drummed his fingers on the table and said, "Life is never boring aboard *Galahad*, is it?"

Triana said, "Not so far, anyway." In her mind she quickly ran through the inventory of current issues. Heating problems, the Kuiper Belt minefield, Alexa's emergency surgery...

And Merit Simms.

The drama from Alexa's appendicitis had distracted Triana for awhile, but she knew that the minute she walked out of the Conference Room she would be walking right back into the controversy that Merit had stirred up.

Gap seemed to read her thoughts. "Just for the record, our troublesome friend came to see me. I have to tell you that I don't care for the tone his little speeches are taking."

Triana shook her head. "I know what you're suggesting, but I find it very hard to believe that he would ever resort to violence."

"It doesn't have to be him, though, does it?" Gap said. "The way he's going about this protest could provoke somebody else to do something stupid. Merit might not even know about it, even though he's to blame."

As much as she hated to admit it, Triana knew that this argument was valid. Tensions were starting to run high and sides were being drawn; an insignificant spark could set off a chain of events that might end in violence. Earth's history was peppered with numerous examples, often with the original instigator out of the picture. And, once it began, it was extremely difficult to stop.

Triana hoped that they had left that particular aspect of human nature behind when they launched. Time would tell.

At the moment she felt the gravity of her balancing act between respecting Merit's right to protest and maintaining peace, order, and productivity among the crew. She immediately recalled Dr. Zimmer's recorded message: "Finding that fair position might seem tough, if not impossible." He had, as usual, been prophetic with his prediction about crew relations; would she now reward his faith in her as a leader?

The logical response to Gap's concern was obvious to her. "The time has come," she said to him. "We'll have a full crew meeting in two days. It's time that we dealt with this issue head-on."

Channy pumped her fist in the air and let out an excited "Yes!" Gap raised his eyebrows and nodded. "Sounds like a good plan to me," he said.

* * *

Hannah walked down the deserted corridor of the ship, keeping exactly two feet from the curved wall. Her eyes remained focused on a spot on the floor ten feet ahead of her. One hand clutched her workpad, the other hung limply at her side. A fellow crew member exited a room directly in front of her, almost colliding, before pulling up and letting her pass. She never saw him.

Her mind was still on the conversation with Bon. The more she thought about it, the more she became convinced that her theory – as crazy as it sounded – might very well be correct. And, if it was, *Galahad* was in more danger than they had originally thought.

So why wasn't she afraid? Why did this excite her when it should have left her terrified?

She realized that the answer lay within her own natural curiosity, a force so powerful it had led ancient mariners to venture out beyond the edge of the horizon, where legend held that the Earth fell away into a void of monsters and devils. The same force had also compelled adventurers to risk their lives to scale the highest mountains, to cross the

Antarctic ice pack, to plunge into the murky depths of the ocean, all in the name of exploration and to satisfy mankind's overwhelming desire to see, to learn, to *know* what was out there.

It had also driven thirty scientists and researchers to the moons of Saturn, where they had mysteriously perished in the pursuit of knowledge.

This same force churned inside Hannah Ross. Fear might lurk somewhere within, but it stood no chance against her overwhelming desire to learn. Bon had helped with another piece of the puzzle; now her mind was in overdrive, trying its best to see exactly what picture this puzzle would produce when all was said and done.

It might not be pretty.

The time had come to meet once again with *Galahad's* Council. She might lack concrete proof of her theory, but her instincts had been right during the crisis at Titan and those same feelings were bubbling around again.

She looked up in time to notice that she had reached her room. Once inside she crossed to her desk, set the workpad down, nudged it slightly to make sure that its edge aligned evenly with the side of the desk, and began to mentally prepare her presentation to the Council before writing it. Snapping on the vidscreen she opened her email account. Before she could compose a note to Triana she saw that the Council Leader had sent out a mass email to the entire crew.

She scanned it quickly. A general crew meeting would take place in two days, 2pm, in the auditorium that they called School.

Things were reaching the boiling point. If Triana was going to address all of the crew members, then she would need to know right away. It could change everything.

-21-

The sounds coming from the hidden speakers in her room mimicked an ocean shore, complete with crashing waves and an occasional gull cry. Although she had spent the majority of her life in landlocked Colorado, Triana loved the soothing atmosphere that was created with these sounds, and was thankful that Lita had suggested them. Lita, practically raised with sand between her toes, had touted the hypnotic background noise as 'therapy for the soul.' That prescription was exactly what Triana needed at the moment.

She scribbled a few words into her journal, but found that her thoughts were scattered and unsatisfying. After a moment of consideration, she decided that was okay; the emotional release from her journaling served a purpose, scattered thoughts and all. She leaned back over the pages.

> With another crew meeting coming up, the perfectionist in me is rearing its ugly head again. With all that has happened in the past couple of days, it's time to give myself permission to NOT have all of the answers all of the time.
>
> If we weren't always moments away from being blasted out of existence, if Merit wasn't practically leading a mutiny, and if Alexa was awake and alert, I'd almost say it was time for a vacation. Just think, it

wasn't long ago that every summer was a
long vacation. Those days are gone.
I could use a mental vacation, that's for
sure. The more I allow myself to think
about it, the more I realize that I do miss
the sun, the wind, the openness of home.
I'm angry that these thoughts even enter
my mind.
But they do. They're real, and I have to
accept them, deal with them, and move on.
Take a break.
So, even though I need to work out exactly
what I'm going to say to the crew…I'm
not going to do that right now. I'm putting
everything on hold for the next hour, and
enjoying the sounds of the sea, maybe
doing some yoga, and simply breathing.

A smile crept across her face. She knew that, for her, this
was a tall order. There was, however, someone who could
help her relax.

"Hey, Roc," she said. "When Roy was programming you,
did he ever tell you much about his past?"

The computer didn't hesitate to respond. "Are you
bored?"

"What are you talking about?"

"You never start conversations with me that way," Roc
said. "What happened to, 'Roc, what's the status on the
Kuiper Belt?' or 'Roc, are the tests finished on those Balsom
clips on Level Six?' or 'Roc, how does it feel to be the ultimate
supreme being in the universe?' You must be bored. Which
seems a little odd with everything going on at the present
time."

"I'm not bored. I'm…" Triana paused. "I'm trying to
decide if I want to meditate for awhile and collect my
thoughts, or distract myself from those thoughts."

"I'm feeling used again," the computer said.

"Quit being a baby," Triana said. "So, did Roy ever tell you that, when he was young, he wanted to be a comedian?"

"He wisely kept that information from me. But I'm not surprised."

Triana slid out of her chair and sat on the floor, propped up against the edge of her bed. She crossed her legs beneath her and pulled her long hair behind her ears. "Would you like to hear one of his jokes?"

"I'm getting worried about you," Roc said. "*You?* You want to tell me a joke? Are you feeling okay?"

"Just humor me, okay?" she said. "A duck walks into a store. He...um, wait a minute."

"Hilarious."

"Just wait a minute," Triana said. "I don't want to mess it up." She murmured under her breath for a moment, reciting the joke to herself. "Okay, a duck walks into a store. He –"

"'And put it on my bill,'" Roc said. "That joke?"

Triana crossed her arms and frowned. "Thanks a lot. You couldn't just humor me for a moment?"

"Sorry. But I know now why Roy was a computer programmer. Good thing you practiced on me and not in front of a packed Dining Hall or something."

"I said it was Roy's joke, not mine."

"Don't be angry, Tree. Friends don't let friends humiliate themselves with unfunny jokes. Next time, try this one: A guy walks into a store with a duck on his head. Wait, did Roy tell you this one?"

Triana continued to sulk. "No."

"A guy walks into a store with a duck on his head. The guy behind the counter looks up and says, 'What's that all about?' And the duck says, 'I don't know, I woke up this morning and he was down there.'"

"And you think that one was funnier than mine?"

"Not necessarily," Roc said, "but you seem to like duck humor, and that's one of the best."

"I'm sorry I even brought it all up," Triana said.

"Would you rather talk about the Balsom clips?"

After a moment of silence, Triana smiled, and then found herself chuckling. "Well," she said, "I guess I got the distraction I was looking for."

"What about the one where the duck goes bowling on crutches?"

"No thanks," Triana said. "I'm off the duck jokes for awhile."

"Okay, then I really will talk to you about the Balsom clips."

"Are you still trying to be funny?"

"Nope," the computer said. "It's actually good news, too. The problem with the heating on Level Six can indeed be traced to the Balsom clips."

Triana sat stunned for a moment. "Wait. You said you had done a complete check – "

"Yes, I did do a complete check," the computer said. "I did a complete check of the clips on Level Six. They're fine."

"You've lost me."

"I'm only telling you this," Roc said, "so you can help me find a way to spin it so that Gap doesn't pull an 'I told you so' and hold it against me."

Triana had to laugh. "This is classic. You're telling me that Gap had it right all along with those silly clips?"

"No. Well, yes. But not the way he thought."

"If Gap had it right, and you told him he was crazy, I most certainly will not help you spin it just so you can save face."

"What if I laughed at your duck joke?"

"No," Triana said. "I might enjoy this moment as much as Gap. Okay, so explain your Balsom clip solution. And tell me quickly. We might get pulverized by a Kuiper object any moment, and I *have* to hear this before the end."

"Never mind," Roc said. "I'll wait until the next Council meeting. Maybe Channy or Lita will be supportive.

Besides..." The computer paused, almost as if contemplating the next thought. "It doesn't make sense. Where the problem originated, I mean. I need time to figure it all out."

The soft chime of the door sounded, and Triana, suppressing a laugh, called out, "Come in." She looked over at Roc's glowing sensor. "This might be the greatest moment of our entire journey."

"Let's not overreact," Roc said as the door opened and Hannah stepped cautiously inside. She looked at Triana, sitting cross-legged on the floor, and stopped in mid-stride.

"Is...this a bad time?" she said.

Triana was still grinning. "On the contrary, it's a terrific time. Legendary, you might say."

"Pay no attention to her, Hannah," Roc said. "She's gone space-crazy."

Hannah's smile seemed uncomfortable and confused. Triana pointed to the chair across from her desk. "Have a seat, Hannah. Roc and I were just discussing how important it is for people to admit their mistakes. Apparently *only* people."

"Um...okay," Hannah said. She sat down and looked around. "I like your room. And I love that sound of the ocean."

"Yeah, Lita turned me on to that."

At the mention of Lita's name, Hannah grew serious. "How's Alexa?"

"Not so good. She didn't wake up from the surgery, and now she's in a coma. I'll be talking about it with the crew in a couple of days. We hope she'll be awake by then."

Hannah looked stunned by the news. "Well, I wanted to talk with you now, before you have that meeting. I suppose it could wait..."

Triana could read the mannerisms of the brilliant girl from Alaska, and knew that this was obviously important. "No, that's okay. What's up?"

"It's a little bit complicated, so you'll have to bear with me. And I don't even know anything for sure. It's just an educated guess."

"Hannah," Triana said. "You have a pretty good track record with your 'educated guesses.' If you think it's important, I'm interested."

With a sigh, Hannah leaned forward, her elbows on her knees. "I've been doing a lot of thinking about the Kuiper Belt, and the way it's distributed."

"You mean the thick patches and the empty stretches?"

Hannah nodded. "It doesn't add up. It should be much more uniform than it is. The fact that it's so heavily populated in some areas was really bothering me. Given billions of years, it shouldn't be so…clumpy."

She looked down at the carpeted floor. "Then I had a funny thought. If it's not supposed to be this way, then *why* would it be this way? What would be the purpose?"

"The purpose?" Triana said.

"Yeah. Gravity shouldn't have made it this way. So what else would be responsible?"

Triana stared at her. "And what did you come up with?"

Hannah looked back at the Council Leader. "The Cassini."

There was a long moment of silence. Finally, Triana leaned forward and clasped her arms around her legs. "I think the Council needs to hear this. Right now."

-22-

"Why do you want to be cranky?"

Gap was leaning against the curved wall of the corridor outside the Conference Room. He glanced down at Channy, who had asked the question, and who was in the middle of one of her stretching routines. They were the first two to arrive for the emergency Council meeting.

"Am I cranky?" he said.

"No, but you will be," Channy said, her face hidden as she touched her nose to her right knee.

"Okay, this is leading somewhere, so I'll play along. Why am I going to be cranky?"

"Because you haven't been to the gym in four days."

"Three," he said.

"Nope, it's four," Channy said, adjusting her torso backwards so that she now lay flat against the floor with one leg stretched out and the other tucked at an impossible angle. "You forget who you're talking with. Four."

Gap rolled his eyes. "I've been a little busy, if you hadn't noticed. Oh, wait, you must have noticed, since you were able to report a snowman up here on Level Six. That *was* you, right?"

A smirk played across Channy's face. "Would I say something like that? Besides, that's not the point. You should be able to find forty minutes out of your day to keep your body from turning to mush. And once it does turn to mush, you'll become cranky and irritable. So, get your tush down to the gym and spare all of us from a crabby Engineer."

Gap performed an exaggerated salute. "Aye aye, Cap'n."

Channy rolled onto her stomach and shifted into a yoga stance called the Cobra. "See, I'm able to find a few minutes to stretch even when I'm waiting around."

"Yes, you're certainly amazing."

"Just like I thought, you're already getting cranky." She pushed up into a different position, then, with a final stretch, jumped to her feet. "So, what do you think this meeting is all about?"

Gap shrugged. "I don't know, but Triana added a little P.S. to my email that said Roc owes me. Whatever that means."

"I'm just happy that she's going to fight back against this Merit Simms nonsense," Channy said.

They looked up as Triana rounded a turn and walked up to the Conference Room door. She said a quick hello, then added, "Seen Bon or Lita yet?"

"Lita called to say that she might not be able to make it," Channy said. "She's still a little overwhelmed in Sick House. I don't know about Bon."

"I do," Gap said. "He grumbled something about 'too many meetings,' then said he'd be here. Just had to make sure first that we all knew he was put out by the whole thing. Now we know."

"Okay, well, Hannah will be here in a minute, too."

"Hannah?" Gap said. "We must have some big news."

Triana nodded. "I wouldn't have called the meeting otherwise. C'mon, let's wait inside."

They had barely taken their seats inside the Conference Room when the door opened and Hannah and Bon walked in together. Although he told himself that the timing was likely a coincidence, Gap couldn't help but bristle. The memory of Bon and Triana embracing flashed through his mind. A moment later he relaxed as Hannah made her way around the table to give him a quick peck on the cheek and took the seat beside him. He shot a quick glance at Bon, who seemed completely uninterested as he filled a cup at the water dispenser.

"We'll get started and catch Lita up later," Triana said. "First, just a quick reminder about the full crew meeting. I haven't heard a peep from Merit since I sent out the email, but I want everyone on the Council to be prepared for any ugly incidents that might occur."

"What do you think might happen?" Channy said.

"Probably nothing. I'm guessing that Merit will use the meeting to take notes on our position, and then go off to work up his response in some sort of dramatic speech. But you never know. He might use the meeting as a platform to recruit more followers."

"Or his cheerleaders might try to disrupt things," Gap suggested.

"Maybe," Triana said. "I don't want us to get worked up over this. Let's treat it like a normal crew meeting, but just keep your eyes open. Remember, we don't want to do anything to fan the flames, right?"

There were nods from around the table, with the exception of Bon, who looked bored.

Triana waited a moment before moving on to the next order of business. "I know that it gets your attention when Hannah shows up at a Council meeting. She started to share some thoughts with me regarding the Kuiper Belt, but I thought it would make more sense for all of us to hear it together."

Aware that all eyes had fallen upon her, Hannah shifted in her seat and kept her eyes on her workpad. When she spoke, her voice was soft.

"As you probably have figured out by now," she began, "I'm someone who really likes order in the universe." There were polite chuckles around the table. "That's why the Kuiper Belt has been so frustrating for me. I'm especially bothered by some sections being as dense as they are, while others are much emptier. Contrary to what we thought, there are no completely empty stretches; there are bits of rock and debris throughout the whole ring. It's just wildly heavier in some spots. I…I couldn't accept that."

She finally found the courage to look up and make eye contact around the table. "I started wondering what that was all about. Then it struck me that it's quite a coincidence that we're hitting one of those rough spots on our way out of the solar system and on to Eos. But…is it really a coincidence?"

The room was heavy with silence. Punching a few instructions into the keyboard before her, Hannah turned on the room's multiple vidscreens. Then she said, "I plugged in a few figures, and was…well, I was a little stunned to see things fall into place."

"Like what?" Triana said.

"Like the fact that any trip out of the system toward Eos would always mean having to go through a 'hot' stretch of the Kuiper Belt."

"What?" Gap said. "That can't be right. The Kuiper Belt orbits the sun, just like the planets. There are bound to be times when a thin stretch pops up."

"That's what I thought," Hannah said. "But in order for us to make the leap to Eos, it requires that we utilize a slingshot maneuver around one of the gas giants. We happened to use Saturn, remember?"

There were nods around the table. Even Bon seemed to be intently listening to the explanation. Saturn had indeed provided the boost that *Galahad* needed to dramatically increase its speed.

"So, when you plug in the numbers – and there are a lot of them – any route from Earth that uses a gravity boost from Jupiter, Saturn, Uranus, or Neptune, and leads to a rendezvous with Eos, would end up going through a dangerous portion of the Kuiper Belt."

When this was greeted with more silence, Hannah continued. "You're probably thinking this is too strange to be true. But I've run the figures so many times that I'm sure there's no mistake. Um...and it gets even more bizarre."

Gap snorted. "How could it be any more bizarre than that?"

"Well," Hannah said, "I decided to check on a few other things. For one thing, the debris in the Kuiper Belt orbits at different velocities. Some clumps are moving much faster than others. Some are barely poking along. This, by the way, contributes to the violent impacts that we've been seeing.

"Next, I took the list we have of known Earth-type planets that are circling stars like our sun, all within a nearby radius of our solar system. When you plug in a route to any of them, using a slingshot boost around the gas giants, you'll wind up having to play dodge ball in the heaviest parts of the Kuiper Belt."

Triana scanned the vidscreen before her. Hannah plugged in courses for *Galahad* using different destinations, sometimes using Jupiter, sometimes Saturn, for a gravity boost. Each time the red line of their route crossed through a dense portion of the ring.

"Do you know what this means?" Triana said quietly.

Hannah nodded. "I know what I *think* it means. The Kuiper Belt is not some random collection of space junk." She paused before adding, "It's a giant fence around the solar system. And it's supposed to keep us inside."

Galahad's Council sat still, absorbing the gravity of the statement. They had come to expect the unexpected, and had been shaken by the discovery of a super-intelligent force on Saturn's moon, Titan. With so many wonders, both beautiful and dangerous, all within the confines of their own cosmic neighborhood, what astonishing discoveries could they expect during the remainder of their journey?

Not to mention what might await them at Eos.

It was Channy who asked the most logical question. "Who built the fence?"

There were glances around the table. Triana said, "Should we naturally assume that The Cassini are behind it?"

"Actually," Hannah said, casting a fleeting look in the direction of Bon, "that's correct."

Triana saw the look and turned to the Swede. "Bon, do you have something that you can add to this?"

He took a slow drink from his cup of water before answering. "Hannah came to see me about this earlier. I am still in some loose form of contact with The Cassini. I…I can't say anything for sure, but I sense that the Kuiper Belt is their creation, yes."

Gap shook his head in awe. "This is unbelievable."

Triana leaned forward. "You say it's just a feeling that you have. Would it be possible…" Her voice trailed off at the same moment she and Bon made eye contact. He answered as if reading her thoughts.

"No," he said. "I won't do that."

Another deep silence enveloped the room. Channy looked from Triana to Bon and back again. "Uh, what are we talking about?" she said.

Gap tapped his fingers on the table and answered, his voice low. "I think we're talking about the translator."

At the mention of the word, Bon stood up and walked over to the water dispenser, his back to the group. Everyone around the table immediately pictured the small, metal device that Bon had used to communicate with The Cassini during the crisis near Saturn. It had turned up among the items recovered from SAT33, the doomed space station orbiting Saturn's moon, Titan.

They called it the translator for lack of a better word, but it worked as a sort of mental connector between Bon and the web-like force that occupied the orange moon. A junction box, it allowed Bon to convey specific messages to The Cassini; without it, they probed his mind at will, picking and choosing the information they wanted.

This connection had been possible because of the unique wavelength that Bon's brain emitted. A dozen *Galahad* crew members had exhibited painful symptoms of this bizarre connection, yet it was Bon who was the most in tune. His brain had become the focal point of The Cassini's attempts to communicate with the shipload of teens.

It had come at a severe price, physically. Bon had been wracked with pain that dropped him to his knees, even causing him to lose consciousness. In the months since that episode, he had been reluctant to discuss it. Without a doubt it was an experience that he wished never to repeat.

And now Triana was asking him to do just that.

She bit her lip, aware of the tension that had settled upon them. "If you'd like," she said, "we can discuss this later."

"We can discuss it now," Bon said firmly. "I don't ever want to make that connection again." He turned to face Triana. "Besides, what purpose would it serve? Suppose we find out that The Cassini *are* responsible for the Kuiper Belt? Then what?"

"Then you ask them how we get through to the other side."

Bon snorted in disgust. "If they did put this…this fence around the solar system, why would they help us out?"

Triana didn't have an answer. She looked at Hannah, who shrugged her shoulders. Gap and Channy also seemed to have nothing to say.

"Listen," the Council Leader said. "I don't enjoy asking you to do this. Believe me, if I could do it myself, I would. But right now we're in serious trouble. We're trying to tiptoe through a minefield where the mines keep moving, we're potentially seconds away from colliding with something, and we have a growing number of people on board who want us to turn tail and run back home.

"The one thing that could help us the most would be a little more information. If there's any chance to get some help, we need to take it. Suppose there *is* an answer to getting out of here?"

Her tone softened a bit. "Bon, I know it's the last thing you want to do. I just don't know if we have any better option."

For almost a full minute he stared back at her. Then, without saying a word, he set down the cup of water and walked quickly out of the room.

Channy looked down the table at Triana. "Oh, boy. Now what?"

"I don't know," Triana said with a sigh.

Gap leaned forward, resting his chin on one hand. "You know what I think? I think he'll do it. He growls a lot, but when it comes down to it, he is just as driven as the rest of us to make this mission succeed. He knows that he's going to be in agony, but he'll do it. Just let him walk around for awhile."

Triana thought about this. Then, rubbing her forehead, she said, "Let me go talk to him." She pushed herself up out of her chair and walked out.

Hannah looked nervously at Gap, who said, "Everything's going to be okay." When neither she nor Channy responded, he said it again. Even to his own ears it sounded unconvincing.

Sheesh, can we ever get away from these crazy Titan aliens? Hey, I watched what Bon went through last time, so I don't blame him for stomping out. Hooking up with those guys is a pain, literally.

Besides, we don't need their help, do we?

-23-

Lita had grown up around her mother's medical practice, so she knew the smell of a hospital better than most people. To her, Sick House didn't have that particular odor, and yet it still carried a scent that recalled memories of patients and procedures.

Not all of those hospital memories were unpleasant. One of Lita's most powerful memories was of trailing her mother, Dr. Maria Marques, during a typical morning round. A nurse had frantically rushed up to them, with news that an elderly man had unplugged his IV and monitor, and was demanding to be discharged to go home. The nurses had tried, in vain, to convince the man that he was in no condition to leave the hospital, and that his doctor was on the way. That doctor, however, was tied up in the emergency room. When the nurse had seen Lita's mom, she had begged her to help in some way.

Lita could still remember the way the old man's room had looked and smelled. A handful of small vases held flowers from well-wishers; a tray, carrying unappetizing breakfast items that had been only picked at, sat near the window; a television, its sound muted, flashed overly dramatic scenes from a soap opera, set ironically in a hospital.

The elderly man sat in his own clothes, his faded hospital gown tossed over the end of the bed. He clutched a small duffel bag in his lap, one toe tapping to a rhythm that played in his head. He fixed his eyes on Lita's mother as soon as she walked in the room. She smiled her electric smile at him.

"Well, good morning, Mr. Romero."

He grunted back, "Who are you?"

"My name is Maria."

"You a doctor?"

"I'm many things. I'm a wife, a mother, a pretty-good cook, a very-good singer, and a wicked canasta player. I do a little doctoring when it fits my schedule."

Mr. Romero grunted again. "I don't want to talk to another doctor. I'm going home."

Lita remembered her mother's patient response. "I don't really like talking to doctors, either. That's why I listed it last." She propped against the bed and clasped her hands together. "Why are you so anxious to get out of here? Aren't they feeding you well?"

The old man stared up at her. "Hospitals are for sick people. I'm not sick."

"You're fighting off a case of pneumonia, Mr. Romero. How would you do that at home? You live by yourself, don't you?"

"I know how to take care of myself."

"I'm sure you do. You're eighty-one-years old, so you must know a few things about taking care of yourself. And I see here on your chart that you retired from the plumbing business, is that right?"

Mr. Romero nodded, his head up, a look of pride and defiance on his face.

Maria continued. "My husband thinks he's a plumber sometimes. He's not. He runs a grocery store. But last year he decided to add another sink in our bathroom, and the next thing you know water was shooting everywhere. It looked like a fire sprinkler system had gone off."

"I've seen it a thousand times," Mr. Romero said. "People always think they know better than a professional. They just end up paying us more to fix their messes."

"And that's exactly what happened," Lita's mom said with a laugh. "I never let him forget it, either. If he had just called you in the first place it would have saved us a lot of time and trouble."

She reached out and took the old man's hand. "So I'm sure you understand that these wonderful nurses here, who have been working so hard to fix you up, would hate to see you try to do their job, right?"

Mr. Romero's eyes darted to the two nurses who stood in the doorway. He made another small grunting sound, then looked back at Maria. She smiled and said, "They're doing such a good job, I'd hate to see them have to work even harder to fix something you've tried to do yourself."

He took one more look at the nurses, then nodded. "They're almost finished, right?"

"I think they'll be able to get you out of here in another three or four days. But if you leave now, it might take them a couple of weeks."

Lita remembered standing quietly behind her mother, listening intently to her words. More than that, however, she remembered the impact those words had on the old man. He stood up and reached for his hospital gown.

"Do you really sing?" he said with his familiar grunt.

"Like a bird. Let these fine women get you back into bed and I'll come back and sing any song you like." Dr. Maria Marques had turned, taken her daughter by the hand, and gone about her rounds.

Now, six years later, young Lita Marques stood in a hospital ward, more than a billion miles from Veracruz, Mexico, and took in the scent that carried a mixture of memories, both tragic and hopeful.

Alexa Wellington was the patient in this case, yet she was in no way able to get herself up from bed. Her condition had not changed. The coma was baffling to Lita, and frightening. Had it been caused by a mistake that Lita had made during surgery? Was there something else wrong inside Alexa, something that Lita had not detected? Was there a solution that Lita had not considered, something that would snap Alexa out of the coma and on to a stable recovery?

The questions tormented Lita. She had dedicated herself to solving the problem, choosing even to miss the emergency Council meeting in order to focus on Alexa. She looked at the monitor as it paced through its readings, looking and listening for something that might make everything clear.

She heard the door open in the outer office, and wondered if it might be Triana coming to recap the meeting. Instead the face of Merit Simms peered around the corner.

"Hi, Lita."

"Hello, Merit. Feeling okay?"

"What? Oh, no, I'm fine. I just wanted to stop by and see how Alexa was doing."

Lita walked past Merit, into the Clinic's office. He turned and followed her. "So, what's the word?" he said.

"I didn't know that you and Alexa were so close," Lita said.

Merit smiled. "I don't know her very well. Does that mean I shouldn't care how she's doing?"

Lita returned his smile. "She's resting comfortably, but she's not up for having visitors right now."

Merit put his hands on the top of a chair and leaned against it, his black hair spilling down around his shoulders. "I heard that she's in a coma. Is that right?"

It would be impossible to keep the news from spreading throughout the ship, Lita realized. Plus, there was nothing to be gained by lying. "Yes, that's right. But I don't expect it to last for long."

"Is she going to be okay?"

Lita fought the urge to snap back. Keeping her voice calm, she said, "Alexa will be fine. Her appendix was definitely the problem, it's been successfully removed, and in time she will heal. The coma is a temporary setback, and, although we don't know exactly what caused it, she's getting the best treatment we can give her, and I expect her to recover completely. Is there anything else you need to know at the moment?"

"You don't want to talk with me about this?" Merit said.

"First of all, Alexa has a right to privacy. Plus, I don't like the fact that you show up here, probing for information, not because you sincerely care about Alexa, but to see if it can help you rally support for your agenda. I consider that despicable. I don't know if I should be angry with you, or feel sorry for you."

Merit scanned her face for a moment, then stood up straight. "Or there's a third possibility," he said. "Perhaps you don't completely understand what's going on. My 'agenda' that you refer to is based on the fact that I care about the well-being of every crew member on the ship, not just Alexa. The fact that she's struggling with a health issue right now is a symptom of our problems, not the problem itself. And, if I'm going to speak for a group of people about that problem, I need to have my facts straight."

"So this is research, is that right?"

He shrugged. "If you want to call it that. But I do care about what happens to Alexa, even if she's not my best friend."

Lita tried to read his face. She was irritated by the trouble he had kicked up recently, but there was nothing wrong in what he was saying at the moment. Like any good motivator, he could be very convincing. How much, she wondered, was sincere, and how much was manipulation?

She felt her earlier doubts returning. Home *did* sound good, never more so than right now. Merit got on her nerves, but underneath it all his promise of better days ahead – on Earth – was tempting. Very tempting.

Rather than let him see the hesitation she forced herself to refocus. "Well," she said, "now you have the facts. Alexa is in a coma, but she's stable and getting good care. I'm optimistic that she'll pull out of this soon, and everything will be fine. Okay?"

Merit nodded. "Yes. And thank you very much for sharing with me. Even though I probably can't be of any real help right now, please let me know if you can think of anything I can do."

"Thanks," Lita said. "I appreciate that. Now, I hope you understand that I'm pretty busy."

"Of course. I'll see you around."

Lita walked back into the hospital ward. Merit watched her go before turning and strolling out into the corridor. Waiting for him were two of his followers, leaning up against the wall. Merit reached them in three quick strides.

"Okay," he said, "you can get started. Let everyone know that Alexa is not only in a coma, but that she's getting worse. Tell them that Lita is worried that she might not make it. Got it?"

The two boys nodded and turned toward the lift entrance. Merit smiled, pushing a strand of hair out of his face.

-24-

She knew exactly where to find him. The narrow dirt path was damp, with a few scattered puddles that had collected the run-off from the morning watering schedule. Most of the tropical fruits were grown in this portion of Dome 2, giving the area a distinct smell that reminded Triana of citrus groves, along with an almost muggy feel to the air. Her shirt clung to her skin. Beads of perspiration had popped up on her forehead, either from the humidity in the air or her nerves. Or both.

She had waited almost an hour, giving Bon time to walk and think. It had also given her time to think as well. It didn't escape her attention that she was asking Bon to step up for the second time in four months, to help the crew of *Galahad* out of a tough situation. Why, she wondered, out of such a large crew, was it him, of all people, who was able to connect with The Cassini?

And why, given his dark and brooding nature, did it pain her so much to ask him to make this sacrifice? He wasn't exactly the type of person who evoked sympathy.

The answer to the first question evaded her. The answer to the second question was much more clear.

Triana could no longer deny that her feelings for Bon were real. She had run from those feelings, just as she had run from other things in her past that had weighed heavily upon her. She didn't want to fall for him; in fact, he seemed to make it difficult for anyone to like him that much. But she was troubled right now because she did care deeply for him, and she was about to ask him to suffer unimaginable pain.

She pushed through an overhang of leaves and there he was, sitting on a metal box that housed an irrigation pump. His long, blond hair reflected the artificial sunlight that poured from the crisscrossing grid above. His shoes and socks were in a pile nearby.

"Thought I might find you here," she said.

"And I was sure you'd come looking," he said.

Triana looked around for a place to sit. The soil was wet, and Bon made no effort to share his perch. She crossed her arms and shifted her weight to one side, trying her best to look at ease.

"If you knew I was coming, then you probably know what I'm going to say."

"Yes," he said, "but let me hear you say it anyway."

"All right. I'd like to ask you to attempt another connection with The Cassini."

He glared at her. "Just like that? You think it's that simple?"

"No, Bon, I know it's not simple, and regardless of what you might think, I'm not making this request lightly. But I'm quickly running out of options."

Bon reached over and picked up a clod of dirt, then crushed it, letting the fragments fall between his fingers to the ground. When he didn't answer, Triana softly said, "Talk to me about this."

"It's not something I can explain to you. You wouldn't understand."

"Try me."

He looked off through the plants and took a deep breath. "It's not a simple matter of 'connecting,' as you call it. And even though the physical pain is staggering, it's not just that." He took another deep breath. "When I...when I make that connection, it's as if my brain becomes filled with thousands of other people. I lose all control of my senses, my emotions, my thoughts. The communication process is very…one-sided."

He looked at Triana. "When I made the connection at Saturn, I didn't think I was going to survive it. I was slowly slipping away, the pain was tearing me apart, and the…" He paused. "The presence in my mind was overwhelming. The rush of sound was deafening. The fact that you took hold of me and helped me relay the message is the only thing that saved me. I couldn't have done it on my own."

Triana felt a pang of sympathy. She knelt down, ignoring the muddy stains that covered her knees. "Maybe…" She reconsidered her thought, then decided to press on. "Maybe it will be a little different this time. Maybe you and The Cassini have established some sort of…I don't know, some sort of relationship now."

Bon shook his head. "You don't understand. They're so far beyond us, so advanced, that they don't form 'relationships.' They do what they do, and they don't make allowances for pitiful little beings such as us. We are like amoebas to them. If they can help us, they will. But they won't change for us."

He closed his eyes and rubbed his forehead. "No, it will be the same."

Triana remained still. She felt that she was making tentative progress, slowly breaking down their own communication barrier, one that had gradually grown between them ever since their one intimate moment months ago. She also realized that she was seeing Bon in a new way.

She had always defined him through his external image, a troubled, brooding young man who built up a tough façade in order to protect himself. She had maneuvered close to him, then backed away, always playing by his rules…or the rules that she perceived were his. She realized that all of her actions toward him had been reactions to his temperament, and not based on her own instincts.

But suddenly there seemed to be a part of Bon that was leaking out from behind that façade. When he mentioned the feeling of 'thousands of other people' forcing their way into his mind, it struck her: *He's as alone as I am.*

Triana couldn't imagine what he was experiencing. She guarded her own thoughts and privacy with intensity, and Bon was clearly the same way. When he made the connection with The Cassini, it wasn't the searing physical pain alone that crippled him; it was the pain of opening every hidden, private cove of his mind to others, of losing all emotional and mental control.

That, she decided, would be enough to bring her to her knees, too. It explained so much about Bon – and the link with The Cassini – that she had never considered.

In a completely impulsive moment, Triana leaned forward, her hand on Bon's knee, and placed a kiss on his lips. When she pulled back, she found his ice-blue eyes boring into hers. After an awkward moment, he put his hand behind her head and gently pulled her forward into another kiss.

"Wait," she said, pulling back again. "I can't let you think I'm doing this to talk you into something you don't want to do. That's not –"

"I know," he said.

"No," she said, pushing away from him. "This isn't the right time for this. It will only complicate things."

He slowly shook his head. "Things are already complicated." He stood up and gathered his shoes and socks. Then, fixing her with a deep stare, he said, "You need to figure out what you really want."

Taking a few steps away, he stopped and looked back. "Get the translator. I'll make the connection." Then he turned and strode quickly down the path.

* * *

Hannah walked alongside Gap toward the Engineering offices, one of her hands looped through the crook of his arm. His head was down, his mind vaulting from one thought to the next, and he was completely unaware that it was she who was guiding them through the corridor, subtly maneuvering them both in order to remain exactly two feet from the wall.

Gap had so far not questioned Hannah any further about her Kuiper Belt theory and The Cassini. It seemed so bizarre, but if the crew of *Galahad* had learned anything on their journey, it was that the bizarre was commonplace in space.

And, as far as he was concerned, if Hannah was sure that it was true, chances were that it was. Her ability to sift through countless mounds of data and somehow make sense of it all was remarkable; that ability had already proven to be a lifesaver during their encounter with Saturn and Titan. Her contributions to the mission were significant, and she wasn't even a member of the Council.

What of his contributions?

A scowl worked its way across his face as he pondered the thought. What exactly *had* he brought to the table? Upon first examination, it didn't seem like much. He had felt almost helpless during the confrontation with the stowaway; in fact, it was Bon who had saved Triana's life, then Triana who had saved the ship.

During *Galahad's* perilous journey past Saturn, Hannah had discovered the mysterious force called The Cassini. Then, once again, Bon had stepped up and helped to deliver the ship to safety.

Now there was trouble within and without as they weaved their way through the treacherous Kuiper Belt, and managed an internal crisis with Merit.

Gap assessed his contributions to this point, and the only thing that stood out was the problem with the heating system. And on that count he had failed so far. He was the Head of Engineering, and yet had no engineering successes to his credit.

No wonder Triana had applied her attentions to Bon. For that matter, what exactly did Hannah see in him? Airboarding lessons only carried so much weight. Would she soon reach a point where she, too, wondered the same thing? Since they had been together she had only seen him fail, it seemed. He hadn't been able to stop the ship's dangerous acceleration around Saturn, and this perplexing heating problem had actually induced laughter from her.

The realization of it all suddenly hit home. Self-confidence had never been a problem for him, which made these doubts even more discouraging. Insecurity was unknown terrain for him.

His mind drifted to home, back on Earth. The days spent with friends at school and in his gymnastics club, the nights spent laughing with family. On one hand it seemed so long ago, a fond but fading memory. Was it possible to go back, to savor the time he had left with his family? If he wasn't contributing *here*...

"Everything okay?" Hannah said.

The last thing he wanted was to allow these doubts to set. In mere minutes Hannah had apparently picked up on his discomfort. "Sure, everything's fine," he said, turning to give her a quick smile. "Just thinking, that's all."

She gave his arm a squeeze.

They neared the Engineering section, and as it came into sight Gap set an intention. He would spend less time on the Airboard track, less time gossiping with friends, less time playing Masego with Roc. From now on he would pay more attention to the duties that his fellow crew members – like Triana – expected him to perform. He would earn his place on the Council all over again.

One way to do it would be to help Triana defeat the rising tide of discontent aboard the ship; that meant defeating Merit. So far it seemed as if Bon was the only person who had taken Merit on. Gap resolved to play a bigger role than he had.

But, first things first. It was time to make his title mean something on the ship. Without fail he would solve the nagging problem of the heating system.

"Roc," he said as they entered the section and walked up to the control panel. "Let's fix this thing once and for all."

The computer wasted no time with a reply. "If you're referring to your fashion sense, I've already told you that it's impossible. You are destined to always match stripes with plaids."

"The heating system, Roc. Let's go back to the very beginning. I want to take a completely new approach."

"I sense that you have not yet visited with Triana," Roc said.

Gap looked at Hannah, then back at Roc's sensor. "What are you talking about?"

"I'm talking about a miraculous breakthrough in the technology of heating systems for interstellar spacecraft. We've decided to shut the whole system down and hand out candles to every crew member. It's a much more reliable heat source, provided we can keep a supply of matches."

Gap smiled. "I'm a little pressed for time, Roc. Quit playing around and let's get to work."

"No work to be done here, my good man. I'm still tracing the original problem, but the system is repaired."

The smile on Gap's face faltered. "Repaired? A temporary fix?"

Roc said, "Temporary in the sense that it will only last us until we arrive at Eos. After that we'll probably cannibalize the system for use on one of the planets."

Now the smile was gone. Gap scanned the control panel, where each of the readings showed normal and steady. "You fixed it?"

"When, oh when, will you realize my powers?" Roc said. "Next up, the common cold."

"Wow," Hannah said. "That's great!" She tugged on Gap's arm. "Isn't that great news?"

Gap paused, aware of the puzzled expression on her face. By all accounts he should be as delighted as she was, and his reaction must have been bewildering to her. He forced a half-smile and replied, "Of course it's great news. Terrific news. One less problem for us to deal with."

He turned back to the sensor. "Thanks, Roc."

For the first time that Gap could recall, the computer had no snappy comeback. Apparently Roc was as mystified as Hannah, and chose to remain silent.

"Okay, well," Gap said to Hannah, "I've got some other things to take care of this afternoon. Want to catch up later?"

She peered into his face, a look of concern coming over her. "Sure," she said quietly. "Maybe we can grab a bite to eat."

"Sounds good," he said. With a quick peck on her cheek he was out the door, leaving her standing alone at the control panel.

-25-

The atmosphere was all wrong. Triana stood near a vidscreen in the Control Room, with a half-dozen crew members working nearby, and she could sense it. The air itself was fine, but a strange vibe enveloped the room, a feeling of conflict and tension. No one said anything; they didn't have to.

Her conversation with Bon had been successful, and yet, once again, it had been clumsy and confusing. She could have gone straight to her room and collected the translator, but instead had chosen to check on their progress through the Kuiper Belt. It seemed imperative that Bon make the connection with The Cassini as soon as possible, but a cooling-off period seemed equally important. She decided to give it one more hour, an hour that would hopefully prove to be peaceful.

It wasn't. An alarm sounded, snapping her back to attention.

"Roc?" she said.

"Collision warning," the computer said. "Not as big this time, but tumbling very erratically. This will take a moment."

Triana bit her lip and waited. There was no sense pushing for more information. She glanced over at Gap's empty work station and wondered where he was.

Roc spoke up. "I'm nudging us a bit."

"You're what?"

"Nudging. You know, pushing, tipping, prodding."

Triana raised her hands. "Fine. Nudge. What's the verdict?"

"Well, that little warning system in the Engineering Section has done it again. With the nudge we'll miss this particular piece of rock by almost a quarter of a mile."

A quarter of a mile. Triana let her breath out quietly, not wanting to appear flustered in front of the other crew members. But a quarter of a mile was less than fifteen-hundred feet. In space, that was nothing. In fact, without the alert from the warning system, and Roc's immediate correction, it meant that mere seconds were all that separated success from destruction.

Seconds.

Triana walked over to Gap's work station and sat down. She could feel the eyes of the crew following her, estimating her stress, her confidence. It was as if she could read some of their thoughts: 'See, Merit was right, we need to get out of here.'

How many were with her? How many had joined the ranks of the yellow arm bands? Who was a friend? Who might be an adversary? The thoughts weighed heavily upon her.

Was she absolutely sure that she was right and Merit was wrong? Another collision warning had only intensified the conflict that bubbled within her. Who was she to say that her way was…

No, she told herself. No! Don't do this. Not now.

She kept her back to the room, punching in mindless computations on the keyboard, meaningless searches for information that had no impact whatsoever on their mission. Anything to keep herself occupied for a few moments while she tried to make sense of everything. If Roc noticed what she was doing, he kept quiet…thankfully.

When the intercom sounded, it came as a relief.

"Tree, it's Gap."

"Yeah, where are you?" she said.

"Could you come down to Level Four, please?"

There were only crew quarters on Level Four, including Gap's. She started to ask him a question, then thought better of it. Instead, almost grateful for the distraction, she simply told him that she'd be right down.

A minute later she stepped off the lift and found a cluster of almost two dozen crew members standing around. Gap waved her over to the side.

"What's going on?" she said.

"Another fight," he said, indicating two boys who waited behind him. "Well, mostly just a lot of pushing and shoving. I just happened to be walking from my room to head up to the Control Room when I heard the commotion." He looked over at the assembled throng. "It certainly drew a crowd."

Triana bit her lip. She turned back to face the crew members gathered in the hall. Their faces reflected a mixture of amazement and concern. "Okay, do me a favor, please?" she said to the throng. "Can you give us a few moments to talk here? Either go back to your rooms, or wherever else you might have been going. A little privacy, please?"

It took a moment to clear out. There were several glances exchanged, some that had an almost challenging look to them. Triana heard more than a few grumbles, and briefly wondered if more drama was imminent. But slowly the crowd dispersed, leaving the two Council members and the two combatants, one of whom, Triana finally noticed, was Balin, one of the two boys who constantly followed Merit. Tall and imposing, Balin eyed her coldly as he readjusted his yellow arm band which had apparently been pulled out of place during the scuffle.

Triana looked at the other boy. It was Jhani Kumar, a normally quiet boy from India. It seemed odd that he would be involved in something like this. She decided to address him first.

"Jhani, what happened here?"

He looked at Balin before answering her. "Nothing."

"Nothing," Triana said. "Uh-huh." She looked at Balin. "Would you care to answer the question?"

Balin gave a dismissive snort. "I'll see you later." He turned and began walking toward the lift.

"Hey!" Gap shouted. "What are you doing? Get back here."

Balin turned to look back at them. "What are you, the police? I don't have to jump when you speak. You might be on the Council, but you can't order me around."

Gap took a couple of steps toward the boy, who, although taller, flinched backward a step. "It's called keeping order," Gap said. "If you're involved in a fight on this ship, it's our responsibility to solve the issue. You know that's true."

"You heard what this guy said," Balin sneered. "Nothing happened. Can I go now, officer?"

Triana took Gap's arm before he could advance again. "Sure," she said to Balin. "You're free to go."

He laughed and spun around. In a few moments he was out of sight.

Triana looked back at Jhani. "Why don't you tell me what happened, okay?"

Jhani shifted awkwardly on his feet. "He's a loud-mouth bully, that's all. I'm tired of listening to it, especially when he's spreading false rumors."

"Like what?"

"He was yelling that Alexa Wellington is about to die. He was blaming you and the Council." Jhani lowered his voice. "Alexa is my friend. I went to visit her just an hour ago. She's not about to die."

Triana stared at him. "No, of course she's not. Where did he say he got his information?"

"He didn't. He just said that she was about to die, and that we would all end up dead if we kept following you."

Triana shook her head, then reached out and touched Jhani on the shoulder. "Okay, that's fine. We'll see you later." As he turned to leave, she added, "And thank you, Jhani."

He nodded and mumbled a response that Triana couldn't hear. Soon she was alone in the hallway with Gap, and was stunned when he turned on her.

"What do you think you're doing?" he said, his face flushed.

"What do you mean?"

Gap pointed towards the lift. "You just let that thug Balin walk away without any accountability at all. It's exactly the same mild-mannered nonsense that's let Merit get away with…with…"

"With what?" Triana said, her tone matching his. "With speaking his mind? You think I should out-bully him? Is that right?

"No, but I think you should show a little more leadership," Gap said. "I'm sick of this. They are stirring up more and more trouble each day. Now they're even lying about Alexa, trying to scare everyone into rebelling. And you let him spit in our faces and walk away."

Triana kept herself quiet for a moment before responding. She didn't want to say something that she regretted later. When she spoke, her voice was low and determined. "I'm just as unhappy about this as you are, Gap. I don't like what they're doing, either. But I'm in no position, even as the Council Leader, to keep them from voicing their opinions. When Balin walked away I didn't know about the Alexa comments. I will address those rumors when I speak to the crew. Until then…" She took a step toward him. "Until then, I will not fight foul behavior with more of the same. I will not stoop to their level. Do you understand that?"

"That's just great," Gap said. "You have no problem talking tough with me, I see, but the creeps on this ship get a lot of sweet-talk."

Triana was speechless for a second. "What is wrong with you?"

Gap didn't answer. Instead he gave her a parting look that seemed full of venom, and marched off down the corridor.

"Gap," she called after him, but he disappeared around a turn.

* * *

Her face was pale. Although it should have looked like she was merely sleeping, something about the expression – was it the eyes, the eyebrows, the set of her mouth? – did not look like sleep. Instead Alexa seemed to be deep in thought, eyes simply closed, pondering a great problem.

And it was unnerving.

Channy stood at Alexa's bedside, one hand stroking Iris, who went about one of her daily cleaning rituals, propped against Alexa's motionless side. Monitors kept a vigil over Alexa, keeping rhythm with her heartbeat, her breathing, her life force. There was no other sound in the room.

Channy shivered. The sight of Lita's assistant, usually one of the more outgoing personalities aboard *Galahad*, now lying in a coma, was surreal. Danger had been a constant companion on the journey, yet this scene carried the force of visual evidence; seeing a friend this close to death made their plight real.

Lita walked into the room and offered a greeting and smile as she moved to the opposite side of the bed.

"It's okay that Iris is here, right?" Channy said.

"I honestly haven't checked it out in the databanks," Lita said, "so I couldn't tell you what the true medical answer is. But in my heart I want Alexa to feel comfort, and if that means sharing some energy with a friendly soul like Iris, then I'm all for it."

Channy nodded, then glanced down at Alexa. "Can she hear us talking?"

Lita considered the question. "Let's just assume that she can, at least on some level. There's conflicting theories on that, too, but I come in and talk to her every hour or so, just in case she can." She looked back at Channy. "You okay?"

"Oh..." Channy paused. "No."

Lita laughed softly. "Well, at least you're honest. Anything specific, or just the whole weight of it all?"

Channy scratched Iris under the chin. "It's just getting so hard, you know? All of the stuff we've been through already, now the Kuiper Belt is trying to smash us into a million bits, and people who are supposed to be our friends are turning hostile. I thought we were all on the same team."

She lowered her voice to a whisper and gestured toward the girl lying between them. "There's even talk about Alexa dying. Have you heard about that?"

Lita said, "Yes. I've had at least a dozen calls, and a few people have even stopped by in person. Word is spreading pretty fast."

"But it's garbage. Don't they know it's just Merit causing more trouble?"

"Of course it is," Lita said. "Don't let it rattle you. It's exactly the effect he's looking for."

Channy stared at her. "I know, I know. You sound like Triana now."

"And Triana is right. Trust in the truth, Channy, it will get us through this."

Iris stood up, turned to face the opposite direction, then plopped back down and resumed her bath, oblivious to the conversation and the drama around her. Both girls watched this, taking in the bizarre visual combination of the fussy feline against the troubled teenage girl.

Channy's face broke into her usual smile. "I don't know what I would do without this silly cat right now."

Lita reached across and tickled Iris behind one ear. "I'm glad you keep bringing her in here. For that matter, I'm glad *you're* here." She stepped back and looked at Channy. "There are a couple of helpers in the next room who will look in every few minutes. I've got to leave."

"What's up?"

"Triana wants me to meet her up in the Domes," Lita said. "Bon is going to connect with The Cassini again, and she thinks it would be a good idea if I was there."

Channy's mouth fell open. "I never thought he would do that."

"I didn't either. I'll let you know what happens."

"Should I come, too?"

Lita shook her head. "I think it would be better if there wasn't a crowd, you know? If you want to help, stay here for a little while and keep Alexa company for me. Don't be afraid to talk to her, okay? I'm telling you, on some level I think it has a positive impact." "

"Umm…" Channy said. "What do you think is going to happen? With Bon, I mean."

Lita exhaled deeply. "You saw what happened last time."

-26-

The evening routine of dimming the lights throughout the ship brought on the imitation of an Earth dusk, and many crew members had come to recognize that the best place to experience it was in the Domes. As the artificial sunlight faded, those who were not on duty or socializing in the Dining Hall or Recreation Room would often sneak away to watch the brilliant starlight emerge from behind the day's glare. It was a popular spot for quiet introspection, a chance to unwind at the end of a work shift.

This evening, however, Dome 2 was closed to the crew. Yellow warning signs blocked the entry with a notice proclaiming that special testing was taking place, and that all traffic should be diverted into Dome 1. One of the Farm workers sat nearby in a folding chair, acting as a make-shift security guard to keep everyone out.

Inside, Triana stood near the center of Dome 2 with hands on hips, a small bag slung over her shoulder. On her face she kept a confident look that she hoped would mask the twisting ball of stress that sat heavily in her stomach. Cleared of other people like this, the dome had a crypt-like silence cast over it, broken only occasionally by the sound of Triana shifting on her feet. To her ears, her breathing was loud and disruptive.

Bon sat peacefully in the dirt a few feet away, his face expressionless, his eyes closed. They were alone.

The setting brought about a twinge of déjà vu in Triana as she gazed up at the spectacle of the Milky Way. It had been only a few months since they had first played out this scene. That fateful connection with The Cassini had taken place in the other dome, with only minutes separating *Galahad* from total destruction. This time...

This time, she wondered, did they even have minutes? It was one thing to have a fatal deadline looming over you, and quite another to live in uncertainty, never knowing if or when the blow might come. It was, oddly, a completely different form of pressure, Triana realized. Both might have the same outcome, yet they worked on the psyche in distinctive ways.

Simply thinking about it brought a sudden sense of urgency into her mind, and yet there was no way she could thrust any more pressure upon Bon. She was determined to allow him to set the pace. She chose, however, to remain standing, if for no other reason than to subtly convey a message of determination.

Bon brought a fist to his mouth and quietly coughed. He glanced up at Triana and spent a moment peering into her eyes. "Is it going to be just you and me?" he said.

"No," Triana said. "Well, maybe to start. But I asked Lita to be here."

He nodded, a look of understanding, mixed with a touch of resignation, crossing his face. They both knew that Lita's medical skills were unlikely to come into play; it was a formality more than anything else. After all, what could she really do?

Another moment of silence passed, then Bon held out a hand. "Okay, I'm ready."

Triana nodded and stepped toward him. From within her shoulder bag she extracted a small, lightweight metal ball. It had four short spikes that protruded from the top, bottom, and two sides, as well as small slits that appeared to be vents. It seemed insignificant, yet had saved their lives once already.

Bon eyed the translator. Before setting it in his palm, Triana reached out and took his open hand. "Thank you," she said.

"You realize that this might get us nowhere, right?" he said.

"Maybe. Or it might help a great deal."

He smiled, a gesture that Triana was unprepared for. She felt a hitch in her breathing and a sensation that often preceded tears; she fought against the feeling. Instead, she returned his smile, let go of his hand, and slowly placed the translator in his palm. Almost immediately his smile dissipated, and he gripped the metallic ball at his side.

It happened quickly. A shudder seemed to pass through his body, his eyes clenched tightly, and his head snapped back. Through his gritted teeth Triana could hear a stifled moan escape, the sound of a wounded animal. She immediately dropped to her knees by his side.

A spasm of pain shook him. His head whipped to one side, then the other, and another cry of torture poured out. A dull red glow escaped from the vents of the translator and seeped between Bon's fingers.

Even though she had witnessed it before, Triana still recoiled in shock when Bon's eyes flew open. They glowed with a brilliant orange color, indicating that the turbulent connection with The Cassini was in full force. Then, moments later, the voices returned.

It was a garbled collection of sounds that spilled from Bon's trembling lips, with an almost hollow echo to them, a mishmash of voices, all communicating at once. The overall effect was frightening: the glow from the translator, strengthening for a brief moment, then ebbing, then picking up in intensity once again; the eerie orange tint from Bon's shifting eyes, eyes that seemed to be looking inward rather than outward; and the voices, stacking upon each other, with a sound that felt as if it might pierce Triana's skull. The Cassini had not only tapped into Bon's mind, but had apparently re-established their link with the other *Galahad* crew members who shared their neural wavelength. Triana wondered what Bon was hearing, what he was seeing. She could only imagine what he must be feeling. It was exactly as it had been four months ago. And then, without warning, it wasn't. Bon let out a cry in his own voice, overriding the multitude of sounds, and his eyes seemed to focus again. They kept their orange shine, but for once it seemed as if Bon was fighting for control. Triana resisted the urge to touch him, to help. Something was happening, and she needed to let it play out without interference, no matter how painful it might be for Bon.

She felt a presence behind her and glanced over her shoulder. Lita stood a few feet away, staring at Bon, her own face a collection of emotions that seemed to include awe, pity, and fear. She held a small medical bag, but let it drop to the dirt.

Triana turned back to Bon just as the unexpected happened. Bon let out what sounded almost like a quick snort of laughter. If so, it was full of pain, too, but when it happened again Triana was sure that it was a laugh. Bon pulled his gritted teeth apart and emitted a long, agonizing groan, followed by a third grunt of laughter.

"Bon," Triana said. "Can you hear me?"

It was difficult, given the shudders of pain that wracked his body, to know for certain, but it seemed as if he nodded once in reply. It was confirmed a moment later when he turned his orange eyes to look directly into her face. He nodded again.

"The Kuiper Belt," Triana said. "Talk to them about the Kuiper Belt. Help us."

Bon blurted out another short, pain-filled laugh, his eyes snapped shut again, and his head rolled back. The voices picked up their intensity. It was as if a battle of wills was taking place, a tug-of-war within Bon's head, each side – or many sides – fighting for control. The translator pulsed.

"The Kuiper Belt," Triana said again. "Bon, hold on. Fight for your identity. Tell them to help us."

She saw him shake his head a couple of times, but not in disagreement. Instead it seemed as if he was wrestling back control. His eyes flickered a few times, then settled back on Triana once more. His breathing became regular, and the voices calmed.

This was also new. Triana held her breath, watching, waiting. Then, a new bolt of fear raced through her when Bon's lips parted with a subdued, ominous laugh. It echoed, similar to the hollow sound that accompanied the voices, but it was distinctly Bon.

Laughter. She felt a chill, and noticed that goose bumps covered her arms. One portion of her brain screamed to get up and run, yet she held firm, anchored to the spot beside Bon. After a moment, he fell silent again. His tremors subsided, but the eyes maintained their orange glow. What felt like an eternity passed, the two of them sitting in the soil of Dome 2, separated physically by less than three feet, although to Triana it seemed like a chasm a mile wide. She completely forgot about Lita standing behind her.

The translator's red light dimmed, then winked out. Bon's grip loosened, and the metallic ball fell to the ground. In less than ten seconds his eyes had returned to their normal icy blue.

It took a moment for Triana to realize that her breathing was almost as labored as his. Her hands were clenched into fists, the muscles in her forearms tight, her entire body clamped and taught as a spring. She willed herself to relax.

Time passed. How much, Triana couldn't say for sure. She kept her attention riveted to Bon's face, trying desperately to read him, to understand what had happened. He gave no indication, and remained silent. Finally, he lay back on the soil with his hands beneath his head, his eyes closed. His hair was matted with sweat, and, for the first time, Triana noticed a light-colored, wispy growth of small hairs on his upper lip.

It seemed odd to her that she should notice something like that at such a critical time, but she found her eyes dipping again and again. Between the faint beginnings of facial hair and the experience that had just concluded, Bon seemed a stranger to her. Kneeling in the dirt beside him, she brought a hand out to touch his leg, but then slowly retracted it.

When the unexpected touch of a hand on her shoulder came, she jumped and let out a small cry.

"Sorry," Lita whispered, kneeling beside Triana. "I didn't mean to scare you."

Triana gave a soundless laugh then swallowed hard. "No, it's okay. I guess I was just so…wrapped up in everything."

Lita indicated Bon. "Well? What do you think?"

Triana glanced down at him. "I don't know. Something's… different, that's for sure." With Lita beside her, she felt confidence return. She reached out and laid a hand on Bon's leg.

A moment later he stirred and opened his eyes. At first he simply stared up at the starlight washing through the dome, his chest slowly rising and falling. Then he turned his head and looked at Triana.

"We're okay," he said.

Triana stared into his eyes, unsure of how to respond. It was such an unusual comment for Bon to make, and not what she would have expected from him. *We're okay.* What exactly did that mean?

Her mind began to decode the simple statement. By *we* did he mean the crew of *Galahad*? Was he referring to the two of them? Or…

The thought flashed through her like a lightning bolt. *We.* Was that Bon speaking? Or…The Cassini?

His connection with the alien intelligence had shifted. Unlike their initial contact around Saturn, Bon seemed to have negotiated with The Cassini this time. He had managed to direct his attention at Triana, he had responded to her, he had…

He had laughed. She was sure of it.

And now he appeared more calm than anyone had a right to be following such an ordeal. He reclined in the soft soil of Dome 2, his head resting on his hands, his pale blue eyes stoically locked onto Triana's. Only the tinge of sweat in his hair gave testimony to the suffering his body had endured only brief minutes ago.

Triana bit her lip, but kept her gaze on him. Finally, she said, "What can you tell me?"

Bon smiled, which only made her discomfort intensify. His voice was soft, but steady. "There's a trick to talking with them, I know that now."

"You had more control, is that right?"

He chuckled. "There's no such thing as control over them. No, it's a matter of not giving yourself away completely."

Triana wrinkled her brow. "I don't know what that means."

Bon turned onto his side and supported his head with one hand. He could not appear more relaxed, Triana noted.

"The first time I interfaced with The Cassini," Bon said, "it was beyond overwhelming. Think of a child opening the door on the world's most wonderful candy store. Except this candy store is brilliantly lit, and it's the size of the universe; it goes on forever and ever, with every aisle carrying upward to the sky, all of it stocked with every delight a child could imagine, and then an infinite supply of delights beyond comprehension.

"It's irresistible. You want to take it all in, you almost *have* to take it in. That's what it's like when I first connect with them. That's probably why it hurts so much." Bon pushed a stray hair out of his face. "When you give yourself over to that amount of sensation, it's impossible to move, to think. The Cassini don't really take over as much as they...I don't know, outshine, I guess. Like a candle sitting next to a supernova."

Triana said, "I get that. But what did you do differently this time?"

Bon shrugged. "The only way I can describe it is that I shut my eyes. My inner eyes, I guess. I didn't allow myself to be completely swallowed by the intensity of their essence. It wasn't a matter of fighting back; it was more like...sipping instead of gulping." He paused, then smiled again. "Yeah, I guess that's the best way to put it."

"I'm sure that's hard to do" Triana said. "It's probably tempting to dive in, right?"

"Yeah. Except..." His smile faded, and he looked down at the dirt below him. "Except that way leads to destruction. We're not equipped to handle that."

Lita inched closer and sat on her heels beside them, but kept quiet. Triana gave Bon a moment of reflection before asking him, "So...did you learn anything about the Kuiper Belt? Can they help us?"

Bon remained focused on the ground. He ran a finger through the soil, back and forth, carving a small trench, then filled it in and began over again. After a moment he looked back up at Triana.

"I think we'll be able to get through," he said.

Triana wanted to smile, wanted to celebrate the news, yet something in Bon's tone held her back. He wasn't telling her everything.

"But..." she said.

"But," Bon said, "I get the feeling that there might be something waiting for us on the other side."

-27-

I like to read. Not in the way you do, probably. I'm guessing you like to curl up with a good book, get really involved with the story and the characters, and let it take you on a voyage of imagination. I appreciate that.

When I read, I am digitally soaking up an entire shelf full of volumes in less than a second. Not too exciting, really. Plus, I can't curl, which takes some of the romance out it.

But I love the knowledge found between the covers of books. Even a work of fiction, which is made up, still has seeds of truth regarding the ways of life. Like, for instance, the fact that just when things seem to be working out okay, you realize that you either left the iron plugged in, or there's something perched outside the Kuiper Belt waiting to eat you.

The corridors on the lowest level of the ship were, as usual, mostly deserted and quiet. A few crew members were likely at the other end of the level, either working out in the gym or taking a few turns in the Airboard room. But this end, which housed the mysterious Storage Sections and the spider bay, sat in muted light, almost a perpetual twilight. It was the only section of *Galahad* that went unused.

At least for now. Once the ship pulled into orbit around one of the two Earth-like planets in the Eos system, it would come alive with activity.

The spider bay held the small transport vehicles that the crew would use to shuttle down to the planet's surface. Known affectionately as spiders because of their oval shape and multiple robot arms, each craft was capable of holding thirty passengers. Plans had called for ten functional spiders to make the journey in the large hangar bay, but as it turned out only eight of the vehicles were completed in time for the launch. The other two were loaded aboard to supply possible replacement parts.

To complicate matters, one of the working eight had been lost in the near-deadly encounter with the mad stowaway. Merit wasted no time reminding his followers that this left only seven spiders to safely deploy more than 250 passengers to the planet's surface. The math, he preached, did not work with eight; to rely on seven was dangerously foolish.

The Storage Sections were a mystery indeed. Loaded aboard the ship just prior to launch, they were sealed and impenetrable. Dr. Zimmer had deflected any and all questions from the young crew members concerning the contents, refusing to say anything beyond "you'll find out when you get there." Tucked into the desolate lower corner of the ship, most of *Galahad's* crew had practically forgotten about the massive containers once the ship was outside the orbit of Mars; that was exactly as Dr. Zimmer had planned.

Just around a bend from the entrance to the spider bay was a lone window that provided a solitary view into space. It was one of Gap's favorite spots, a secluded setting that offered a rare break from noise and company.

He stood there now, leaning against the window with his arms crossed, scanning the spectacular star field. It often struck him as odd that there was no sensation of movement, how the stars seemed almost like a painted backdrop that never changed, even as the ship flashed through space faster than any human-built device ever conceived. He wondered if he would catch a glimpse of one of the Kuiper objects, perhaps a tumbling boulder, as it wound its way around the sun.

His temper had finally cooled. He scolded himself for lashing out at Triana, yet at the same time he recognized that many factors had played a part in his anger. Anxiety, fear, frustration, and self-doubt. They had all mixed together to create a vicious mood, and once again his emotions had bubbled to the surface, overriding his rational side.

Perhaps guilt had played a part, as well. He had vented to Triana about Balin and Merit…and yet he, himself, had entertained thoughts of turning back. He had fantasized about reuniting with his family and friends, then took out his frustrations on Triana.

The outburst still troubled him, maybe because one other emotion – one that Gap had thought was suppressed – kept clawing its way to the top, demanding attention.

There was no time for such thoughts.

He heard the soft approach of footsteps, and turned his head to find Hannah walking toward him, a tentative smile on her face.

"Your favorite place," she said. "You would be the world's worst hide-and-go-seek player, you know?"

"You're probably right," he said, forcing a return smile. "But it's still the best place to get away and think."

He felt a rush of feelings that surprised him. Part of him was glad to see Hannah, one of the sweetest people on the ship. She was so easy to get along with, so understanding, and so caring. He had to admit that his mood could swing pretty rapidly, and yet she had weathered his shifting emotions without once complaining.

If he began to catalogue her other qualities, they would be impressive. She was brilliant, artistically talented, kind, and even sported a dry sense of humor. On top of all of that, he was attracted to her looks, too. She had so much going for her, and he knew that he was a lucky guy.

So why, when she came around the corner, had he also felt a touch of annoyance? It wasn't simply that he wanted time to be alone; it was *her*. He hadn't felt this way before. In fact, *he* was the one who had insisted on spending so much time together, who had pushed the relationship perhaps faster than it would have normally progressed. And now he was irritated when she showed up? What was that about?

He tried to rationalize the feeling. His inability to solve the ship's heating problem, coupled with all of the contributions that Hannah had delivered, might be causing a temporary surge of jealousy. Or his heated argument with Triana had opened an old wound. Or maybe it was simply the combination of those issues, along with the added stress of a crew in turmoil.

In any event, something was different. Complicating things even further was the twinge of guilt that overlapped his feelings. Hannah had done nothing wrong, so why was he pulling away from her now?

He decided to ignore the conflict for the moment, especially since he suddenly found her head resting on his shoulder. He draped an arm around her.

"It's beautiful," she said, staring out the window. "You would think we'd be used to it by now, but it still leaves me in awe every time I see it."

"That's why it's so easy to find me," Gap said. "I hope I never get tired of it."

They were quiet for a minute, each taking in the scene before them. Then Hannah pulled her head back and looked up at him. "Is there anything you'd like to talk about?"

Now he was caught. He knew that he was lousy at camouflaging his feelings, and to say no would be an obvious lie. He chewed on his thoughts for a moment before responding.

"You'll think it's silly."

"I'll think it's silly if you don't talk about what's bothering you."

He sighed, an uneasy smile playing across his face. "Listen, you're putting me in a tough spot, because no guy likes to show weakness, you know?"

Hannah shook her head. "Do you think I want you to be a machine or something? It's nice to know that there are genuine human emotions floating around inside there." She grinned. "Okay, so I like the strong side of you, too. But a little sensitivity from time to time is…attractive. Get it?"

Gap shrugged. "Sure. I get it." He withdrew his arm, walked across the corridor and leaned against the far side, his hands behind him. Hannah leaned against the window and faced him.

The slight distance between them seemed to help him. It was a buffer zone, of sorts, and he found that the words began to flow out of him.

"It was an honor to be selected for this mission. For all of us. I remember how proud my parents were. Even though they were sad, they were also happy, you know? Then, to be named to the Council, I thought my mom was going to burst with pride. When I wrote to her with the news she wrote back to say, 'Dr. Zimmer has put a lot of faith in you; he sees what I have always seen in you.'"

"She was right," Hannah said.

"Was she? I think I've talked a pretty good game so far, but when you get right down to it, what have I really done?"

Hannah stared across the corridor at him, a look of irritation spreading across her face. "What are you talking about? Stop it right now."

Gap ignored this. "What did I do when we were confronted by the stowaway? What did I do when The Cassini almost did us in? What have I done with this whole Merit Simms trouble? Nothing. Now my one job was to repair the heating system, and I couldn't even finish that. Roc took care of it without me."

He dropped his chin to his chest. "Tomorrow I'm going to meet with Triana and talk about resigning from the Council."

Hannah covered the distance between them in a flash. She pulled his chin up in her hand. "What is wrong with you?" she snapped. "Where is this coming from? Remember when I said that a little sensitivity was attractive? Well, *this* is not."

He gave her a wry smile. "Great. So I'm failing with you, too."

She let go of his chin and took a step backward. "I can't believe this is the same Gap I fell for. Are you listening to yourself? If you can't be the hero all the time, or the knight in shining armor, or whatever you want to call it, you suddenly sulk and quit? I don't believe that."

Gap had no response.

"Hey," Hannah said, her voice softening. "Whatever you're going through right now, let me help you. Don't be this way."

After another moment of silence, she stepped up and encircled him with her arms. He waited a few seconds, his arms dangling at his sides, before slowly returning the embrace. He looked over her shoulder, toward the window and the backdrop of starlight.

* * *

Every eye turned to watch as Triana and Bon stepped out of the lift into the Control Room. Every conversation abruptly ended.

Triana noted with a quick glance that Gap's station was once again vacant. Given more time to reflect on it, she might have been angry that he was consistently unavailable lately. But with more pressing matters at hand she dismissed the concern for the time being, while making a mental note to deal with Gap as soon as possible. Their last meeting had turned nasty, and she wondered if that played a part in his absence.

The room remained quiet as she and Bon walked up to the interface that allowed direct programming access to Roc and *Galahad's* ion drive. Triana looked at the Swede.

"Do you need me to do anything?"

Bon shook his head. He had spoken with Triana as they made their way from the Domes down to the Control Room, but had only begun to give her a brief description of what would have to take place in the ship's navigation. He didn't understand all of it himself, but an almost eerie sense of the task at hand was imprinted upon his mind; an hour earlier none of it would have made sense.

"I think I can handle it," he said, inspecting the vidscreen before him. He pulled up a chair and placed his hands on the keyboard. "I'll need Roc for some of this."

"I'm happy to lend a hand," the computer countered, "but would it be asking too much for you to fill me in on what's about to happen?"

Bon looked around the room at the crew members before looking up at Triana. She read his thoughts. "It's okay," she said, "they'll all find out sooner or later. Tell him."

Sitting back in the chair, Bon looked at the glowing red sensor. "I'm going to patch in a code that will help us maneuver through the Kuiper Belt without smashing into something."

"Okay," Roc said, "and when you're finished I'll plug in a code that will make rabbit poop turn into jelly beans."

Bon smiled. "You don't believe me?"

"Of course I believe you. Trillions of chunks of rock and ice, all bouncing off each other, without any pattern to their movements whatsoever, and you have the magic formula to slip past like they weren't even there. Why would I possibly question that? By all means, change the course settings. If you guys need me, I'll be over here putting my will together."

Triana leaned on the console. "Roc, the code comes from The Cassini."

"Oh, you mean the same Cassini that tried to blow us out of space a few months ago? Why didn't you say so? I feel better already. Listen, most wills use the phrase 'sound mind and body.' Do I lose points by not having a body?"

"You know that the problem at Saturn was a misunderstanding," Triana said. Then, looking at Bon, she added, "Don't mind him. Go ahead, do what you need to do."

"Um, may I ask a question?" Roc said. "How will this affect our course to Eos?"

"To be honest with you, I can't worry about that right now," Triana said. "The big issue is avoiding a collision; getting back on course once we leave the Kuiper Belt will have to be secondary."

She was aware that the conversation was having a troubling effect on the assembled crew members. The tension in the room was obvious, and out of the corner of her eye she noticed Mika, one of Merit's followers, lean over and whisper something to the boy next to her.

Triana tapped Bon on the shoulder once and nodded at the panel. He leaned forward and began to type on the keyboard. Slowly at first, with several pauses, then a little more. For a moment he closed his eyes and furrowed his brow, as if he was trying to remember something. Triana could only speculate as to how he was retrieving the information from The Cassini.

She started to ask him about this, when suddenly an alarm sounded. The loud, pulsing tone made her jump and grab onto Bon's shoulders for support. "What did you do?" she yelled over the alarm.

"Nothing," he said back to her. "I'm only doing preliminary work. I haven't even uploaded anything yet."

"It's not Bon," Roc said. "It's the collision warning system down in Engineering."

"What about it?"

"It just failed. It's out completely."

Triana's eyes grew wide. "How could that happen?"

"Checking," Roc said. "It may take awhile to track down."

Bon turned and looked up at Triana. "That means we're flying blind right now."

She felt her breath catch in her chest. There was no way for them to know what was coming at them, or where it was, or how to avoid it. They were completely vulnerable.

She looked back at Bon, then pointed to the keyboard before him.

"Hurry," she said.

-28-

The red ribbon that she often used to tie back her hair was still missing, and Lita looked around her room for the third time since that morning. 'Why,' she wondered to herself, 'do we always look in the same spot over and over again?' It was not in the room. She sighed, opened a dresser drawer, and dug around until she came up with a pink ribbon. Close enough for now, she decided.

As she stood before the mirror, adjusting the ribbon, she thought about the episode with Bon in the dome. It had rattled her a little bit, but on some level she realized that maybe she was becoming almost numb to the bizarre events that piled up during this journey. Each strange occurrence made her aware that the universe was not only vast, but was full of more wonders than the human mind could comprehend.

And what of Bon? He seemed fine when he and Triana had left for the Control Room…but was he? There was an odd change in him that Lita had noticed, but it was so vague that it wasn't worth commenting on. She kept it to herself, mainly because she wouldn't have been able to describe it anyway. It was simply a feeling. He was the same Bon as before, yet *not* the same Bon. What was happening to him each time he connected with The Cassini?

The only thing to do, she decided, was to wait and watch. Perhaps others would notice it, too. Channy, for one. It was hard to get anything past her.

She turned to examine the room, which could use some tidying up. But she also felt a need to get back to Sick House as soon as possible. The decision was made for her a split-second later when the alarm sounded. The loud, pulsing tones jolted her for a second. Her first instinct was to call Triana, but she also knew that the Council Leader and Bon were already in the Control Room, and undoubtedly were in the middle of whatever was taking place. Instead, she quickly grabbed the medical kit that she had carried up to the dome, and dashed out the door.

Three minutes later, with the alarm now muted, she stood at her desk in Sick House. Two of the clinic's workers had questioned her immediately, but no, she told them, she had no more information than they. It was hard to concentrate on the mundane tasks that faced her while her imagination worked through all of the possible emergency scenarios. Finally, she tossed her stylus pen onto the desk and walked into the hospital ward to check on Alexa.

Each time she had entered the room in the past few days her heart ached. Although she had done everything with textbook efficiency, her friend and co-worker lay unconscious, and the feeling of responsibility was heavy. Lita stood beside the bed and smoothed the covers. Once again she briefly wondered if Alexa sensed what was going on around her, and again felt certain that she must.

"You should have seen it," Lita said in a soft voice. "Bon did his mind-merge trick again with The Cassini." She smiled as she gently pulled Alexa up, adjusted the pillow beneath her, then laid her back again. "I guess they gave him the key to the back door out of the solar system. But an alarm went off a few minutes ago, so I hope he knows what he's doing."

She took a step back and looked at the monitor which reflected Alexa's vital signs. "Of course, I suppose we should be lucky that we have a Cassini ambassador aboard the ship, right? Somebody who speaks their lingo, anyway. Although I have to tell you, this time when he connected he – "

Lita stopped short when she heard it. A small hiss, barely audible. She stepped closer to the monitor to see if it was coming from there, then looked behind her to see if someone had entered the room. But they were alone.

When it happened again she was startled to hear a high-pitched moan underneath the sound. She quickly darted back to the bed and looked down into her patient's face.

Alexa's eyes were open halfway.

Lita felt her heart race. "Alexa!" she said, grasping the blonde girl's hand. "Alexa, can you hear me?"

Again she heard the hissing sound, with more of the moan, and this time there was no doubt it was coming from Alexa. "Hey, Alexa. C'mon, you can do it. C'mon."

She grabbed a cool wash cloth that was on the night stand and patted Alexa's forehead. It was something her mother had always done for her whenever she was sick, and it just seemed…right.

"Alexa?" she said. "Do you know where we are?"

Alexa's eyes drooped shut for a moment, then opened again, this time a little more than halfway. She seemed to be staring into nowhere, until seconds later her eyes shifted and made contact with Lita's. Lita felt a surge of excitement.

"Hey, welcome back. Did you have a nice nap?" Her emotions began to take hold of her again, and she could feel tears roll down her cheeks. She didn't care. Keeping one hand holding onto Alexa's, she leaned over and pressed the call button to summon some of her help from the other room. Two of her assistants quickly scampered into the hospital ward, their eyes growing wide when they saw Alexa.

"Run a scan on her right away," Lita said without taking her eyes off her friend. "Blood, respiration, cardio-vascular." She paused, then added, "And neural. I want a brain scan, too."

While the workers began their preparations, Lita leaned close to Alexa's face. "You've been asleep for awhile. Are you able to talk?"

The wheezing sound came, but no words at first. Then, as if she was thinking hard about something, Alexa scrunched her eyebrows and closed her eyes. Her lips moved, but she seemed to have difficulty forming words. One of the assistants handed Lita a cup of small ice chips, and she gently put one into Alexa's mouth.

"Not too fast," Lita said. "Your mouth is probably like a desert."

Alexa's face relaxed as she moved the ice around her mouth, then asked for another by opening wide. Lita smiled and put two more chips in.

Soon Alexa was able to make more sounds. She moaned, not in a painful way, but as if she was working out her vocal cords. She took two more ice chips, then looked back up at Lita and croaked her first word.

"What?" Lita said, leaning forward. "Say that again."

Another croak. Lita looked up at one of her assistants, Mathias. "Did you catch that?"

The boy shrugged. "Sounded like 'Santa.'"

They both looked down at Alexa, who frowned and slowly shook her head. She licked her lips and, mustering her strength, clearly said, "Sedna."

"Sedna?" Lita asked. "S-e-d-n-a?"

When Alexa nodded, Lita and Mathias exchanged glances again. "Doesn't mean a thing to me," he said, then went about his work.

Lita chuckled at her friend, then fed her another ice chip. "Are you loopy?"

Alexa cleared her throat, and this time her voice was much easier to hear. "You...asked where we were. We're... at...Sedna."

"Well," Lita said, "I don't know anything about Sedna, wherever that is. But if that's where you're hanging out right now while you get well, then I'm okay with that." She smiled at her friend. "What if I got you a cup of tea? Remember, nothing comes between you and your tea."

Alexa didn't answer. Instead, she closed her eyes and appeared to rest comfortably. Lita helped gather the data on *Galahad's* first-ever coma recovery patient, and was pleased with the information. Alexa seemed to be fine physically, and her neural scan displayed no brain damage, either. There was a slight arch in one wavelength that hadn't been there before, but nothing significant.

She was just finishing up when the intercom buzzed. It was a call from Triana. Lita walked over to her desk to answer it.

"Hey, I was just about to call you," she said. "We've had some excitement down here, and I forgot all about the alarm a while ago. What was that about?"

Triana said, "The collision warning system in Engineering went out."

"It went out? You seem pretty calm about it."

"That's because it popped back on again," Triana said. "Without us even doing anything. So we flew without any warning system for almost ten minutes."

"And Bon? What about his code, or whatever that was?"

Triana let out a long breath. "Well, he uploaded something. I'll be honest, it's a total leap of faith, because it has taken us off course, and I'm a little nervous about that. But supposedly it will get us through the Kuiper Belt."

Lita thought about this for a moment. "So we won't need the warning system, is that right?"

"I don't know. I'm trying to have faith in our little friends back at Titan, but I'd just as soon have the warning system as a backup, you know? Anyway, I'm going to address all of this at our crew meeting in a couple of hours. Wanted to see if you were going to be there. What's this excitement you mentioned?"

Lita smiled. "Our sleepy-head patient has come back online."

Triana digested this for a moment. "You're telling me that Alexa is awake again?"

"That's right."

"That's great!" Triana said. "And she's okay?"

"As far as I can tell. A little disoriented, maybe. She mumbled something strange, but I think it's probably just like waking up after an intense dream. She probably couldn't tell the real world from the dream world, I'm sure. But yeah, she seems fine."

"Congrats to you and your staff," Triana said. "What a relief. I can't wait to announce *that* at the meeting."

Lita grew serious. "Yeah, I was thinking about this meeting..."

"And?"

"And I'm just curious how you're going to handle it. After everything that's happened lately, I'm a little worried that it might turn ugly."

Triana paused before answering. "The only way to handle it is to be honest."

"That doesn't seem to buy much with some people anymore," Lita said.

"Yeah, I know," Triana said with a sigh. "But I've had this discussion with Gap already. There's no other way to go with it. It's not like I won't be firm, but regardless of what happens I can't abandon my ethics. I know that emotion often overpowers rational thought, but where would we be if we all ditched reasonable and logical thinking just to battle someone else's emotional outburst?"

Lita had been standing during the conversation, leaning against her chair. Now she pulled the chair out and sat down. "Listen, you're the Council Leader on this ship, but you're also my friend. You know I support you one hundred percent. I just..." She hesitated before finishing. "I just worry that always taking the high road in all of this will only lead to us plummeting off a cliff at some point, you know?"

Triana said, "I'll ask you the same thing I asked Gap: What do you suggest?"

Lita sat quietly. She picked up a little glass cube on her desk, one of her personal mementos from her hometown. It was filled with sand and pebbles from the beach at Veracruz, a visual reminder of the seashore that had supplied so many of her happiest memories. She had spent countless days running through the surf with her family, and had also spent several evenings alone with her mother, sitting in the sand, watching the moon rise over the water. She cherished those memories, as well as the wisdom that her mother had worked so hard to transfer to her oldest daughter. So much of that wisdom involved dignity and moral decisions.

Triana's steadfast determination to fight disorder with dignity reminded Lita of her mother's lessons. How could Lita possibly find fault with that?

"You're right," she said to Triana. "I'm just...never mind."

Triana chuckled, then said, "I never knew how passionate this Council was. Channy wants to get tough, Gap wants to fight, you're a little feisty, and Bon punched someone in the mouth. Maybe *I'm* way off base."

"No," Lita said. "We're lucky to have you in charge. If it was up to us there'd be chaos by now. You've been steady. Then there's me..." Her voice trailed off.

"You've had a lot to deal with," Triana said gently. "Don't beat yourself up for thinking about turning back. We've all thought about it."

Lita sat back, surprised. She had never considered that Triana, of all people, would have those feelings. Yet why not? There was a sense of comfort there, compared to the harsh reality they faced each day in space. Of course Triana would feel that, too.

It was selfish, Lita realized, to assume that no one else could experience what she was going through. Yet before she could respond, Triana changed the subject.

"So, will you be at the meeting? It starts in two hours."

"Are you kidding?" Lita said with her own laugh. "If you can't control all of us thugs, I'll need to be there with my little medical kit."

"Things will be fine," Triana said, then, after congratulating Lita again for the good news on Alexa, signed off.

Lita swirled the sand around in the cube, then put it back on the desk and walked into the next room to check on her lone patient.

-29-

In the seven months since leaving Earth, there had been only three previous all-crew meetings aboard *Galahad*. Triana believed strongly that not only were they unnecessary in most instances, but that too many meetings would dilute their significance. She instead encouraged department leaders to make their own decisions as they saw fit, and to report any problems or concerns to the Council, which usually met about once per week.

As she walked into the large auditorium, Triana felt an oppressive heaviness in the air. The usual chatter and laughter of the assembled group was restrained, much quieter than one would expect from a gathering of more than two hundred teens. Triana felt the gaze of each eye as she made her way to the front of the room, much as she had when she watched Merit's speech in the Dining Hall. Her path down the aisle took her past many friendly faces, and several crew members greeted her with a smile and a wave.

But it seemed that just as many either frowned or looked away.

She approached the front row of the room and was relieved to find Lita, Channy, and Bon seated, talking amongst themselves. Or, to be more precise, Channy was talking, while Lita and Bon sat passively.

There was no sign of Gap. This time the irritation within her quickly swelled into anger. Whatever issues he might be experiencing, Triana could not accept that they warranted his continual absence. She looked around to see if he might be seated nearby, but although she spotted Hannah about five rows back, Gap was nowhere to be found. She decided that her first order of business after the meeting would be to locate the Council member and have a serious discussion about his future in a leadership role.

For now, however, it was important that she focus on the crucial meeting at hand, and not let Gap's apparent lack of maturity disrupt her thoughts. All of her concentration would be required to overcome the hostility of Merit and his disciples.

Her eyes were drawn to a knot of activity toward the back of the auditorium, and she knew at once that it had to be Merit. He was all smiles, shaking hands with everyone around him, waving to others nearby, and playing the role of popular underdog to the max. Triana felt her heartbeat accelerate, and forced herself to remain calm. This would undoubtedly be her toughest test of the journey, and she could not afford to let him throw her off track.

She walked up to her fellow Council members. Channy jumped out of her seat and gave Triana a hug.

"I am so glad this is finally happening," the Brit said. "You'll be great, I know." Triana smiled, but couldn't think of anything to say in return.

Lita spoke up from her seat. "Alexa sends her regards, and says that she wishes she could be here to cheer you on."

"She still doing okay?" Triana said.

"She seems to be fine, except for that disorientation I mentioned. Guess that's a pretty good tradeoff for waking up, though."

Triana agreed, then looked at Bon. "Have you seen Gap?"

He shook his head. "No. Is there a problem?"

"I honestly don't know. Just wondering why he's not here."

All three of the Council members gave her a blank look. Finally, Lita said, "I'll try to hunt him down after the meeting. Maybe I can find out what's bothering him."

Triana nodded, although she knew that the responsibility was hers. She turned and walked up the steps to the auditorium stage, positioned herself behind the podium, and stared out at the suddenly silent room. The only crew members not present – other than Gap and Alexa – were those whose duties kept them from attending, and they were watching on vidscreens around the ship. When she spoke, Triana was pleased to hear her voice come out loud and strong.

"I won't pretend that everything is happy and peaceful on this ship today."

She noticed that the words had the immediate effect she had hoped for. Her objective of speaking honestly and forcefully was intended to, at the very least, maintain the respect of the crew, regardless of their position. She certainly had their attention right away.

"A growing number of you have questioned the mission that we trained very hard to accomplish. Many of you have expressed dissatisfaction with the Council and its decisions. And some of you have also requested that we discuss the option of turning around and plotting a course back to Earth. I have called this meeting to answer these concerns and requests."

She took a deep breath. "I will also fill you in on our latest connection with The Cassini, and how they're helping us through the Kuiper Belt."

Triana paused to let this sink in, and to allow the inevitable buzz to ripple across the room. Those wearing yellow arm bands had used the concept of Cassini support to back their campaign of a return to earth; if the mysterious alien force was now suddenly helping to pilot *Galahad* to safety, it was a blow to Merit's movement. Triana took a quick glance at him, and their eyes met briefly. He wore a faint smile, as if he recognized the strategic move Triana had successfully executed, elevating their battle to a new level. When the murmurs died down, she continued.

"I must admit that I have found it personally disappointing that a few of us have so quickly abandoned the spirit which powered our mission from day one. Each of us made incredible sacrifices to be here; we left family and friends behind because we believed in what we were doing. We believed that it was our destiny to take the human race to the stars.

"Of course it hasn't been easy, and I won't stand up here and lie to you and promise that the worst is behind us. We don't know what lies ahead. And, even more sobering, we have no idea what awaits us at Eos."

She paused again and took in the entire room. "Every one of us knew this when we made the decision to leave. We were strong, then. We also knew that we were leaving behind a future that promised only disease and death, and chose instead to create a future filled with hope. I'm saddened to think that, even though we have conquered every challenge presented to us, a number of us would prefer to give up."

Triana could sense the unease that her words created in the room. She knew that Merit's message had never been portrayed in this manner before; no one had equated his movement with the concept of quitting. Her goal of presenting the R.T.E. idea in a new light was having an effect. She pushed on.

"There has been growing criticism of the Council, spearheaded by individuals who seek to trumpet their ideas while disregarding the concept of order and discipline when it doesn't serve their purpose. The Council was never created to rule as a monarchy; you have the rights and abilities to change the Council as you see fit. But, bear in mind that when you begin to eliminate any sense of organization, and rush to alter the governing body every time it disagrees with your personal agenda, you're encouraging chaos. Order and discipline must always be preserved, or we'll be no better than animals when we reach our destination, be it Earth or Eos."

Another low murmur spread across the room as the impact of Triana's words hit their mark. In the front row Lita subtly nodded her approval to her friend. Bon stared up at Triana with a look that she could only interpret as respect. It strengthened her resolve.

"I have taken note of the recent suggestion that we turn the ship around," she said, and again the room fell silent. "There are three points I would like to address. One, the dangers involved in attempting to turn around within the Kuiper Belt are statistically greater than maintaining our straight path. Two, there has been no contact from Earth that suggests any change has taken place in regard to Bhaktul's Disease. Where is the sense in fleeing from death, only to allow insecurity and fear of the unknown to lead us right back into its grip?

"And third, some have implied that The Cassini would fix all of our problems on Earth, painting a picture that resembles the Garden of Eden awaiting us. This is the lowest form of propaganda, because it plays on your emotions rather than your rational senses. Its goal is to get you to feel, rather than think. It's dangerous, and can not be backed up with facts of any kind."

Triana took a deep breath. As she began to speak again she looked up to see Gap enter the back of the room. He stood by the door for a moment, then slowly made his way down the aisle to the front row. Triana watched him, trying to make out the expression on his face. He appeared to be calm, and, as he sat down beside Channy, looked up at Triana and nodded once.

She looked across the sea of faces. "As we make our way on this voyage, we find that we are truly children. Not just in a physical sense as individuals, but as a race of beings. Our experience with The Cassini taught us that we have so very far to go, so much to learn, and probably quite a bit that needs to be un-learned. If we allow it, it can frighten us and prevent us from expanding our knowledge and our intellect. If we allow it, it can destroy us, rather than teach us how to live in the galactic community. Those decisions are up to us.

"Three hours ago Bon re-established contact with The Cassini. He specifically requested their help in navigating through this dangerous ring called the Kuiper Belt. Twenty minutes later he used their response to program a new course for *Galahad*, one that will put us on a safer track, and will speed us onward to Eos. There are too many details to try to share in this meeting, but we will post all of the information on the ship's intranet. You are encouraged to examine the specifics, and to submit your questions and feedback."

Triana looked back at Bon for a moment. "But there is so much more that we have learned from this particular exchange, much more than we discovered during the incident at Saturn. I've asked Bon to speak to you about it. I think you'll find it...fascinating."

She stood aside. Bon hesitated, then rose from his seat in the front row and slowly climbed the steps to the stage. As he walked to the podium the room remained deathly silent. This was something completely unexpected; Bon, renowned for his quiet demeanor and often-surly attitude, had never addressed any gathering of crew members beyond his duties in the Farms, and was something of a mystery aboard the ship. His bond with The Cassini also lent an aura of wonder about him.

He reached the podium and, for the first few moments, kept his gaze down. Then, he slowly looked up and addressed the crowd.

"It's difficult to explain my communication with The Cassini. I have tried to describe it to Triana as a complete surrender to an energy that we can't possibly begin to understand. I get the sense that they are far older than our solar system, possibly as old as the universe itself. We could probably talk for hours about their history and their purpose. But, for the sake of time, let me tell you the essence of The Cassini."

He looked back down for a moment, and appeared to gather his thoughts. Triana noticed that no one in the auditorium moved; they were as captivated as she in the mystery of it all.

Lifting his gaze to the assembled crew, Bon continued. "For lack of a better word, I believe The Cassini are... policemen."

Yet another rumble spread across the room, as crew members looked at their neighbors and attempted to decipher the meaning behind the statement. Bon remained passive on the stage, apparently content to let them discuss the possibility. When they again fell silent and directed their attention at Bon, he resumed.

"We are a flawed species. It's impossible for us to imagine a life form – if that's even what we can call The Cassini – that has evolved to the point of near-perfection. As the universe has expanded outward, they have progressed with it. I get the impression that they now exist...well, everywhere. They might actually be one immense life form, with segments scattered across the universe.

"One could ask, after so much time and evolution, what is left for them to accomplish? My best guess is that they now reside in star systems like ours, as a kind of guardian for the life forms there. They create various barriers around the systems, and monitor movement. That means monitoring movement both into and out of the system."

Bon paused and licked his lips. This was the most he had spoken at one time since boarding *Galahad*, and to Triana he seemed to be reaching his maximum tolerance level. She decided to assist him.

"What that means," she said, stepping up beside the Swede, "is that when we imagined the Kuiper Belt to be a harmless, natural phenomenon of our solar system, we couldn't grasp the idea that it was an intentional ring of debris and chaos, created to pick off anything attempting to enter or leave. It might seem, on the surface, to be a rather primitive defense system, but consider this: We have an incredibly sophisticated warning system and navigational tools at our disposal, and we have barely slipped through the first third of the Belt."

Bon picked up on this thought. "The Cassini, as I see it, have witnessed a mind-boggling number of civilizations in the universe come and go throughout their billions of years. They obviously are superb judges of what is best for each of those civilizations. Because of our violent history, it's no wonder that we've never received visitors from another world. The Cassini have chosen to keep us isolated.

"And now, we have the opportunity to leave the nest, to experience life in another part of the galaxy. The Cassini must evaluate us and make an important decision."

He looked out at the crew of *Galahad*. "They are deciding if we're worthy of survival."

-30-

Triana allowed the crew to chatter for a few moments. Bon's theory of The Cassini as galactic policemen had stunned them at first; his suggestion that they might also operate like a judge and jury, determining which species survived and which were either isolated or terminated, created mild panic. Triana had predicted this response. She noticed that, amidst the commotion, Merit sat still and spoke to no one. She could imagine that his mind was working on this new information, preparing a pitch that would use it to his advantage.

After two minutes, Triana asked for quiet. Although scattered pockets of conversation continued around the room, she spoke over them.

"I'm sure you have questions. We will try to answer them as best we can."

A boy in the middle of the room stood up. "You say The Cassini are trying to decide if we're worthy of survival," he said. "Yet they gave Bon some sort of key to navigate out of the Kuiper Belt. Doesn't that mean they have given us a green light?"

Triana looked at Bon. He seemed increasingly uncomfortable on the stage, but he answered the question.

"It's not a one-time course correction. The fact that I connected with them again bought us some time, but we'll need multiple adjustments in our course over the next few weeks. During that time I get the distinct feeling that we'll be...observed. Don't ask me how. If we fail to live up to their standards – whatever those might be – my guess is that we'll be left on our own. Which means almost certain destruction."

Another question came from the third row. "Are The Cassini fixing things back on Earth?"

This time Bon needed no prompting. He said, "They are obviously very powerful, but they are not gods. They don't wave a wand and clean up a planet's atmosphere. The term I used was policemen. They are able to keep track of what comes into and what leaves the solar system, but I do not see them stepping in to save our planet. There is a cycle of life in the universe; some civilizations survive, some do not. Their job is merely to insure that one does not negatively impact another."

Triana jumped into the discussion. "Remember, they have reached a level of evolution that we can't begin to comprehend. Simply by trying to study our little human machines, they essentially squashed the research station at Titan, and almost 'helped' our ship to destruction. Fixing little problems is not their focus."

A third question was raised. "How do you know all of this for sure?"

"They don't!" came a shout from the back of the room.

Heads turned, and crew members strained to see who had called out. But Triana knew immediately who it was.

Merit was on his feet. "Of course they don't know any of this for sure," he said, this time in his natural speaking voice. He took a few steps out of the row and stood in the aisle. Triana knew that it was to afford a better view of himself to the assembled group, and to allow him to move while he spoke, which was his style.

"Am I allowed to speak?" Merit said, looking up at Triana. "Or, is this meeting similar to one of your Council meetings, where we must beg an audience with you?"

Triana felt a surge of anger. She opened her mouth to speak, then happened to catch sight of Gap. He mouthed something to her, then repeated the gesture to make sure she understood what he was saying. 'Let him talk.'

Puzzled, she looked at Merit, then back at Gap. He nodded once to her, then turned his attention to the back of the room like everyone else.

This was a surprising turn. Of all the people on the ship, Gap would be the one who would want to stifle Merit. Why would he want the crew to hear Merit's message? Her instinct told her to play along, as dangerous as it might be.

"You are free to speak," she said, "as long as this becomes a dialogue and not a speech."

Merit smiled and began a leisurely walk to the front of the room. His pace was measured, and looked to Triana to be almost rehearsed for effect. After a few steps he stopped and spread his arms wide and spoke in a commanding voice.

"I want to thank all of you, my friends, for your presence today, because it forces the all-powerful Council of *Galahad* to listen to ordinary crew members, like me. Believe me, if you were not here as witnesses, none of our voices might be heard. We're making progress."

His smile widened and he took a few more steps down the aisle before again stopping and addressing the crowd.

"How very convenient that only one person on this ship is able to communicate with The Cassini, and that person happens to be on the Council. I'm reminded of the ancient civilizations that followed their high priest, the only person deemed capable of talking with the gods. Of course, no one dared question the high priest, for fear that the gods would smite them if they disobeyed."

Triana felt her temper flare again. Gap glanced up at her, this time gesturing with his hands to calm down. He turned back toward Merit.

"In the past week or so," Merit continued, "more and more of you have considered our dilemma, as well as our possible choices. You have made it clear that you would prefer to abort this dangerous journey and return to Earth.

And I can see from the many armbands on display today that those numbers increase daily."

He took a few more steps toward the stage, putting his hands behind his back and lowering his gaze to the floor. The pose, Triana was sure, was calculated to give an appearance of deep concern and heavy responsibility.

"But now," he said, "we are told that, according to a Council member, The Cassini can not help anyone on Earth." He paused and looked up, arching his eyebrows. "Does anyone in here remember the amazing power that we witnessed back at Saturn? Is there one among you who believes that The Cassini are powerless security guards?"

There was a small hum of discussion throughout the room. Triana saw several clots of crew members nodding their heads in agreement.

Merit took another step, then spun and faced the stage. His voice grew stronger. "Should we ask our fearless leader, Triana, why we should believe her? Should we ask her why we should once again place our lives in danger, zigzagging through a deadly minefield billions of miles from home?"

Triana forced a smile onto her face. "Thank you, Merit, for taking a breath, and allowing me to respond to your campaign speech." There was a smatter of chuckles, but many in the room looked up at her with distrust.

"There were multiple witnesses to Bon's first connection with The Cassini," she said. "The results of his first contact speak for themselves, and we owe our lives to that bond."

"We are discussing his latest chat," Merit said. "Would you mind telling the crew who witnessed *that* little talk?"

Triana realized that she had walked into a trap. She knew that her hesitation in answering had already damaged her. Her only recourse was the truth.

"This latest connection was in the Farms, witnessed by me and by Lita."

"Of course," Merit said. "You and yet another Council member."

"I was not aware," Triana responded, with more acid in her voice than she had intended, "that during a time of crisis we needed to gather representatives from groups that have a grudge with the Council." She took a breath to calm herself. "Until a majority of the crew elects to change the Council membership, we will continue to act in the best interests of everyone aboard this ship."

"Of course, of course," Merit said, again pacing toward the stage. "We're all aware that we have no choice – today, at least – but to have total and complete faith in the high priestess of our colony."

Triana made eye contact with Gap again. He seemed to read her mind, knowing that she wanted to verbally spar with Merit. He shook his head slowly. Triana was perplexed by his actions, and grew increasingly nervous that he was encouraging her to accept this assault. She bit her lip and remained quiet.

Merit had reached the steps, and now methodically climbed up to the stage. He stood ten feet to Triana's right, then pivoted to face the crowd.

"Why don't we try some easier questions?" he said. "Besides the obvious threat outside the ship, have we forgotten about the problems within? One of our friends lies in a hospital bed, and has just today awakened from a coma. A coma!"

Triana was startled that Merit already had the news of Alexa's recovery. It was another brilliant tactic on his part: take some of the only good news that Triana might deliver, and deliver it himself – keeping the attention on him – while spinning the news to paint a dire picture. One card that she had hoped to play, and he had already trumped it.

"We need heat to survive," Merit said, "and until recently we had no idea why the temperatures were falling on the crucial sixth level."

On the front row, Gap cracked a faint smile. Triana stared at him, but he kept his eyes on Merit, seeming to enjoy every minute.

"But forget about freezing to death," Merit said, again spreading his arms in a dramatic gesture. "That would be a slow, excruciating death. We would at least know what was happening, unlike the biggest danger we face: being instantly disintegrated by a giant boulder smashing into us with no warning."

Gap's smile grew more distinct.

Merit said, "I wonder how many of you have any idea what happened earlier today. I'm sure you heard the warning sirens, but you might not have had time to learn what that was all about."

Heads turned in the auditorium, and there were more whispered exchanges. Merit took two steps toward Triana and gave her a look that she swore resembled a predator's face closing in on the kill.

"Let me tell you what that alarm signified," he shouted over the buzz in the room. "We have one tiny weapon in our battle against the Kuiper Belt's treachery. A sophisticated warning alert system that tells our ship if we're about to get obliterated by a massive rock. Well, that warning system went down today for a few minutes. All of us were completely vulnerable. It's practically a miracle that it came back online before we were hit."

The room exploded in sound. Several crew members were on their feet, pointing at Triana and yelling. Even the crew members who had remained loyal to her and the Council appeared shaken. In the front row, Lita and Channy seemed stunned at the hostility directed toward the ship's Council leader.

Beside them, Gap was laughing.

A lightning bolt of fear raced through Triana. Suddenly it dawned on her: Gap's behavior, his angry confrontation with her in the hall, his absence from duty...

He had rebelled, and obviously joined the opposition. True, he had seemed to be no fan of Merit Simms...but how else to account for what had just happened. He had stifled her attempts to debate with Merit, placing her in an almost defenseless position now. She had no idea how the Council would survive this catastrophe.

She stared down from the stage, oblivious for the moment to the shouting and screams coming from the crew. She felt the rage of betrayal as she watched him laugh. And within that rage she felt a burning sense of pain. Although they had never connected in the manner she knew he had desired, Triana never doubted that Gap cared for her. To think that he would destroy her like this was agonizing.

Her lip trembled and she clenched her fists. Merit assumed a passive stance on the stage, obviously aware that his mission had finally been accomplished and that no further words were necessary at this point.

The uproar in the auditorium began to settle. Unsure of what to do or say, Triana glanced at Bon who seemed to be as startled as she. Lita and Channy were doing their part, apparently engaged in heated discussions with several crew members in the row behind them. Something needed to be done.

Just as Triana opened her mouth to speak, she spied Gap standing and raising his hands. He was yelling.

"Excuse me! May I say something, please? Hello? Can I please say something?"

What was this, Triana wondered. The final dagger in the heart?

"Excuse me," Gap yelled again. The room began to grow quiet. Gap moved to the steps and joined Triana, Bon, and Merit on the stage. Triana couldn't help but notice the look of curiosity on Merit's face. He apparently was as clueless as she about Gap's motives.

"If I could have just one moment of your time," Gap said, and the room's noise level dropped enough for him to be heard. "Thank you," he said. "I want to say a few things about what Merit has told you today. He could not be more right about the warning system. It is, indeed, our last layer of defense out here."

Gap looked at Triana, the slight remains of the smile lingering on the corners of his mouth. She couldn't decide what his look meant, but it almost appeared...vindictive.

"And Merit is right that it failed today. It was down for about ten minutes. That means ten minutes where we could have been blown right out of space."

He walked over and stood next to Merit, who shifted his gaze out over the crew, much like a king surveying his subjects. He nodded to indicate that Gap was speaking the truth.

"But that's not all," Gap said. "You don't know the whole story yet."

Triana's chin dropped to her chest and she closed her eyes. Inside, she felt her heart break.

-31-

There was no sensation of time. Triana stood quietly, her head down, but her mind was whirling. Besides the crushing weight of despair, she couldn't help but question everything. How could this have happened? How could she have better handled the crisis with Merit? Was there some way she could have steered the ship through the Kuiper Belt without the near-collisions, the drama, the fear?

Could she have managed the Council better? Could she have taken more of a leadership role in the eyes of the crew as they wound their way through the minefield? Was there some way she could have prevented the near-catastrophe with Alexa?

All of these thoughts tumbled across her mind, sending her down a tunnel of doubt and insecurity. Yet, when she came out the other side, she found, to her surprise, that her confidence and dignity took over. She raised her head again and looked out toward the crew.

'No', she told herself. 'I have not mishandled this in any way. My father taught me well, Dr. Zimmer taught me well, and if I had to do it all over again, I would not change one thing. I have the courage to stand here now, to face my peers, and to know that I have done the best that I could.'

She steeled herself for whatever Gap was going to say. She crossed her arms and held her chin high.

"I should have realized this from the start," Gap said to the audience. "When the problems with the heating system on Level Six came and went, it was odd to me, but I thought it was a defective part that had been built into the ship. "I just spent some time in Engineering looking at the culprit." He reached into a pocket and pulled out a small metal block, slightly grayish in color. It fit into the palm of his hand. "This is called a Balsom clip. I don't expect you to know anything about it, so I won't bore you with too many details. But it's a sensor that regulates the temperature on the ship. Each level has a series of them. They work in connection with each other. It's so complicated, I didn't even really know how they played off one another until recently. But when one breaks down, it might not create a problem until farther down the series."

Triana was confused. Where was he going with this? Roc had told her that the problem definitely came from a faulty clip, but what did that have to do with this meeting?

Gap continued. "This little bugger right here was the problem. Funny, isn't it, that something this small could cause so much trouble?" He held it up to the crowd and slowly swiveled it, letting them get a better look.

"But guess what?" he said. "Each of these parts, including the replacements, is numbered and coded. And this," he raised the Balsom clip again, "is not one of the clips that was in place when we launched."

The room was quiet. This information seemed important, yet produced only looks of puzzlement from the crew. Triana took her eyes off Gap for a moment when she noticed that Merit's shoulders had slumped ever so slightly. He certainly no longer held a kingly pose. She bit her lip. The significance of Gap's revelation began to dawn on her.

"This," Gap said, indicating the clip, "was a spare part seven months ago. But a few hours ago I pulled it out of the heating controls for Level 5. It's been tinkered with. Not enough for a full breakdown, but enough to cause it to flicker on and off."

Triana suddenly understood. It was sabotage.

"We'll probably never know who did this," Gap continued. "But I think I know why it was done. Nobody on this ship would want to have the heating fail completely, but a consistent breakdown would cause an awful lot of distress among the crew. Isn't that right?"

Triana continued to watch Merit, who looked speechless. She couldn't recall ever seeing that before.

Gap placed the clip back into his pocket and said, "This made me wonder: what other part of the ship was so crucial to our comfort and safety? Well, in this shooting gallery called the Kuiper Belt, isn't it obvious? The collision warning system. And don't you find it interesting that it went down for ten minutes, and then popped back on?"

Looks were exchanged between the assembled crew members. Gap stood quietly while they seemed to mull this over. Before he could continue, however, Merit raised his hands and addressed the room.

"I see what's going on here, don't you?" he said. "First we're supposed to believe that somebody sabotaged the heating system, and now – conveniently – someone has tampered with the warning system." He crossed his arms and looked at Gap while shaking his head. "So this is the best you can do, is that right? Rather than admit that we're in serious trouble, you manufacture a villain." He looked back at the crowd. "But we're not falling for it this time."

Triana watched him closely, analyzing the way in which he worked the room, rallying his troops. But the assembled crew members seemed confused, torn.

Merit raised his voice for emphasis. "I suppose we have another stowaway, is that what you're saying, Gap?"

Gap shook his head. "No, it's not a stowaway. It's you."

There was an instant stir in the auditorium. Merit's arms fell to his sides, and a look of disbelief covered his face. "Me?" He began to laugh. "*Me?* Oh, Gap, you might have been able to confuse people at first, but this?" His gaze shifted to the crowd. "Do you see what you're dealing with now? When they can't solve a problem, this is how they react."

A loud buzz enveloped the room. Triana stood still, watching, waiting. She concentrated on Gap's face. He seemed calm, and very sure of himself. She was sure that he wasn't finished yet.

When the room began to grow quiet again, Merit took a couple of paces toward Triana. "Are you behind this nonsense?" he asked her. "Was this your idea? To have your pawn attack while you sit back?"

It was Gap who answered. "No, Triana doesn't know about this. Only you and I know the truth here."

Merit whirled. "That's right. We both know the truth, that you're lying, doing anything you can to deflect responsibility. Tell me, Gap, what is your evidence? Usually when one makes an accusation like you have, they have some evidence." He faced the crew. "I think we'd all love to see your evidence."

Slowly another smile worked across Gap's face. "Evidence? I think I can do that." He cast a quick glance at Triana, then back toward the rows of crew members.

"We don't use video surveillance on this ship," he said. "We haven't thought it was necessary. I mean, who would want to cause harm, right? But..." He paused. "But protecting this crew is part of my job. It's why I'm on the Council. After realizing that someone had messed with the heating system, I programmed a remote camera to watch over the warning system."

He turned to Merit Simms. "Merit, you weren't even on duty this morning in Engineering. Can you explain to the crew what business you had opening the warning system's front panel?"

Merit fell motionless on the stage. Every eye in the room bored into him, and the silence was deafening. He fidgeted, unable to speak for almost half a minute. Gap waited patiently, then said, "If you'd like, we can lower the screen and play the video for everyone."

Triana's heart beat faster. Everything – *everything* – had changed in a flash. She stood frozen in place, taking it all in, hardly believing what she was hearing.

Seconds ticked by. Merit clenched and unclenched his hands. He stared at Gap, who stood with his arms crossed, his weight on one foot, displaying a look of complete control.

Finally, Merit looked up to face the crew. "I need you to understand that I never once meant to harm anyone. You have to believe me." A strand of black hair fell across his face. He left it there. "I knew the heating problem would be repaired. And the warning system should only have blinked out for a few seconds. That's all...a few seconds. I...I don't know what happened."

"I'll tell you what happened," Gap said. "You almost killed every one of us."

Merit didn't respond at first, then slowly nodded. "I know. And...I am truly sorry. All I ever wanted to do was...was scare you into doing the right thing." He pushed the stray hair back and addressed the crew. "You have to understand. I still believe in my heart that this journey is too dangerous. I'm...I'm afraid. Every day could be our last day, don't you see?"

A low chorus of boos began to roll across the room. In a moment a yellow arm band flew through the air, landing at Merit's feet. Within a few seconds a handful more fell to the floor.

"What I did was wrong, but you have to understand my motives," Merit said, his usually strong voice collapsing into a whining plea. "Please, you have to listen to me. We could die out here, don't you understand? I just...I just want to go home. Don't you? We need to..."

The boos grew louder, cutting him off. He started to speak again, then closed his mouth. Without looking at Gap or Triana, he walked down the steps, then briskly up the aisle toward the exit. More yellow arm bands fluttered towards him, many striking his chest and face before dropping to the floor. He pushed open the auditorium door and was gone.

Triana realized she had been holding her breath. She let it out with a whoosh, then walked over to stand beside Gap. "I...I don't know what to say," she said.

Gap's gaze remained on the door at the top of the room. "Not necessary," he said softly. "Besides, this could have gone very badly."

"What do you mean?"

He turned to look into Triana's eyes. In a low voice that only she could hear he said, "There is no remote camera near the warning system."

She stared at him, dumbfounded. A moment later Gap turned, hurried down the steps, and exited the room to a round of applause and many slaps on the back.

* * *

Thirty minutes later, Triana walked into the Control Room. The crew members who had remained on duty during the meeting, and had watched on video monitors, quietly went about their business. Nobody said a word to her, but the atmosphere had dramatically changed. Everyone seemed especially alert as they went about their duties; there was a crispness in their movements that hadn't existed two hours earlier.

Bon was sitting at the interface panel, rapidly punching strings of code on the keyboard. Triana sidled up beside him and watched for a moment, reluctant to interrupt his work. Then, with a final flourish, he hit ENTER and sat back.

"That should take care of the next leg through the Belt," he said. Turning to look at Triana he added, "After this, I'll have to connect again to receive another update."

"How do you feel about that?" she said.

He shrugged. "It's not the most pleasant experience in the world, but I can handle it now."

Triana studied his face for a moment, trying to see through those ice-blue eyes and read his thoughts. Had he really accepted the idea of the Cassini connection so easily? Just a few hours earlier he had been unwilling to attempt it; now he was quick to acknowledge that it would be happening again, possibly several times.

It was more than that, however. Bon's attitude wasn't one of tolerance. It was...anticipation?

A new – and frightening – thought came into Triana's mind. Did Bon now *enjoy* that connection? She had wondered, even during the first encounter around Saturn, if the link to the Cassini caused damage to Bon's brain. But what if it was a sensory stimulation that created a dependence? Could Bon slip into an addiction to the power of The Cassini?

She mustered a smile that felt forced, and held out her hand. "You still have the translator on you, right?"

Bon looked puzzled. "Yes. It's in my pocket. Why?"

Triana said, "I just think I should hold onto it for you."

She could tell from his expression that Bon wanted more of an explanation. He made no move to extract the metal device from his pocket.

"Listen," she said, quickly rationalizing her request. "We have no idea what might happen each time you connect with them. I think it would be a good idea if I held onto the translator, to make sure I'm there when it's time." She smiled at him again. "Just a safety measure, that's all."

Bon silently stared at her. She knew that he didn't buy the explanation, but she also knew that he wouldn't have his own reason for keeping the translator, either. A moment later he placed it into her open palm.

"Thanks," she said. "How much longer until you need to hook up with them?"

He mumbled something that sounded like, "I don't know yet," then stood, preparing to leave. Triana felt an awkward moment pass between them, and felt that something needed to be said.

"Thanks again for everything. I mean that." When Bon only nodded a response, she added, "I'll see you at the Council meeting in the morning." He walked past her toward the lift.

Triana turned to watch him, and was startled to see Mika standing beside her. The Japanese girl had left her post and was quietly waiting for a chance to speak to Triana.

She also no longer sported a yellow arm band.

"Hi, Mika."

"Triana, I wanted to…to apologize for any anxiety I might have caused in the Control Room." She appeared to fumble for words. "I…I was too quick to…to lose faith in our mission, and I…feel like I let you down. It won't happen again."

Triana offered a gentle smile. She reached out and put a hand on Mika's shoulder. "I appreciate that. Don't worry about what happened. You were never disrespectful or rude. We simply…disagreed. But you did your job, and never let our differences interfere with your work. I'm glad you're here."

A visible look of relief crossed Mika's face. She nodded acknowledgement of Triana's comments, then walked back to her post.

Triana spent another five minutes checking in by intercom with all of the various departments on *Galahad*. Again she noticed the crisp response from each crew member who answered her call.

She was once again in command.

-32-

Once upon a time, back when I was a little baby computer, I had a long talk with Roy, my creator. I asked him what the hardest thing was about building the world's most incredible thinking machine. That's me, by the way.

He said, "It's not the building. It's the rebuilding."

Meaning that it was one thing to put me together. When he had to take me apart to fix things, however, it was always a little more difficult getting things back to normal.

And isn't that the truth with just about everything?

What are we going to do about Merit Simms?"
The Council sat around the table in the Conference Room, and Lita's question hung in the air.

"I mean," she continued, "we don't have a jail on this ship. We could confine him to his room for a while, but, really, what good does that do?"

"We could throw him off the ship," Channy said with a grin.

Triana had already considered the issue for hours. Tossing and turning during the night, she had reflected on several choices, including Lita's idea of detention. It seemed almost silly, however, to send Merit to his room. Was that really the way bad behavior would be dealt with during the journey? Even dangerous behavior?

Dr. Zimmer had done his best in planning the system of government on *Galahad*, yet had assumed that only minor squabbles and differences would require disciplinary action.

He – nor anyone else, for that matter – had imagined a crew member recklessly threatening the lives of everyone on the ship.

Although Merit's actions had been designed to only induce fear, and to manipulate the crew's loyalties, they could have spelled disaster. He had not been seen in the eighteen hours following the meeting in the auditorium. Triana assumed that he would lay low for at least a few days.

In the meantime, it was up to the Council to determine the punishment, if any.

"May I make a recommendation?" Bon said from the end of the table.

Triana was startled. Bon never offered suggestions; in fact, he usually needed prodding to even open his mouth during a Council meeting. "Uh, sure," she said.

Bon leaned forward, his elbows resting on the table. "I don't believe that we should reward this person by giving him a vacation, even if it's in his room. I vote to put him right back to work, with perhaps an extra shift each week. And, when his next rotation of rest comes around, he should forfeit that and immediately report to his next station."

Triana smiled. Bon's work ethic was unquestionably the strongest on the ship; of course he would advocate hard work for any misconduct. She looked around the table for reaction, and was greeted by looks of thoughtful approval.

"It makes sense, really," Lita said.

Gap nodded. "I agree."

"If you won't boot him off the ship," Channy said, "then okay, put him to work."

The unanimous decision helped, but at the same time Triana realized that the lack of a policy dealing with dangerous behavior could come back to haunt them. A world of no consequences would only mean chaos. Her to-do list had suddenly picked up a priority item.

She moved on to the next item on the agenda. "Tell me about Alexa."

"I think she's going to be fine," Lita said. "It might take her a couple of weeks to get her strength back, but physically she's okay. The only thing…" She let the sentence fall away, seemed to think about it, then continued. "Well, she doesn't seem to be the same Alexa as before the surgery."

"What do you mean?" Channy said.

"Um…I can't really put my finger on it. She seems pretty…serious."

Channy laughed. "You think? She just had emergency surgery, then lay in a coma for a couple of days. You want jokes or something?"

Lita smiled. "It's not that. Her personality seems a little different." She looked at Triana. "I'm not saying anything's wrong with her. Her brain scan is normal, no apparent damage. But this has changed her somehow."

Triana thought about those words for a moment. Finally, she looked at Lita and said, "I think we've all changed, you know?"

The discussion moved to a lighter topic for a minute, as Channy announced that her plans for a dating game would now continue. She enthusiastically predicted at least a dozen crew members would participate. There was a mixture of groans and chuckles when she raised her eyebrows and looked around the table for volunteers.

Gap had been relatively quiet throughout the meeting. Triana had noticed, and wondered if she should later meet privately with him. For the time being she asked him for an Engineering update.

"The heating unit is working perfectly," he said. "If there's any silver lining to what Merit did to make it malfunction, it's that we now know exactly how the Balsom clips behave when they're damaged or failing."

"How did he do that, anyway?" Channy said.

"He's on his second tour of duty in the Engineering section these days, and he had a lot of time to study up on what he needed to do. Plus, it's not like we sat there guarding the heating system, right? He could have done everything in the middle of the night, or whenever. Nobody would have thought twice about him being there."

Lita said, "So we shouldn't be worried about those clips going bad?"

Gap shook his head. "No. I would be surprised if we ever have to pull out a spare clip again on the rest of the trip. It's a pretty solid unit, which is why the malfunction was so frustrating in the first place."

"But you figured it out," Triana said, doing her best to soothe whatever issues were apparently still festering inside Gap.

"Well…" he said, looking uncomfortable. "I didn't think to check the clips for another level, and that might have saved us a lot of time."

"Quit being modest," Triana said with a laugh. "You did a good job. You even outsmarted Roc."

"Can we talk about something else?" the computer chimed in.

"Yes, we can," Triana said. "What's the status on the warning system?"

"Same story as the heating unit," Gap said. "Merit loosened a key circuit within it, knowing full well that a back-up circuit would kick in. It's just that the warning system didn't identify it as a complete malfunction, and instead tried to either repair the first circuit, or go around it. It caused the unit to completely shut down rather than use the back-up."

"It's been reprogrammed," Roc said. "From now on, at the first indication of any problem, it will use any and all back-up systems. It's not anyone's fault, really. The system was a brand new invention, and obviously nobody on Earth had ever needed one before. Plus, who knew that we would be driving through such heavy traffic?"

"Speaking of which," Triana said, "The Cassini's secret path through the Kuiper Belt seems to be perfect so far." She looked at Bon. "Any thoughts yet on when you might need to check in again?"

Bon sat still for a few moments before answering. "It's a feeling, that's all I can really say. As strange as it sounds, I think they'll let me know when it's time to talk. In the meantime, we'll just have to trust that they're...okay with us."

Lita looked worried. "Meaning...they still haven't decided if we get a pass, is that right?"

Bon nodded. "Yeah."

"But they must be happy about how things have turned out now," Channy said. "I mean, there's no more fighting on the ship, and...and..."

Triana cut in. "We don't even know what they're looking for. We can't assume that they only grade us on how we get along. In fact, I would think it *has* to be more than that."

"You're right," Bon said. "For a species to grow and prosper, in their eyes, not only must they be civilized, but they must prove that they have something to offer to the rest of the universe before they can reach out and affect others."

Channy looked glum. "Well, what would we possibly have to offer?"

There was silence for a few seconds, and then Triana began to laugh. "Oh, Channy, don't be that way. What if we're judged on positive energy? You usually bring more of that to the table than any two crew members combined."

A smile spread across Channy's face. "Hey, you might be right. Okay, positive energy it is." She turned to Lita. "You know, love is the most positive form of energy there is. Just think how much we would glow if you joined the dating game."

There was laughter around the table. Triana began to feel better than she had in a long time. She looked back at Gap, ready to wrap up the meeting.

"One last thing," she said. "Our course has changed through the Kuiper Belt, so we'll need to begin plotting a correction eventually. But I guess we'll need to figure out where we are before we figure out where we're going."

"Yeah, I've already started that process," Gap said. "We're running in something like a zigzag pattern through the Kuiper Belt right now, only a little more complex than that. There is one thing that's pretty cool, though, and it can't be a coincidence, I don't think."

He punched a couple of buttons on the keyboard before him, and all of the room's monitors pulled up a tracking view of the Kuiper Belt. "If things don't change too much in the next week, we'll get a pretty good view of another dwarf planet, similar to Pluto."

"Hey, that's awesome," Lita said. "What is it?"

Gap highlighted a small, reddish dot on the screens. "It's one of the last major bodies in the Kuiper Belt. Not as big as Pluto, but still interesting. I think we'll zip by close enough to get some great pictures, at least."

Triana raised her eyebrows. "Maybe The Cassini use it as an anchor for the secret passageway, eh? What's it called?"

Gap looked up at her. "It's called Sedna."

Lita had been raising a cup of water to her lips. She froze, her eyes looking over the rim of the cup at Gap. "What?" she said loudly.

"Sedna. S-e-d-n-a."

Triana saw the look of surprise on the Lita's face. "What's the matter?"

Lita slowly put the cup on the table and said, "Oh my God."

"What is it?"

Lita didn't answer at first. She said to Gap, "And we would never have come anywhere near this...this Sedna... before we changed course?"

Gap shook his head. "Not even close."

Triana grew concerned. "Lita, what is it?"

The young girl from Mexico slowly turned to face the Council Leader. "I knew it. I knew there was something different about her."

"What are you talking about?"

Lita took a deep breath. "Remember when I said that there was something different about Alexa? There was a funny blip on her neural scan when she came out of the coma. I couldn't explain it, but didn't think it was important. But now..."

She took a couple of minutes and told the story of Alexa's foggy comments upon awakening from the coma.

"You said she was mumbling," Triana said. "Are you sure it was Sedna?"

"I spelled it, just like Gap did."

Gap and Triana exchanged glances. Channy whispered, "This is too weird. She...she's become psychic. The coma turned her into a psychic!"

Bon looked away, deep in thought.

-33-

Dusk arrived on *Galahad*. They had gone to dinner together, and now, as the lights slowly dimmed, Gap and Hannah strolled down one of the paths in Dome 2. During the meal he had caught her up on some of the details of his day in Engineering, but had repeatedly steered the conversation away from any mention of his success at thwarting Merit.

He also did not mention the bizarre circumstances unfolding around Alexa.

Hannah walked slowly, staying two feet from the edge of the path. Occasionally she would brush her hand against Gap's, but he made no move to grasp it.

This was their first time alone since the tense moment in Engineering. He had not volunteered any information regarding his decision to leave the Council, and she wondered if he had discussed it with Triana. Finally, during a lull in the conversation, she brought it up.

"I haven't decided for sure," he said. "I want to think about some things."

"You realize," she said, "that the crew thinks of you as a hero right now. It wouldn't make any sense for you to quit."

"I'm not a hero," he said. "But let's not talk about this right now, okay?"

She nodded. They walked in silence for a few more minutes, passing other crew members who had also chosen a walk in the dome for the ship's version of a sunset. In the distance they heard the sound of irrigation pumps beginning their nightly chores, a low, rhythmic thump that reminded Hannah of a heartbeat.

The awkward feeling between them was not getting any better. Hannah felt torn, wanting to discuss how she was feeling, how *he* was feeling about the two of them, yet not wanting to inflame the already sensitive aura that had somehow descended upon them. She was confused about what had happened. One day everything had been fine, and now...

"I want to apologize if I've been difficult lately," Gap said, nudging her out of her thoughtful state. "I know it hasn't been much fun for you."

"That's okay, I understand," Hannah said.

"You've been terrific, as always," he said. "It's just that... things have been tough, you know?"

She nodded, keeping her head down.

"I don't know what's going to happen with me and the Council. I don't even know if I should be in charge of Engineering right now. Maybe somebody else could bring a fresh view to the Council, shake things up a little bit."

They walked in silence another minute before he spoke again. "I guess what I'm trying to say is that I'm a little overwhelmed right now, a little confused about what I need to be doing, you know? And..." He paused. "And I think, to be fair to you, that you and I should take a break right now, too."

Hannah stopped in her tracks. It took Gap a few seconds to realize that she had dropped back. He turned and walked back to her.

"What are you saying?" she said. "You're breaking up with me?"

"I'm just saying that I'm really confused right now-"

"You're confused?" she said. "That's it? You're dumping me because you're confused?"

"I'm not dumping you," Gap said. "I'm not very good company right now, and you deserve a lot better."

Hannah stared at him, her lower lip quivering.

"Please," Gap said. "I just want you to understand."

"Understand? You're dumping me. At least have the guts to be honest."

Gap shook his head. "I really don't want this to get ugly. I'm not saying I don't want to be with you, but it's just not a good time for me right now. It's not a good time for *us* right now."

Hannah stared at him, tapping a finger against her leg. After a few moments she slowly shook her head.

"I thought the whole 'it's not you, it's me' speech only happened in books and movies," she said. She started to walk away, then turned back. "You know, when things are going tough, the last thing you should sacrifice is the one person who knows you best and cares about you. You should lean on them, Gap, not push them away." Her voice cracked as she added, "Sometimes the answer – and the right person – is right in front of you."

This time when she walked away she didn't look back.

* * *

Lita didn't look up from her work when she heard the door to Sick House slide open. It wasn't until she felt the presence of someone hovering at her desk that she raised her head to find Bon patiently standing there.

He looked uncomfortable. Lita was sure that he associated the clinic with his own hospital stay several months earlier, and she wondered what could have brought him down here from the Farms. When she asked, he nodded toward the hospital ward.

"Any chance I could visit with Alexa for a minute?" he said.

"Uh...sure," Lita said. "She's awake. I think she just finished dinner." She stood up and walked around her desk. "C'mon, I'll take you in."

"Any chance I could visit with her alone?"

Lita stopped and looked into Bon's face. "Well..." She quickly sorted through all of the possible arguments, but really couldn't find one that didn't come back to the fact that she was simply curious about his request. "Yeah, I guess that would be okay." She waved him ahead. "Just five minutes, okay?"

Bon thanked her, then walked past her into the ward. Lita stared after him, her mind racing. She had already wondered about the changes in Bon; now he had come to visit Alexa, who also was no longer the same person she had been days ago.

She felt the hairs on the back of her neck stand up.

* * *

Sweat was dripping from Channy's face, and she loved it. The workout had been full, the largest attendance for an evening session in months. Now she sipped from a cup of water and exchanged greetings and jokes with several of the crew members as they filed toward the locker rooms.

"Is that all you got tonight?"

"What are you talking about? I saw you stop and rest a few times when you thought I wasn't looking."

"Hey, Channy, not so fast after dinner. I thought I was going to hurl."

"Maybe you should skip the second helpings for a while, you think?"

Kylie, her roommate, walked up to her, a smile covering her face. "I can't remember the last time I saw you so happy."

Channy shrugged. "Why not? The workouts today have been terrific. The crew seems pretty happy, too."

"I think they're embarrassed," Kylie said, helping herself to some water.

"What, you mean because they put their faith in a scoundrel when they should have been supporting Triana all along?"

Kylie laughed. "Yeah, something like that."

They were interrupted by Addie and Vonya, who approached slowly, their eyes darting back and forth between each other, as if pooling their courage.

"Uh, hi," Addie said, glancing at Channy and then looking at Kylie.

"Hi," Channy said. She could tell that they likely wanted to speak with her in private, but she also remembered their last encounter after a workout. They had had no problem speaking in front of Kylie when their attitude had been confrontational, so it would have to be okay this time, as well. "Is there something on your mind?"

"Well, yes," Addie said, throwing another look at her friend, pleading with her eyes for support. Vonya chimed in.

"We just wanted to let you know that we apologize for being so...so snippy with you. Things were a little crazy, and we...we didn't handle it very well."

Channy took another sip of water without taking her eyes off Vonya's. She could have bailed them out by quickly accepting the apology, but she decided to let them dig their way out a little longer.

"Yeah," Addie said. "You've always been great, and we treated you pretty badly. Can we move past all of that?"

Channy stared at the two girls for a moment without reacting. Then, a smile slowly crept across her face. "That means a lot to me. Thank you, both. And yes, we're still friends, so no worries, okay?"

A visible look of relief spread through Addie and Vonya. They each mumbled a thank-you, then hurried off to the showers.

Channy turned to Kylie and raised her eyebrows. Kylie wiped some perspiration from her forehead with a towel and said, "You look like you're about six inches off the ground."

"It's better than you think."

"What do you mean?"

"When it comes time to do my dating game," Channy said with a grin, "people will sign up out of guilt. I'm sure to have a full house."

* * *

Bon stepped into the hospital ward and could see that Alexa was the only patient in the room. He immediately flashed back to his own stay, back when the connection with The Cassini was fresh...and painful.

Alexa turned to look at him, and kept her gaze on him as he walked from the door to her bed. Something in her look registered with Bon, a sensation that hit him right away and remained constant. There was a power radiating from her, something that he wouldn't have been able to explain to anyone else. It was something he wouldn't have understood himself until recently.

He stood beside her, quietly, for a minute. They simply looked at one another. He heard a trilling sound, and noticed that Iris was curled up beside Alexa, sleeping soundly.

"How are you feeling," he finally said, and when she smiled he realized how rehearsed – and unlike him – it sounded.

"I'm fine," she said. "Ready to get back to work, to tell you the truth."

"I understand," he said. "Uh...do you mind if I talk to you about something?"

"No, that's fine. What is it?"

Bon indicated the edge of her bed. "Okay if I sit down?"

Alexa looked amused by the request. "Sure."

He perched beside her. Iris woke up, yawned, then tucked her head back under her leg and closed her eyes. "I'm just a little curious about how you're feeling after waking up from the coma," Bon said. "Or, to be more accurate, *what* you're feeling."

She looked into his left eye, then his right, then back again. "Explain."

Bon took a long breath, then began to tell her about the ship's zigzag course through the Kuiper Belt, and how they had just discovered that their path would take them near the large body known as Sedna. He watched to see her reaction when the name was mentioned. There was none.

"You referred to Sedna when you came out of the coma," he said. "Can you tell me how you knew about it?"

A brief smile flickered across Alexa's face, then she looked away. "I don't know how to answer that. How do you know your birth date? How does anyone know their parents' names? I just…" She trailed off.

Bon considered that for a moment. He glanced at the sleeping cat, then back into Alexa's face. "May I ask a favor?"

"Sure."

"Would it be all right," he said, "if I touched you?"

This time her smile remained. "Are you going to heal me?"

"Just humor me."

Alexa shrugged again, and held out her hand. Bon hesitated, then grasped it.

His eyes went wide. His body went stiff, shaking slightly. A minute later he gently placed her hand onto the bed, then he stood up.

"You felt that." It wasn't a question.

"Yes," she said. She licked her lips nervously, then reached down and began to scratch Iris behind the ears. The cat lifted its head, yawned again, then stretched.

"I can't explain what I'm feeling," Alexa said. "But when I go to sleep, I wake up with a very…strange sensation. Like I've been somewhere while I was asleep."

Bon didn't reply, so she continued. "When I woke up from a nap about an hour ago, just before dinner, I knew that you were coming to see me."

"Are you afraid?"

She appeared to think about the question. "No. Not really. Just…intrigued, I guess. I don't know what's happening."

Bon leaned against the bed and crossed his arms. "I…I understand. Probably better than anyone else could, actually. I haven't felt…normal since we left the space around Saturn."

He paused, shifted his weight to his other foot, and continued. "I don't think you and I are experiencing the same thing, necessarily. But…" Another pause. "But it's nice to know that someone else has changed."

Alexa took a few seconds before answering. "Maybe we should use a different word. I think I'm the same person I was yesterday; I've just been…modified."

"Fair enough," Bon said. They stared at each other for a moment before he added, "Any other visions, besides the one about my visit?"

Alexa moved her hand from Iris's ears to her chin. "Yes. But it was more of a feeling, rather than a vision."

"Would you like to share?"

She looked up and met his gaze. "We're going to make it through the Kuiper Belt just fine."

Then she paused before finishing the thought. "But there's something waiting on the other side."

-34-

It was close to midnight, the end of a very long – and interesting – day. Triana put on a long t-shirt and eyed her bed, but knew that sleep would never come until she emptied the receptacle of thoughts that was filled to the brim. She sat at her desk and spent a few minutes leaning over her journal.

> Once again I can't help but think of everything that has happened and wonder what lessons I might have learned. Dad always said that there were lessons in life every day, and that it was up to us to find them.
>
> I know that I stayed strong with my convictions, and I did not sacrifice my beliefs in a time of crisis. But if that almost cost us the mission, what lesson do I extract from that? It's so hard sometimes, so hard.
>
> I do know one thing for sure: we have so many obstacles in our path, and yet over the next four years the biggest challenge will likely be in learning how to deal with each other.

She set down her pen, stood up, and stretched. There was more to say, but she wasn't sure how to put it into words.

"Oh, just say it," she muttered to herself, and sat back down.

> Bon and Gap are two perfect examples. They have both changed in the last few days. For Bon, I'm starting to worry about the effect that his connection with The Cassini is having on him. It's not his fault, that's for sure. I asked

She marked these last two words out and started the sentence over.

> I begged him to re-establish contact with these super beings, or whatever they are, so now I can't come back and fault him for what it might be doing to him. I know that we probably would not have survived this ring of fire called the Kuiper Belt if they hadn't shared their code with us. I just wonder what long-term effect this is going to have on Bon.
> And, once again, I have to wonder where we stand personally. We have kissed now, and I can't deny that I liked it. A lot. But what does that do to our situation? Anything? Nothing? I am more confused than ever about all of that.
> And then there's Gap. His inner turmoil is surprising, but at least I understand it. I've experienced more than my share of that, too. All I will say right now is that I miss the fun Gap we were lucky to have on the Council, and I hope he comes to grips with his insecurities. Is there something I should be doing to help this? Or is this

such a personal issue that I need to mind my own business?

And Alexa...

I honestly don't know what to make of her. I'm going to give her at least a couple of weeks before I begin to worry about her condition.

As for myself, I have to be honest and admit that Merit Simms accomplished more than he thinks he did. I have put on the brave face since day one, and yet I'm scared, too. He at least stood in front of two hundred of his peers and came clean. I attributed all of his motives to a lust for power, when perhaps most of it was much simpler than that: He's just afraid. His mask might take a different form than mine...but we both apparently wear them.

And finally, I hope that, as a team, we're able to live up to the expectations that The Cassini have in order to be considered true 'citizens of the galaxy.' I suppose it's another example of their code, only this time it's a code of conduct. Of course I'm concerned about that, but they can't demand total perfection, can they?

Triana set her pen down again and thought about that last line. Total perfection. If that was the standard needed to venture out to the stars, then the human species was never destined to make it. Surely, she thought, The Cassini were not unreasonable keepers of the galactic passes.

She closed the journal and made her way to her bed. She lay back with her hands beneath her head and stared up at the ceiling, waiting for the peaceful rescue of sleep. As she often did, she began to mentally critique her own job performance over the last few days, wondering if her dad would be proud of the way she had handled things. Or Dr. Zimmer, her mentor and stand-in father figure after her dad had passed away. He had warned her about handling crew controversy. What would he think of her decisions? Would he at least be proud that she had rejected Roc's offer of secret recordings? Would he –

She suddenly sat up. The thought had flashed into her mind so quickly, something that she had buried in all of the recent turbulence, and now it screamed for her attention. How could she have forgotten about this?

Dr. Zimmer and his video message replayed in her mind.

For a moment she debated whether to get up and add a postscript to her journal entry. Instead, she lay back down and bit her lip. This, she knew, would keep sleep at bay for at least another hour.

Somewhere on *Galahad*, she remembered, a fellow crew member had the blood of Dr. Zimmer coursing through their veins.

I remember one of my earliest conversations with Gap, so many months ago, long before we left Earth. He asked me an interesting question, and for Gap that's quite an accomplishment.

He wanted to know if I was ever jealous that I wasn't human. Sounds like a question that Gap would ask, doesn't it?

Let me think about this for a moment. You humans sometimes get so caught up in your emotional crises that you almost destroy each other. I, on the other hand, remain calm and rational. You make mistakes, some of which can cost you your lives, while I am practically flawless. You go from happy to sad to anxious to overjoyed to depressed, all within the space of an hour. I am reliably stable at all times.

So what do you think? Am I jealous?

YES! Please don't tell Gap, but it's true. Something about you crazy humans, and your unpredictable swings, is strangely appealing to me, and I can't begin to tell you why. The only thing I can assume is that it's what lets you know that you are truly alive, and THAT is something I will never experience. So, yes, I'm a little envious. Just a little. If given the chance, like Pinocchio, to become a real boy, would I?

No. And not just because of that whole freaky nose thing. SOMEBODY has to think clearly around this place, and it might as well be me.

Having said that, I do wonder about your ability to get along. I've been thinking about that, and I've reached this conclusion. Yes, you can, but it takes compassion, trust, and patience. Oh, and one other thing: empathy. Lots and lots of empathy.

Which, I think, our little space voyagers will need in large supply as they continue their journey. Seems that we're seeing a few changes in the moods and attitudes of our fun bunch, and I'm pretty sure it's only the beginning.

What a time to be tested, if that's really what The Cassini are doing. And yet, when you get right down to it, aren't all of you being tested on a daily basis? Think about it.

Actually, think about it later, because right now you should be thinking about what's on the other side of the Kuiper Belt. Alexa might have 'the vision,' as some people call it, but could she go back to sleep and try to dig up a few more details, please? If I understand the whole idea of The Cassini's ring of debris, it's meant to not only keep us from leaving the solar system until we're ready...but it's also supposed to keep things out that don't need to be here.

Just how angry are these visitors who have been waiting at the front door, ringing the bell for who knows how long? You don't suppose they would try to take it out on our innocent little Earthlings, do you?

I guess we won't know until Galahad 4.

Let's meet back here, okay?

About The Author

Dom Testa, of Denver, Colorado, has been a radio show host since 1977, and currently is a co-host of the popular "Dom and Jane Show" on Mix 100 in Denver. A strong advocate of literacy programs for children, he regularly visits school classrooms, where he hosts writing workshops. Dom began the "Big Brain Club" to encourage students to overcome the peer pressure that often prevents them from achieving their true potential. Find out more at www.DomTesta.com, or at www.BigBrainClub.com.

Join Club Galahad!

What does it cost to join?
Nothing!
What do you get?
Plenty!

- *Be the first to get Galahad updates!*

- *Find out about special Galahad events!*

- *Links to other great sites!*

- *Monthly trivia contests for prizes!*

You get it all when you join Club Galahad. Just visit:
www.ClubGalahad.com

To order all of the books in the Galahad series, visit:
www.DomTesta.com